IN HELL

L. Marshall James

In Hell
By L. Marshall James
Copyright 2013 by L. Marshall James
Front cover illustration by Victor Lammert
Editing by Jennifer Zaczek

ISBN-10: 0-9897974-0-6
ISBN-13: 978-0-9897974-0-5

First Publishing 2013
Highwater Publishing

To those who wander.

0

The monster was the best friend I ever had.
—Boris Karloff

In a lot of ways, I was just an average American guy. I loved my family but spent far too little time with them. I had a decent job that I inherently disliked. I tried to cook and eat healthy but usually resorted to eating fast food and drinking beer. I enjoyed guns, sports, and the occasional sexy-times with a lady, and I had one hobby that bordered on a gleeful, irrational, childish obsession: I loved zombies.

Ever since the day I sat down with my dad and watched my first zombie flick at the ripe age of seven, I had been spellbound. Some father-son pairs would play catch, go fishing, or watch World War II documentaries. My dad and I would shut off all the lights and hunker down in the windowless basement as legions of zombies flooded the earth. The endless onslaught of the undead became something of a bonding experience for us, replete with blood, gore, tragedy, and horror. I didn't care if it was old school or new school, A-list or B-list, high budget or low; as long as it featured rotting, homicidal cannibals craving flesh and brains, I watched with slack-jawed fascination.

Once I grew up and moved out, the infatuation not only remained but grew into something more intense and all-encompassing than the casual interest my father had. Instead of playing video games or collecting panties from the local talent, I studied zombie movies, collected posters, action figures, and undead memorabilia, and amassed a small but respectable weapons stash. I don't think I ever genuinely expected a zombie apocalypse; it was only fantasy. Still, I had thought that if the time came in which I had to defend myself or my loved ones from a world of brain-dead murderers, I was prepared. I would be ready.

But things never pan out like you expect. You make assumptions, you make mistakes, you have to improvise, and no matter how hard you might have tried, there is no way to prepare for a reality you've only experienced through your imagination or the magic of Hollywood. Things fall apart, and instead of saving lives and salvaging what's left of the world, you find yourself struggling just to keep yourself together and keep going. When you consider the oft-predicted apocalypse, you think of it as happening all around you, with yourself existing within but somehow separate from, and immune to, the chaos, death, and madness of the end of the world. You never realize that as a piece of this world, you are a necessary part of its entropy. Some lessons have to be learned the hard way.

I hear labored breathing, and the barrel of a pistol is pressed against my head. The pool of blood near my feet is slowly spreading and will soon reach me. My heart is beating wildly, my ears are ringing, and I am splattered with blood, none of which is mine. Someone is screaming nearby, but he no longer matters. As my finger tightens on the trigger, I know I was wrong: it wasn't just fantasy.

And I was never ready.

1

I sighed as my bladder evacuated like an over pressurized squirt gun. Mother of the gods, that felt good.

"I can't believe they broke up already," Zack said from the other room.

"Are you kidding me?" Alex responded.

"What? Yeah," came his reply. "You're not surprised?"

"Dude, that was obvious a mile away," Terry said.

"Seriously," Alex agreed. "I mean . . . I love the guy, but he's really kind of an asshole."

Zack laughed. "Yeah. I guess I figured it would take her at least a month to notice though. She lasted what, two weeks?"

"She's a smart one," Terry muttered.

I shook off and flushed. As I washed my hands, someone knocked on the bathroom door.

"Hey, Paulie!" Terry yelled. "You want another beer? You're almost empty."

"Yeah," I called out. "Get me another of the same."

"You're a classless son of a bitch, you know that?"

"Pshh," I said as I dried off. "I only drink the good stuff when I'm with your mom."

"Fair enough," he called back. "At least you're treating her right."

I pulled open the bathroom door and stepped out as he disappeared into the kitchen.

"If he doesn't get his act together," he said as he opened the fridge, "he's never going to keep a"—he paused to sneeze before finishing the sentence—"girlfriend."

"If you're not careful," Zack countered, "you're going to give us all the South American flu!"

Alex and Zack laughed as I sat down and picked up my cards.

"It's not the flu. It's the goddamn stray cat on the porch," Terry yelled back.

"Bullshit," Alex said. "Now we're all infected, and I'm going to get fired for missing more time."

He laid down a card and turned to me. "Draw two, asshole."

"We also might die, or something," Zack added.

"Shit," I said, and drew two cards from the pile. "What are you guys talking about? You spreading the HIV all over my house?"

"Yeah, Terry is sneezing his AIDS all over your leftover burritos."

"I think he teabagged the milk too, dude."

"Guilty," Terry said as he came back into the living room, a beer in each hand. "My bad."

"Goddamnit, Terry," I said.

He held a beer out as he passed me en route to his chair. I grabbed the can and laid a card on the table as he sat down.

"Dine on dicks," I commanded. "Draw four. The color is blue. So what's this South American flu? Is that the latest scare?"

Alex turned to me and shook his head.

"Dude, seriously?" he said. "Do you ever bother with anything aside from zombie movies? Like the news, for instance?"

"Yeah," I said. "Sometimes, I watch zombie TV shows instead. But no, I hate the news. It's fucking depressing."

"Fair enough," Alex responded, "but if you spent five minutes paying attention, you might have at least a vague idea of what's going on in the world."

"You know zombies are dead, right?" Terry interrupted.

"Undead," I corrected.

"No, I mean they suck," he replied. "They've been killed by overexposure. You need a unique hobby, like animated snuff films or Bigfoot erotica. An untapped market."

"Are those untapped or nonexistent?" I asked.

"Same thing."

"It's been all over pretty much every media outlet for a week or two, at least," Zack said.

"At least two weeks," Alex said. "And not pretty much every media outlet—all of them. My nephew is fully up to date on the situation, and he can't even speak full sentences."

"Ah, sorry," Terry said. "What's wrong with your nephew?"

"What?" Alex answered, sounding either confused or defensive. "Nothing. Why?"

"You said he can't speak sentences," Terry replied.

"Oh. Well, he's an infant. He's not supposed to."

"Then how can he know about the South American—"

"The point is," Alex interrupted, "that Paul is so out of touch with reality that the biggest health scare in fifty years has passed completely under his radar."

Terry nodded at his cards, his brow furrowed.

"That is a pretty good point," he agreed.

A silence fell over the group as everyone except me stared at their cards. I glanced around, hoping for elaboration. My eyes settled on Alex, who only glanced back momentarily before laying down another card and focusing again on his hand.

"So . . ." I prompted.

"His nephew is fine, Paulie," Terry assured me without looking away from his cards. "Like he said, he's only a baby, so it's okay that he doesn't talk."

"Yeah, he's fine," Alex agreed. "Don't worry so much."

"What? Yeah, I know," I persisted. "What about the flu?"

"Flu?" Alex replied. "He doesn't have the flu."

"The . . . no, the—" I started, then caught myself.

I looked at each of them as they stared at their cards, their poker faces fully engaged. Zack's poker face, however, was not as practiced or tempered as Alex's and Terry's. As a result, a grin wriggled at one corner of his mouth.

"I hate you guys so much," I said.

Zack let loose a brief giggle.

"Uh-oh, Zack has the giggles!" Terry announced.

"That's stage two of the flu!" Alex claimed. "Stage one is chortles."

"Stage three is belly laughter," Terry continued. "Stage four is death."

"It takes such an unexpected turn for the worst," Alex lamented. "I think that's why it spreads so fast."

Zack giggled again, and I struggled not to join him.

"Seriously," I said with as much indignation as I could manage through a grin. "What is it?"

"It's—" Zack started, then giggled and abandoned his effort to explain.

I looked to Alex, who nodded again as he tried to suppress a smile.

"It's some kind of crazy-contagious flu going around Brazil or Venezuela or some shit," Alex said.

"Both, actually," Terry said. "Brazil and Venezuela. It's been spreading from there I think. The CDC is doing their 'wash your hands and avoid public places' bit."

"Man," I said. "I don't know the details, but I can absolutely guarantee it's the exact same deal as the bird flu, the swine flu, or whatever else. The chances of you coming down with one of those was the same as getting hit by lightning while winning the lottery."

"Eh, I don't know," Terry insisted. "This thing is actually going around like crazy. I heard Madagascar shut down its ports."

"They have ports?" Zack asked.

"Only one."

"Wild. Red."

"Fuck."

"My boss wants us to wear those medical mask things to work," Zack said. "I'm going to end up with fucking mask tan lines."

Terry barked a laugh, then promptly broke into a coughing fit. We watched him struggle to form words in between coughs, then abandon the effort. When he finally recovered, he gestured toward Zack with his whiskey glass.

"You are so gay," he said finally. "Wild. The color is . . . emerald. Or green."

"Hey, you don't have to be gay to hate tan lines on your face, asshole," Zack replied.

"Aw, Zack. If I wasn't so straight, I'd throw you a bone just to make you feel better about all the gay jokes we make."

"Pshh, you're not straight," Zack retorted.

"Yeah, probably not," Terry agreed. "I do have a curious fondness for dick, after all."

"North Korea is sealing their borders," Alex redirected.

"When aren't their borders sealed?" I asked.

"China and Japan are closing their borders too," Alex continued. "Supposedly, this flu is worse than both the swine and bird flu combined."

"Meh," I said. "Flu season comes every year. A bunch of babies and old people die, then it's always back to normal. I never get a vaccine, and I never get sick."

"Wait, what?" Zack asked. "Since when are you one of those anti-vaccination fucktards?"

"I'm not," I replied. "I just never go to the doctor."

"Uno," Terry said as he laid down another card.

"Ah, you bastard!" Zack exclaimed.

"It's the flu," I said. "Everyone I know who ever got the swine or bird flu is still alive. It's the same every year."

"It's definitely serious," Alex contended.

"Bullshit," I retorted. "What are the symptoms?"

6

"I heard some people have died," Zack said.

"That might have been because of riots though," Terry said.

"Riots?"

"Yeah, I saw it on the news. There were riots and fires and such. Something about flu shot availability."

"Wait, what?" I asked. "People were rioting about flu shots?"

"Apparently."

"Wow," I said. "People really will use any reason to riot."

"Still a better reason than sports," Terry replied.

"Touché."

"Speaking of vaccines," Zack broke in, "I heard some morons are saying the vaccines are causing the outbreak. Is that even possible?"

"Definitely," Terry said. "South American flu, autism, Ebola, dysentery, 9/11 . . ."

"Vaccines caused 9/11?" Alex asked.

"Yes," Terry responded with certainty.

"I knew it."

"So, what are the symptoms, other than flu-like symptoms?" I asked.

Alex thought for a moment before shrugging his shoulders.

"Exactly," I said as I laid down a card. "Wild. The color is blue. This whole thing is another annual government media blitz to get you to flip the fuck out and pay attention to anything but the men behind the curtain."

"Communists?" Zack asked.

"No," Alex claimed. "The Illuminati."

"Aliens."

"Pagans."

"No, me," Terry concluded with authority. "Suck it long and hard, fellas."

Everyone groaned as he laid down his last card. I threw my cards down in mock disgust as he sat back in his chair and calmly sipped his whiskey.

"Son of a bastard," Zack said. "You'll rue this day, Terry."

"Doubtful."

"Yeah, I know," Zack accepted sadly.

"We'll get you back, Torino," I said. "One way or another."

"Okay, I should probably get running," Alex said. "Workie workie."

Zack looked at his cell phone and groaned again.

"Yeah," he agreed. "I better head out too."

"Balls!" Terry exclaimed. He finished the last of his glass and wiped his face with the back of a hand. "I guess since you poor losers are all taking off, I might as well leave too."

"All right," I said. "So I'll see you all tomorrow night at the Boulder House, yeah? Pierogies and pizza?"

Everyone agreed as they collected their things and migrated slowly through the house. I walked with them to the front porch and hugged them each in succession.

"You need a ride, Terry?" Zack asked.

"Nah," Terry answered. "Not a far walk."

"All right. Don't piss on any homeless people on the way home."

"No promises."

2

I woke to the urgent beeping of my alarm clock. Disoriented and confused, I slapped blindly at the noise until it stopped, then glared stupidly at the offending device until I remembered what it was. As my consciousness slowly returned, I managed to decipher its strange numeric symbols and determine that I should have left for work five minutes prior to waking up.

"Shit."

I crawled out of bed, stumbled to the bathroom, and gargled mouthwash as I urinated, which was a multitasking method I learned from the Internet. I continued to gargle as I got dressed, then spit, made my way outside, and ran to the bus stop. I checked my watch with growing anxiety throughout the bus ride, the short walk to my building, and the painfully slow elevator ride up to my floor, but my hopes of slipping unnoticed into my cubicle were dashed when the doors finally opened. A huge gaggle of people, apparently my entire department, had gathered in the common area between the cubicles and the elevators. I tried to act casual as I joined the group and sought out my friend Erin. I spotted her near our cluster of cubicles and made my way over to her.

"Hey," I said. "I know I'm five minutes late, but what the hell is going on?"

"Eh, I'm not sure yet," she shrugged. "I guess management called for some sort of meeting. We're probably all going to get fired or something. Executed by firing squad, maybe."

"Yeah, sounds about right."

I scanned the crowd.

"Where's Todd?" I asked.

"Sick. Flu."

I eyed her and wondered for a moment if she was serious. I had only found out about the flu the night before, and suddenly Todd had come down with it?

Erin was focused toward the front of the crowd but met my gaze when she realized I was looking at her.

"What?" she asked.

"Todd is sick?"

She began to answer but a loud and authoritative voice interrupted her.

"Morning, everybody!" a voice called out.

Erin nodded quickly to confirm what she had said, then looked for the source of the voice. I joined in the search and spotted the face of Dickson Laugherty, our group manager.

"Thank you all for coming in," he said. "Now that everyone is here, I have some news to discuss with you. I'm sure all of you are aware by now of the South American flu, a.k.a. the Brazilian flu. Now, as with the swine and bird flu viruses, we have some informational pamphlets ready to hand out to you. But unlike before, we've been advised by several sources to take some additional safety measures. Those of us in management have thought long and hard about this, and in light of how serious this flu seems to be, we've decided to temporarily reduce working hours. We're going to run on a skeleton crew until this blows over to help cut down on the possibility of infection."

The group fell silent.

"Don't worry," he continued. "No one is getting laid off. The Centers for Disease Control and Prevention is recommending this sort of thing for all large offices, and we've come to the conclusion that this course of action is in everyone's best interest. I understand money may be tight for some of you, but rest assured that this will be over soon enough. Once things are back to normal, we'll have some catching up to do. You can talk with Brenda about makeup time. And before anyone gets worried, this will not affect your benefits."

Dickson turned and nodded to Lindsay, his secretary, who picked up a box and stepped forward to stand beside him.

He reached into the box as he spoke.

"In addition to the pamphlets, everyone gets one complimentary bottle of hand sanitizer and one of these fashionable masks."

He held up a surgical mask with a smiley face on it.

The crowd groaned.

"I know, I know," Dickson said. "But our Asian counterparts wear them all the time, and I can't recommend them highly enough for safety. So, Lindsay is going to leave this box on the table here. Just take one for now, and if there are extras later, feel free to take more as needed. We'll have a few more boxes set out this week."

He whispered something to Lindsay, then continued, "You'll find your amended schedules on the bulletin board. Those of you not scheduled for today, please enjoy your day off and we'll see you tomorrow. And as always, make every day a productive day."

I rolled my eyes and looked over at Erin, who made a jackoff motion with her hand. We moved along with the crowd as it surged toward the board.

"The boss man hates me," I said. "I guarantee I'm going to get cut down to zero hours."

"Hey, at least you'll still have health insurance," she said.

"Yeah, I guess. And hand sanitizer."

"And a sweet mask."

"I'll treasure that especially," I said. "Man, this whole thing is stupid."

"I hope so."

We fell silent as we drew nearer to the bulletin board and searched for our schedules. Erin caught sight of her name and schedule first.

"Hey!" she exclaimed as she read it. "I'm off! That's f—" She paused as Dickson brushed past, and she remained silent until he was beyond hearing distance. "Awesome," she finished.

"Nice," I said. I kept looking until I found my schedule. "Balls, I work today. Oh, but I get a four-day weekend!"

"Sweet."

"Ah, shit," I heard Chuck say from beside me. "I work this whole week."

"Why is that bad?" I asked. "You'll have a hell of a stretch of days off!"

"My daughter's school closed this morning. My mom is watching her today, but she's coming down with a cold and doesn't want to give it to Sara, so I don't know what I'm going to do with her. She can't be by herself."

I started to respond but hesitated as I processed what Chuck had said. Schools were closing too? My mind jumped to my sister and her daughter, who lived south of the city.

"How old is she?" Erin asked.

"Six."

"Oh yeah," she said. "Still a little too young. Poor kiddo."

"Which schools are shutting down?" I asked.

"I'm pretty sure they all are," Chuck responded. "All schools and preschools, I think."

"Shit," I said, and made a mental note to call my sister. "Well, good luck, man."

"Thanks," he said. "Well, I'm gonna go get started. Catch ya later. Bye, Erin."

"Adios, Chuck," she said, then turned to me. "All right, I'm going to head home. I'll see you when this blows over, eh?"

"I guess so," I said. "Stay safe."

I forgot to ask again about Todd.

3

The workday went smoothly enough, but without Erin or Todd to talk to, it seemed to last forever. I managed to avoid Dickson for the rest of the day, though I'm not sure if I was lucky or if he just left after the group meeting. It didn't matter either way. I was three blocks away from the building by the time the clock hit five, and since there was much less traffic than normal, I managed to get home earlier than usual. I dialed Terry as I entered my house through the front doors. As the phone rang, I made my way to the kitchen and grabbed a beer from the fridge. Terry answered after a few rings.

"Hello?" he croaked.

"Hey, dude! You all right? What's up?"

"Eh, not much. Slowly dying."

"Aw, shit," I said. "So it's more than just allergies?"

"I don't know what it is, but I'm not enjoying myself. I'm not going to be able to come out tonight. I already talked to Alex. I guess he's out, too."

"Seriously? Is he sick too?"

"No, he just can't afford to take more time off and doesn't want to risk coming down with the bubonic plague."

"Shit," I said. "My company cut down on hours today. They even handed out medical masks to everyone. Is it really as bad as it's starting to look?"

"You know, if you checked the news more than once a decade or had normal conversations about current events, you would have seen this coming. You should consider picking up a newspaper or checking out a friggin' weekend special or something."

"It's the flu, dude," I retorted. "At the worst, you have the equivalent of the bird flu or swine flu, which infected like six people combined in the

United States. I'll bet all my money on the regular flu, which is easily treated with more whiskey."

"Eh," he said. "I'm definitely out. I'm gonna chug a bunch of water, take some PM pills, and sleep until I'm better. You could try to convince Alex and Zack."

I sighed.

"Yeah," I said. "Maybe I'll give them a call. Shit."

"Sorry, dude."

"Nah, it's cool. Get better, man. I'll buy you a beer or three when you do."

"I'll take you up on that offer as soon as I stop feeling like a raccoon took a shit on my vital organs."

"Excellent. All right, well, sleep tight for now. Call me up when you're not dead."

"Will do, definitely. Talk to you later."

"See ya."

I hung up the phone and tossed it across the couch, then grabbed the remote and turned on the TV.

"Fine," I said to no one, "I'll check the news."

The TV blared to life, and I was greeted by a sweaty, bulging athlete who was preoccupied with fighting a fiery demon of some sort.

"—hard and play harder!" a narrator screamed. "This is the deodorant that will—"

I hit the mute button and changed the channel, searched until I found a news station, then unmuted it.

"Two decapitated bodies were found in an abandoned SUV in a parking lot in East LA, where authorities say they could have remained undiscovered for days before being reported."

"Ffffffuuuuuuuuuuuuuuck," I muttered. "How do you even decapitate two bodies in a car?"

"The identities of the two victims are still unknown, and police are investigating possible gang ties. In international news, the World Health Organization has officially reclassified the South American flu from its previous state as an epidemic to a pandemic. Cases of the illness have now been reported in more than twenty countries, and efforts to stem the spread of the infection appear to be ineffective thus far. Raoul Escobar of the WHO spoke with reporters earlier today at a press conference in Madrid."

The camera cut to a shot of a chubby, stern-looking man in a dark-gray suit. I vaguely recalled his face, though I wasn't entirely sure. He seemed strained and tense as he stood at a podium and waited for the low din of the audience to fade. The video skipped slightly to footage of him speaking.

"While the symptoms of the so-called South American flu have so far only mimicked classic flu symptoms, the spread of the virus and its resistance to treatment has caused significant concern. As usual, the elderly and the very young are the most at risk, but we advise all individuals to take extra precautions, to avoid crowded places, and maintain strict personal hygiene. Frequent use of disinfectant is highly recommended, as well as the use of medical masks to avoid contamination."

The camera cut back to the reporter, who blinked several times before speaking.

"Many local schools, afterschool programs, and day care centers are closing temporarily due to the large number of cases reported in the area. Flu shots are available for the young and the elderly, as well as other high-risk individuals. All others are encouraged to contact their local doctors and add their names to the statewide waiting list for vaccinations. For more information on both access to flu vaccinations and a complete list of school closings, please visit our website at Burgh news dot—"

My cell phone rang from the other side of couch. I grabbed it and muted the TV again as I picked up.

"What's up, sis?"

"What's happening, Paulie?"

"Not much. Watching the news, trying to hold down my beer. The world is a scary place apparently. South American flu is the new big thing."

"Yeah, you're not kidding. I think I got it."

"What?" I responded. "Are you serious? Like, the actual South American flu?"

"Well, I'm experiencing flu-like symptoms," she replied, "so that's my guess, yeah."

"Shit. How's Kaylee? Is she sick too?"

"No, she's fine. But her day care closed today. They used the word 'indefinitely,' so I'm not sure what I'm gonna do with her."

"Are you still working?"

"I don't think so, no. I'll probably take some time off if our office doesn't close, but I don't want her to get it from me."

"Ah, right. What about Mom and Dad? God knows they'd love to spoil her for a few days."

"Well, Mom twisted her ankle last week, so I don't think she'd be up to it—"

"Oh yeah," I said. "I forgot."

"—and Dad's on some sort of business trip until Monday."

"Shit, forgot about that too."

"Yeah," she said. "So I'm kind of in a bind."

I hesitated. I loved the kid, but I was never a fan of being a babysitter, especially on weekends and days off. I valued my freedom too much. Aside from my bouts of semi-voluntary abstinence, freedom was a huge part of why I didn't have any kids. Still, if I could help Shelly out . . .

"I can babysit her later this week, if you need," I said.

"Huh? Aren't you working?"

"Nah," I said. "Bad news, good news. The bad news is that my company is cutting down hours because of the flu. The good news is that I have a four-day weekend to get drunk and neglect your child."

She laughed. "I'm glad you can spare some time for neglect."

"Of course! But yeah, I'm off Thursday and Friday, so I can pick her up Wednesday night or something. And I can watch her until Sunday night, if you need. I work again Monday, but I could maybe drop her off somewhere else."

"Oh God, that would be awesome. Thank you so much, Paulie. That takes such a load off."

"No problemo. I got your back, Sheesha."

"Sheesha?" She snorted. "Damn your nicknames, Paul!"

I laughed.

"Yeah, sorry," I said. "Anyway, I gotcha. Let me know when and where ya need me, and we'll go from there."

"Okay. I'm going to start calling around and get this figured out as soon as I can, so I'll keep you posted."

"All right. I'll be here."

"Okay. Thanks again, Paulie."

"Not a prob, sis. Get better soon."

"I'll try. I'll talk to you soon. Love ya."

"Love ya."

I hung up, tossed the phone back across the couch, and unmuted the television.

"—smell like a man's man and a woman's dream so you can work hard and play harder. This is the deodorant—"

I shut off the TV.

4

At first, I enjoyed the relative quiet of the nearly abandoned office. Without the typical distractions, I managed to get into a bit of a groove and power through more work than usual. Still, and despite the reduction in income, I was excited by the prospect of a four-day weekend. As time dragged on, I became more uncomfortable with the ghost town that the office had become. When Wednesday finally rolled around, I was ready to escape to my own home and relax; I just hoped Kaylee would let me.

A friend of Shelly's dropped Kaylee off around nine o'clock on Wednesday, and the possibility of a peaceful night seemed likely. She had spent the afternoon and evening playing with a few other kids, so she was ready for bed by the time she arrived at my house. I started up a movie for her in the guest room, made sure she brushed her teeth, then laid her down around ten. She was asleep before I shut the door behind me. I had already settled into a comfortable spot on the couch when Shelly called. I stuck a thumb in the book I'd been reading and closed my eyes as I spoke.

"Yellow," I said.

"Hi, Paul."

"How's it going, Shells?"

"I'm okay. How about yourself?"

"Not too bad, doing a bit of reading. Kaylee is already passed out."

There was a long pause on the other end.

"She's asleep?" she asked.

My eyes opened, and I hesitated to answer; in only two words, Shelly suddenly sounded furious. Something was wrong. I sat up.

"Yeah, she was pretty tuckered out," I said finally. "Why, what's wrong?"

"Oh, nothing," she said, her tone no less acidic. "I just figured I could talk to my fucking daughter, that's all."

"Oookaaay," I said, drawing the word out. "Well . . . I can wake her up, if you like."

There was another pause during which I suspected that she had realized the ridiculousness of her hostility.

"No, no. Let her fucking sleep," she said.

I waited for her to say more but was met with nothing but silence.

"Is something wrong?" I asked.

"Nope."

"You sure about that?"

"Yep."

"Mmhmm," I said, nodding. "Okay."

I cradled the phone between my head and shoulder as I shifted into a sitting position, then replaced my thumb in the book with the illegible strip of paper I used as a bookmark. Shelly remained silent as I set the book down, took a deep breath, and sat back.

"All right, sis," I said. "Talk to me—"

A loud crack sounded through the phone. Reflexively, I jerked away and let the phone fall to the couch, then picked it back up and listened. I heard a few seconds of scrabbling, followed by silence.

"Shelly?"

"Yes?" she responded.

She sounded strangely indignant, even malicious.

"What . . ." I started. "Did you drop your phone?"

"Nope."

"Did you . . . throw it?" I asked, only half-kidding.

"Yep," she said matter-of-factly.

"What are you, five?" I snorted. "What the fuck is wrong with you?"

There were a few seconds of silence before she answered.

"Paul?"

"Yeah?" I responded.

"Fuck," she said, and paused for effect, "you."

The line went silent, and I listened for a full five seconds before realizing she had hung up on me. I looked incredulously at the phone and had almost laid it down when it beeped with the receipt of a text message from Shelly. It read,

go kill urself

"What . . .?" I said aloud.

I closed out of the text and held in Shelly's speed dial until it started to ring. As I waited for her to pick up, I wondered what the hell could have been going on. PMS? PCP? Bath salts? I decided to give up on speculation and wait for her to give me some semblance of an explanation, but her voicemail picked up. When I hung up and dialed her again, it went directly to voicemail without even ringing. I set the phone on the table and stared at it, still half-expecting another text or call with an apology, an explanation, or a continuation of her ridiculous behavior . . . something. When a few minutes passed and nothing else happened, I got up, grabbed another beer, then thought twice and retrieved an extra before I sat back down and reopened the book.

5

After Shelly's unexpected outburst, I was nervous about talking with her or allowing her to talk to her daughter. As a result, I spent a good portion of the next day trying to distract Kaylee from thinking about her mother. Aside from a trip to the park, most of the mixed success I had was due to her keen interest in the various zombie paraphernalia littered throughout the house.

"What's that?" she asked.

She was pointing at a picture hanging on the wall. It was a still frame from the first zombie movie I had ever seen.

"That's a man who fights zombies," I said.

"What's the thing on his arm?"

"That's a chainsaw."

"Why does he got a chainsaw?"

"Uh . . ." I hesitated. "For cutting down trees, silly."

"Why does he have to cut down trees?"

"So he can build forts to keep the zombies out."

"Oohh," she said, apparently satisfied with my answer. She pointed to an action figure that stood foremost among many others in a china cabinet.

"Is that him too?"

"Yup," I said, cringing slightly.

"What is he holding?"

"Uh . . ."

"It looks like a face."

"Uh, yeah," I said in faux surprise. "That looks like a zombie's head."

"How come he is holding onto a zombie's head?"

"I guess he found it," I said, grasping for explanations.

"Oh," she said. "Did the zombie die?"

"Uh, no . . ." I said. "Zombies are pretty tough."

"Oh," she said, and wiped her nose on her sleeve. "Okay."

"You need a tissue?"

"No, I'm okay."

"Hmm," I said. "I think I'll get one for you. You don't want to have boogers all over your shirt, do you?"

She looked thoughtfully down at her sleeve, as if imagining what it would look like if covered in mucus.

"I guess not," she concluded.

"Okay."

I walked upstairs and grabbed a box of tissues from the bathroom. As I made my way back down, her voice wafted up the stairwell.

"I can't hear you, kiddo," I said.

She didn't respond, and only as I entered the room did I realize that she was talking on my phone.

"Yeah, okay," she said, holding the phone to her ear with both hands. "Uncle Paulie is teaching me about zombies."

I set the box of tissues beside her as she continued to talk.

"Um, we went to the park. I played on the swing set. Uncle Paulie played too."

I walked to the kitchen to grab a beer, then shook my head and filled the electric tea kettle instead.

"There was a man who was being mean to his doggy," she continued. "He was hitting it. Uncle Paulie took me to the car, and he went up to the man and the man left."

I waited for the water to boil as I listened.

"Okay," she said. "Okay. Bye. I love you, Mommy. Bye."

The phone clattered on the coffee table as she laid it down.

"Kaylee," I called out. "Was that your mom on the phone?"

"Yeah," she responded.

"Is she feeling better?" I asked.

"Yeah," she answered. "She told me to listen to you while you're watching me."

"Oh, okay," I said, and peeked my head in the living room. "I guess that means you can't tickle me anymore, huh?"

She giggled.

"I'm not gonna tickle you!" she said.

"Oh yeah? Well, maybe I'll tickle you!"

She squealed and ran. I roared monstrously and gave chase through the hall toward the stairs.

"I am the tickle zombie!" I yelled.

She continued to squeal at an unthinkable pitch as she accelerated up the stairs and I roared again as I stomped up after her. I stopped at the top of the stairwell and watched her run into the guest room, still screaming even as she closed the door behind her. I trotted across the floor on all fours with all the grace of a drunken cow and knocked gently on the door.

"Yes?" she answered from behind the door.

"Can I come in?" I said in my friendliest monster voice.

"No!" she said.

"Pleeeaaase?" I asked. "I wanna . . . have a tea party."

"No!" she said again, the word edged on both sides by giggles.

I reached up, turned the doorknob, and started to push. It gave slightly, then she started pushing back.

"Nooooo!" she screamed.

I continued to push, and her feet slid on the carpeted floor even as she placed her whole weight against the door.

"I just wanna play dollhouse," I said as I reached an arm in toward her through the door opening. "And do cartwheels . . . and maybe . . . tickle you!"

I fell into the room as she abandoned the door entirely and ran for the closet.

"You'll never escape!" I roared. "I'm gonna tickle you forever! And then—"

I stopped and made a shocked "O" shape with my lips as she pulled a foam sword out of the closet.

"Uh-oh."

I turned and clomped away, but there was no escape. I collapsed helplessly beneath a ceaseless barrage of slaps and shrieks as she wrought a swift and just vengeance.

L. Marshall James

6

A whistling ringtone infiltrated, then interrupted my dreams. I blinked at the glow of the screen in the darkness of my room, picked up the cell phone, and accepted the call without bothering to check the caller. If it were Shelly on the other end, maybe she had rediscovered sanity.

"Hello," I mumbled.

"Paul, tell me you've seen the news."

In the residual haze of deep sleep, I tried to place the voice. "Alex?" I queried.

"Tell me you've seen the news," he repeated.

I rubbed at my eyes and tried to stamp down a tinge of annoyance. "What news?"

"The"—he sighed—"the fucking news, Paul. For fuck's sake."

My annoyance was replaced by dull fear from the tension in his words and the silence that followed them. "What's wrong?"

"Turn on the TV, check the news, and call me back in ten minutes. Okay?"

"What's going on?" I asked.

When I heard nothing else, I squinted at the phone. He had already hung up.

"What the hell?"

I pushed to my feet and stumbled toward the stairs, took a detour to the bathroom, then continued down to the living room. I made a beeline for the couch, turned on the TV as I sat down, and switched through the channels until I spotted a newscaster.

"—you, Brandy. Ladies and gentlemen, the footage we are about to show may not be suitable for immature audiences, as it contains graphic violence. We strongly recommend that any children leave the room immediately."

The anchor stared blankly for an awkwardly long period of time before the screen cut abruptly to what appeared to be a helicopter view of several city blocks that were thick with movement. Masses of people swarmed in the streets, smoke poured from buildings, and cars burned amid the flashing lights of police cars and ambulances. At first, I thought a riot had grown out of control, but as the camera zoomed in, an element of serious violence became apparent. The mobs weren't just destroying public property and flipping vehicles; they were fighting among themselves. People in the crowds tore and beat at each other, even as smoke and tear gas floated around them. One man raised something—a pipe or a crowbar—high over his head and brought it down on what appeared to be a body lying prone in the street. Several people pulled on the legs of someone who was holding desperately onto something inside a vehicle, even as fire raged under the hood. In the middle of a street was a massive pile of bodies that at first appeared to be composed of corpses. Upon closer inspection, I noticed movement; each of the bodies moved, clawed, and punched wildly.

The feed cut back to the news anchor, whose gaze was lost somewhere behind the cameraman. In the silence of the broadcast, an insistent whisper rose and grew louder before culminating in a single yell that recaptured the reporter's attention. He returned his focus to the camera and took a deep breath before speaking.

"Ladies and gentlemen, that was genuine footage recently captured in San Antonio, Texas. This is not the only location of such an occurrence. What at first appeared to be spontaneous, isolated riots are now being reported in many cities in the United States and numerous other countries. These riots, for which there is currently no official explanation, have become increasingly violent, resulting in catastrophic damages and death all over the world. Though communication with our worldwide correspondents has become sporadic, death toll reports range from the thousands to the hundreds of thousands to the millions."

He paused, took a deep breath, and continued.

"Though the cause is still uncertain, it seems clear that the riots are in some way related to the South American flu that has quickly spread across the globe and recently attained pandemic status. Authorities recommend at this time that you remain in your homes. If you witness any unexplained violence, please call 911 immediately. Avoid—"

The cell phone rang, and I flinched, then answered the call and held it to my ear as the broadcast continued.

"Alex?" I said.

"Yeah."

I took a deep breath.

"Look, I don't want to sound stupid, but . . . the footage I just saw . . ."

"I know," he said.

"It looks like . . ."

"I know."

I couldn't bring myself to say what I was thinking. I felt wide-awake, but I couldn't help but think that I was dreaming. It had to be a hoax or a practical joke.

"I saw a fight today between a cook and some girl in a diner," he said. "And someone was murdered today. I saw them die."

The intensity and quaver of his voice told me that it was not a joke. I fell silent as I tried to process what he was saying and what it meant. He continued before I could think of a response.

"I was sitting at a red light, and I spotted this guy on the side of the street, walking like he had an ass to kick, yelling shit. I couldn't tell what he was talking about, but he was pissed off about something. He stopped at the corner and waited for the light to change, but the longer he waited, the angrier he seemed to get, until he just snapped. He just . . . walked into traffic. Toward the oncoming vehicles, like he wanted to pick a fight. He just . . ."

He trailed off.

I didn't need to know exactly how the story ended to know what it meant: the chaos depicted on the news had already reached Pittsburgh.

"We have to leave," he said.

I started to agree, then stopped.

"Shit. I can't," I said.

"What? Why?"

"Kaylee is here."

"Who?"

"My niece."

"Why?"

"My sister's sick."

The realization hit me like ice water.

"Oh God."

"She has the flu?"

"Oh God. I have to call her."

"Paul—"

"I'll call you back," I said, then hung up.

I brought Shelly up on speed dial and listened with dread as it rang five, six, then seven times before going to voicemail. Two redials yielded the same result. I held my head in my hands and tried to organize my thoughts. Shelly wasn't picking up. When I talked to her last, she had been not only sick but also oddly and unreasonably hostile. I couldn't remember her ever acting like that. Not since we were kids, probably.

My mom and dad popped into my head, so I dialed their number and waited. When the voicemail picked up, I hung up and tried again. Voicemail. I left a message.

"Hey, Mom, Dad. It's Paul. Uh, call me as soon as you can, okay? I . . . it's important. Love you. Bye."

I hung up and stared down at the phone for a moment before dialing Alex.

He picked up on the first ring.

"Okay," I said. "We leave in the morning. Get packing."

"Okay. Where should we meet?"

"Uh, shit," I said. "Where are we going?"

"I don't know."

A rush of calm flooded my mind. In my infatuation with all things zombie, I had prepared for this. I knew what to do.

"Okay," I said. "We can head to my parents' house. It's pretty secluded, about thirty miles north of the city."

"Thirty miles?"

"We can make it," I said. "I've already figured it out."

Silence, then: "Okay. Should I come to your place? When?"

"Get here as soon as you can. I'll get my things ready in the meantime. When you get here, we'll figure the rest out. Don't bother packing too much. Bring only the bare essentials. Some clothes and something to defend yourself until you get here. I can give you whatever else you need."

"Okay."

"Should we call the guys?" I asked. "Have you talked to anyone?"

"I already tried them," he said. "No one is picking up."

I took a deep breath and willed myself to remain calm. They could still be okay.

"Okay," I said. "Pack up. Get your ass here. Hurry."

The phone fell silent. For a moment, I thought Alex had already hung up.

"Paul?" he said.

"Yeah?"

"Are we fucked?"

He wasn't asking me to comfort him; what he wanted was my honest assessment. Still, I had to contemplate my answer for longer than I was comfortable with. I had planned for this kind of emergency. I'd spent countless hours collecting supplies and scouring maps of Pittsburgh and the surrounding landscape for the best possible escape routes in the event of a zombie pandemic that would never happen. I had gone through so much planning, but I realized suddenly that I hadn't really given it my due diligence. I had never taken survival classes, read up on how to survive in the wilderness without a food supply, taken weapons training, or bothered to keep myself in prime mental and physical condition. I had never gone to the effort of renting a house outside the city limits instead of where I was or considered whether I could really protect a child if I had to. I had always assumed that I would be alone and that it would be me against the horde until I found a stronghold. Planning out strategies for the zombie apocalypse had been a game, something to amuse myself and give me something to do. Compared to actual survival strategies, my efforts were a joke. We were fucked.

"Nah," I said. "We're fine. But hurry."

L. Marshall James

7

I killed the TV and returned to my room. I had already prepared a "go bag" filled with camping and survival supplies, just in case I ever had to leave in a hurry. The bag was stocked, but I checked it anyway to make sure I had what I thought I'd need. It had all the basics of camping: tarps, a sleep sack, cooking materials, a water purifier, and various other essentials I had used on countless hiking and camping trips.

Beyond that, I had the weapons and equipment we would almost certainly need. As far as firearms, I had a 9 mm pistol and a pistol grip shotgun with a collapsible stock for myself, as well as two spare pistols for whoever needed them. In addition to the guns, I had two kukris, which are like heavy-duty machetes but with inwardly curving blades. One of the kukris, which boasted a wooden handle and a leather sheath, was my chosen melee weapon. Alex could have the other, which was still a formidable weapon despite its cheaper construction.

Aside from the weapons and supplies, I had a couple of tricks I had thought up awhile back. The first involved a few small, cheap air horns and some zip ties. The idea was to tighten a zip tie around the trigger of one of the horns, then throw it. With any luck, the blare of the horn would attract the undead and allow me to slip past them undetected. It was a half-assed idea conceived in a whiskey-induced haze, and I had never expected to use it, but recent events dictated the horns might be of some use. I strapped them to the side of my pack and pocketed some of the zip ties.

The second idea, which seemed a bit more practical, was a folding slingshot. I figured that at the very least, I could use it to fire rocks or ball bearings to distract the infected. It could also be used as a last-ditch weapon, though I hoped my situation never became that desperate.

I checked, then double- and triple-checked my things. Once I was satisfied, I set out an extra hiking pack and spread out a bevy of supplies on the floor for Alex to choose from when he arrived. I wouldn't make Kaylee carry anything. She'd be stressed enough as it was unless I somehow convinced her that it was only a game or a camping expedition.

I looked down at the weapons spread out across the bed and shook my head. Game? Camping expedition? Not even a four-year-old would buy that. But really, all that mattered was that I could get her safely out of the city.

A loud bang came from outside. It seemed to come from the alley between my house and the next, but I couldn't be certain whether the source was in the alley, the street, or my backyard. I turned off the bedroom light, moved to the window, and looked down. I couldn't see anything, but there seemed to be more noise coming from the street.

I grabbed my pistol and slid a magazine in, then loaded a round and decocked the hammer so that I couldn't accidentally fire a round. No need to get too antsy. Not yet. I made my way down the hall and peeked out the front window. At first I couldn't identify anything that was wrong, but something seemed to be amiss. The noises I'd heard had since gone quiet but had been replaced by another noise, faint but continuous. I eased the window open, rested my ear beside the gap, and listened. After a few seconds, I realized the source of the sounds and my confusion gave way to alarm. Somewhere in the distance, several sirens wailed in and out of sync. Some were police sirens, and others were ambulance sirens.

I started to pull the window shut but stopped at what sounded like a scream from the street accompanied by the faint slap of shoes on concrete. I looked again, and a man crossed into my line of sight. He was running in a dead sprint, and it was clear that he was running from something. Before I could discern what was chasing him, something flipped end over end through the air behind him and hit the back of his head with a dull thud. The object clattered to the asphalt as the man went limp, collapsed face-first, and did not move.

I turned and ran down the hall to the stairs, held the banister with one hand as I leaped down three and four steps at a time, and rushed to the front doors. I opened each of the front doors in succession, ran out to the porch, and skidded to a stop.

The man lay in the street, unmoved and untouched. Beside him was what had hit him: a thick metal pipe. Less than ten feet away from him was a group of four people who stood facing each other as they exchanged blows. They said nothing as they fought. They were silent, aside from grunts of effort and the muffled thuds of fists on flesh. A helicopter flew low overhead, its searchlight off, perhaps a hundred feet from the ground. It quickly disappeared, and I wordlessly returned my focus to the scene in the street, unsure of what to do, if anything. A door slammed in or near the house adjacent to mine, but when I turned, nothing was there. As one man in the group collapsed amid frenzied blows to the head, I took a step back toward the outermost door.

Suddenly, the front door of the neighboring house swung open, and an older woman, Marge, stomped out onto her porch. The rollers in her hair bounced on her head as she stopped a few feet from her porch steps and glared at the still-brawling group, her hands on her hips. It was immediately apparent from her facial expression and her body language that she was furious. She didn't know the danger; I had to warn her.

"Marge!" I whispered as loudly as I dared. "Marge!"

She turned to me, and I held up a hand to wave her back into her home even as I looked back and forth between her and the scene in the street.

"Go back inside," I said. "Lock the—"

"Fuck you!" she exploded.

I started to reply, then stopped and stared at her.

"Fuck you!" she screamed again.

I stood there with the pistol in my hand and said nothing as she glared at me, her face twisted with contempt. I held out my empty hand to try and signal peaceful intent.

"Marge," I said again.

Her face contorted into something almost unrecognizable on her usually placid face, and she broke into a hobbling run toward me. A wavering growl escaped her lips, grew steadily louder, and fell abruptly silent when she impacted the porch railing and tumbled over it. Even as she fell, her eyes remained focused on me. Though I couldn't see her hit them, I heard the trash cans topple and scatter in the alleyway between our houses. I stepped quickly to my front door and grabbed the handle.

"Hey!" a voice sounded from the street, as much a roar as a yell.

I turned toward the source and fell back against the door. One man stood alone in the street, splattered with blood. He wore nothing but boxers and a tank top that hung from him by a few tattered threads. Littering the ground around him were the inert bodies of the others he'd been fighting. He stared at the alley where Marge had fallen. In one hand, he held the metal pipe.

"Fuck you, cocksucker!" she screamed.

"No," I whispered, too quiet to be heard. "No, Marge."

But I didn't move, even when he ran toward her, even when Marge's head rose into my line of sight, then disappeared briefly again as she ran at him. They collided at the edge of the street, and his greater momentum carried her back toward the alley where they fell out of my view onto the sidewalk. After a moment's scuffle, the bloodied pipe rose into view, then disappeared. She screamed, and it again swung into view and disappeared. Metal clanged on concrete, and he emitted a loud grunt, though I couldn't tell if it was of pain or effort.

A door creaked open across the street. An elderly man, probably in his sixties, emerged from his home with a double-barreled shotgun. He stopped at the railing of his porch and focused on Marge and the man as they continued fighting, unaware of his presence.

"Hey!" he yelled.

If they heard him, they didn't acknowledge it. I held my hands out toward the man and waved, desperate to get his attention but too afraid to call out. A gunshot would be heard for miles, but any noise risked attracting the attention of the two in the street.

"Hey!" he yelled again, louder.

When they continued to ignore him, he turned and walked down his porch steps. I ran to the edge of my porch. By the time I finally caught his attention, he had already reached the sidewalk. He squinted as I waved him back inside. He looked almost indignant.

"What in the hell is going on?" he screamed.

"I don't know," I mouthed.

I shook my head and continued to wave him off.

He glanced down at my pistol, then back at me. Finally, he turned and walked back onto his porch. As he did, a car turned onto our street with a squeal of rubber. I felt a touch of relief at what I saw: it was a police cruiser, its lights and sirens off. If the police were still in service, then maybe there was still hope.

The cruiser rode up onto the sidewalk to avoid the pile of bodies, then continued down the street and swung around the next corner without even slowing down. The old man's gaze shifted from the dark intersection back to me, his eyes wide. Abruptly, he looked toward the alleyway and lifted the shotgun to his shoulder.

"Stay back!" he yelled.

The man in the alley rose silently into my line of sight and walked with large, determined steps toward the old man, the pipe at his side. He had just stepped over one of the bodies in the middle of the street when the shotgun erupted and sent him flying back out of sight. In the ensuing silence, the old man turned, ran into his house, and slammed the door behind him. I turned to follow suit and gasped at the sight of Kaylee, who was standing in the hall just inside the doors. As casually as I could manage, I shoved the pistol into the back of my pants as I walked inside, closed the outermost door behind me, and locked the deadbolt.

"What's wrong, Uncle Paulie?"

"Nothing, honey," I said.

As I closed and locked the innermost door, another gun sounded off.

"What are all the loud noises?"

"Just fireworks, kiddo."

"Oh. Can I watch them?"

"No, not right now," I said. "They are too dangerous."

I walked to her and knelt down.

"You need to go back to bed, bugaboo."

I held out a hand. She grasped it, and I walked her at an agonizingly slow pace back up the stairs to the guest room. I knelt beside the bed as she climbed under the covers, then tucked the blankets around her as she settled in. She sniffled.

"Don't cry, kiddo. I'll take you to see fireworks another time, okay?"

"It's okay," she said. "I'm not crying."

A pang of fear struck me.

"Do you feel sick?" I asked.

She shook her head.

"Were any of the kids you played with yesterday sick?"

"I don't know," she said.

I put my hand on her forehead, but I couldn't tell if it felt any warmer than normal. I leaned over and kissed her on the forehead.

"You get some sleep, honey," I said. "Sweet dreams, okay?"

"Sweet dreams," she echoed.

L. Marshall James

8

I closed the door behind me and made my way downstairs to the back door. After making sure both locks were secured, I pulled a cabinet across the linoleum until it rested against the doorframe. It wasn't much of a barricade, but it was better than nothing. Hopefully, the back door wouldn't be much of a target. The front of the house, on the other hand, would almost surely be a problem. I walked to the front doors, unlocked the innermost of the two, and moved the bench that sat just inside the entryway until one end rested against the inside of the outermost door. Once I closed and locked the inner door, the space between the two doors and the bench was no more than a few inches. Anyone who tried to open the outer door would also be pressing against the bench and, in turn, the inner door. Since the doors and the bench were solidly constructed, the entryway was more or less impregnable without intense, sustained effort or machinery of some kind. That hardly mattered, though, since anyone who wanted to get in could just step ten feet to their left and break through the giant front window. At six feet wide and five feet tall, it was a gaping hole in the physical security of the home.

The sounds of another scuffle came from the street. I was hidden behind the blinds, but the close proximity of the noises still unsettled me. If anyone wanted to get inside the house, all they had to do was try. There was almost nothing I could do to stop them. Even if I had the supplies to build a proper barricade, they would hear me and attack well before I could manage to do so. The most I could do was try to quietly block the window off from the inside, lock the French doors that separated the front room from the hallway, and hope for the best.

My eyes settled on the entertainment center against the far wall. At around three and a half feet wide, it wouldn't quite span the window and would topple easily if someone made the effort to break the glass and press through, but if I managed to slide the thing into place without attracting attention, the house would be at least marginally safer. I stepped toward it, crouched by the side near the window, and listened.

Footsteps slapped the street, grew louder, then quieted again before disappearing altogether. A scream sounded from somewhere; it was quieter than the nearer voices, so it might have been one street down or maybe two. In the distance, various sirens continued to wail.

I wrapped each hand around a leg of the entertainment center, lifted enough to get them off the floor, and pulled. The other two legs scraped against the floor as I eased it slowly toward the window. With a few pauses to listen and peek out the blinds, I finally maneuvered the wooden bulk until it was centered more or less in the middle of the window. I took a step back and surveyed what I knew was a shitty barricade.

"Shit," I whispered. "We gotta get out of here."

Though I doubted it would work, I pulled out my cell phone and tried calling my sister again. When it beeped without ringing, I hung up and tried again.

"We're sorry," came a prerecorded message. "All circuits are busy at this time. Please try again later."

I hung up and dialed my parents' phone.

Beep.

"Fuck, fuck, fuck," I whispered.

"All right, calm down. Finish packing. Make sure everything is in order. Wait for Alex."

I walked to the hall, closed and locked the French doors, and returned to my bedroom upstairs. I stared uselessly at the equipment strewn about the room. There wasn't much I could do until Alex arrived.

Alex.

How would he get in? I'd blocked all the doors. Hopefully, he knew enough to go around back, but even if he did, the door was blocked off and the phones might not work. If someone followed him around back, I would need to open it and let him in quickly. I couldn't afford to have to pull the cabinet out of the way and unlock the door before letting him in; if he was being pursued, there wouldn't be time. I turned to head back downstairs and jumped at the sight of Kaylee. She looked up at me from the doorway, her hair matted and her face flush. She looked miserable.

"I don't feel very good," she said.

"Are you feeling sick?"

"I'm cold."

I knelt in front of her and noticed a sheen of sweat on her forehead. For her sake, I forced a smile.

"Well, you should stay under the blankets, silly-pants."

"They don't help."

Against the back of my hand, her forehead felt hot. Too hot.

"I'll go get some medicine. Do you want some water?"

She nodded.

"Okay. You go sit on the bed, and I'll bring you some water. Okay?"

She nodded again and walked back to the other room. I stood, grabbed a cup, walked into the bathroom, and filled it in the sink. I tried to hide my growing dread as I carried it to Kaylee and handed it to her. She sat slumped on the edge of the bed as she took the cup with both hands.

"Thank you," she said, her voice scratchy.

"No problem, kiddo. I'll go get some medicine, okay?"

She nodded and raised the cup to her lips. I turned and walked out of the room, then closed the door behind me and stared down at the end of the hall. There was nothing there but shadows. I closed my eyes and breathed deeply. Kaylee was not infected by whatever the people outside were sick with. She had something else. Anything else. She had the regular flu, the common cold. She would be fine.

"Medicine," I said aloud and opened my eyes.

In the bathroom, I found the cardboard box that served as my all-purpose medicinal container. I pulled it to the floor and scoured through it, tossing irrelevant items aside as I searched for something to fend off her fever. Half-empty bottles of generic painkillers, expired poison ivy gel, muscle rub . . . I sighed in relief at the sight of a half-empty bottle of cold and flu liquid medicine. I set it on the counter and continued searching. If we were going to travel thirty miles, we would need as much help as we could get. After a few more minutes, I found nothing else except for a mostly empty box of cold and flu pills. That would have to do until I found more. If I had to, I'd ransack a drugstore or raid a house. Kaylee would be taken care of. I would make sure of that.

She had finished almost all of the water by the time I returned with a measured dose of medicine, and she held what was left on her lap as I brought the small measuring cup to her lips. She drank some, then stopped and grimaced as she swallowed.

"I know it tastes bad, but it's good for you, okay? It will help make you feel better."

She nodded and swallowed the rest.

"Atta-girl. Now lie back down, okay? You need to get plenty of sleep."

With a nod, she lay back down.

"I'm too hot now," she croaked.

A few strands of hair stuck to her face. I pushed them away, then leaned over and kissed her on the forehead as I tried to think of some way to help her cool down.

"I'll go get a fan for you. That will help. I'll be right back, all right?"

"All right."

I grabbed a flashlight, then made my way down to the first floor. At first, I left the light off and tried to make as little noise as possible, mostly out of fear that something may have already sneaked inside. When I reached the bottom of the stairs, I listened for movement.

Silence.

I walked over to the closet under the stairwell, opened the door, and turned on the flashlight. Two box fans sat side by side next to a pair of ancient dumbbells and a pile of miscellaneous items. I pocketed the flashlight, grabbed each of the fans by the handles, and lifted them carefully from the floor. The dumbbells rolled and the pile shifted, clanked loudly, and settled back into silence. I froze and listened. It was unlikely that anyone outside heard anything, but I didn't want to take any chance.

After I heard nothing, I set the fans down at the bottom of the stairs, returned to the rear of the house, and pulled the cabinet away from the back door. It wouldn't be as safe without the barricade, but the lock would provide some defense and warning in the unlikely event that one of the crazies came around back and tried to work their way inside. It also wouldn't take much time to unlock it once Alex arrived. It was a risk worth taking.

Kaylee had already fallen back asleep by the time I returned with the fans. I set them up a few feet from her, plugged them in, and adjusted the knobs to the highest settings as they whirred to life. I walked back to my room and checked the time. 3:35 AM. I thought again of Alex. As far as I knew, he could arrive at any time but I was getting tired and our journey was going to be long and taxing. If I wasn't at the door to let him in when he arrived, he would be left outside with God only knew what else. Sleep would be too risky. I dialed his number and held the phone to my ear.

Beep.

"We're sorry. All cir—"

I hung up and walked to the window by Kaylee's bed, which overlooked the scant backyard. My mind raced to figure out what I needed to do. If I slept in the room with Kaylee, I would be in a good position to defend her if necessary and I would be able to hear Alex if he called out. But if Alex was being pursued, I had to be able to get to him in time. I made my way back downstairs, found a marker, and scrawled on a sheet of paper: BACK DOOR.

I taped the note in the small window of the outermost front door, then returned to the back door and hesitantly unlocked it. If Alex needed to get in fast, he could get in and lock the door behind him. As long as I heard him, I would most likely be able to make it to him in time to help barricade the door against any pursuers. The chances of someone breaking in were greater than before but still not high. My house was only one among hundreds and thousands of others. If it gave Alex a greater chance of survival, I was willing to take the risk.

I grabbed an armful of blankets and pillows and laid them in a pile below the window at the foot of Kaylee's bed. For a few minutes, I stood in the darkness and watched her sleep. I had known her since the day she was born, and in all the time since then, the only emotions I had ever felt for her were love and fear. But as powerful and valid as my fears had seemed before, they were suddenly faint, meaningless, and irrelevant. I tried to override the feeling of creeping dread as I lay down, closed my eyes, and fell into a shallow sleep.

9

I jerked awake, pushed myself into a sitting position, and pressed my back against the wall. It was quiet. Rays of sunlight streamed in through the blinds of the window on the other side of the room. On any normal weekend, that would have been a good thing; it might have indicated pleasant weather. On this morning, the weather didn't matter. My nightmares faded immediately from memory as I emerged into consciousness, leaving behind only the familiar residue of fear. I wondered how much of what I remembered of the previous night had been true and how much had been purely imaginary. I glanced over at Kaylee, then down at the pistol in my hand.

Fuck.

I made my way out into the hall and surveyed my room from the doorway. Yes, that part of the last night had actually happened. I had definitely begun packing for a hasty exit from the city. As for the zombie apocalypse . . .

I stepped back over to Kaylee's door and peered in. She was still sleeping; I had no intention of changing that. I quietly closed the door, and as I walked through the hall to the front window, I tried to reconcile my surreal memories of the previous day and night with how normal the world seemed in the quiet of my house. More likely than a zombie apocalypse, it seemed entirely possible that I had suffered a mental breakdown. It happens. Nothing to be ashamed of, though explaining it could be difficult.

Yes, Shelly, I had an episode and starting packing for a zombie apocalypse while Kaylee was sleeping. Yes, I loaded all my weapons and set them in a place where she could easily access them. Yes, I agree that I need to see a doctor, a psychologist, or both.

I stopped a few feet from the front window and listened closely for any noises that seemed out of the ordinary: a siren, a scream, a gunshot. But I heard nothing. It was like any normal day. Still, I hesitated to pull back the curtain because I was afraid to see what I felt increasingly certain I would: chaos, blood, and gore. All I wanted to see was an empty street with the occasional passing car, the postman begrudgingly delivering junk mail, and Marge smoking pot on her porch like it was legal. Sure, it would mean I might have fallen off my rocker, but that would be okay; at least it would mean the world hadn't.

I took the last few steps to the window and carefully peeked out from behind the curtain. Bodies littered the street. Some were badly mutilated, others slightly less so. As far as I could tell, they were all dead. That settled that.

I checked my phone to see if anyone had called, then checked it again for the time. 8:15 AM. Shit. I grabbed the pistol from my room and started to walk out, then thought twice and hid the other weapons on the uppermost shelf of the closet before heading downstairs. With the pistol gripped in both hands, I made my way to the back door.

Slowly and carefully, I looked through the blinds of the rear window. The backyard area looked completely unchanged. Nothing out of place. No new, decomposing lawn ornaments. I opened the door a crack, then all the way and stood in the doorway, pistol at the ready as I scanned the bushes at the back edge of the yard for any glimpse of cloth or skin.

"Alex!" I whispered.

After a few seconds passed with no response, I whispered his name again. When I still heard nothing, I descended the steps and looked down through the row of backyards in both directions. Nothing stood out, and aside from a few scattered bangs and screams in the distance, there was no noise. I eased over to the corner of the house and looked through the alleyway toward the street. Marge's body was lying in a heap on the sidewalk, right as it had been the night before. Though I was a good distance away, I could tell that the top of her head was caved in and surrounded by a massive puddle of blood. I looked away when I realized I was staring at it. No point in dwelling on the dead.

I sneaked over to the bushes in the back of the yard and looked behind them with the hope that Alex was simply asleep and hadn't heard me. No dice. Just grass, dirt, and a pile of dog shit.

I went back inside and sat down on the couch, then set the pistol down on my lap and turned on the TV to see a black screen. I changed the channel, but it made no difference. As I shut it off, I wondered briefly if the Internet was still working, then concluded that it didn't matter much and it wouldn't change much if it was. I needed to get out of Pittsburgh. Nothing would change that.

After trying Alex's number again, I sat and lost my mind in thought for a while, only rousing when the sound of tiny footsteps caught my attention. Kaylee padded into the room in her flower pajamas and stopped in front of the coffee table to look at me. I wondered for a moment how she was coping, then remembered that she still had no idea. I sat forward and laid an arm across my lap to conceal the pistol.

"Hey, kiddo. Are you feeling better?"

She shook her head.

"Do you want some water?"

She nodded.

As I stood, I slid the pistol around my side, then tucked it into the back of my pants as I walked to the kitchen. I grabbed a glass from the cabinet and tried to think of some way to explain why we had to leave when Alex arrived. It was still too early to explain to her what had happened, but she was going to find out the truth sooner or later, regardless of my efforts to protect her from the awful reality of the situation. The best I could hope was that she was able to adapt, but for the time being, my priority was simple: survival.

"Go ahead and sit down, honey," I said as I filled the glass. "I'll bring the water to you and get you some medicine."

"Okay," she replied.

I winced. Her throat sounded painfully dry. When I walked in with the glass of water, she was sitting on the edge of the couch, staring at the floor. When I held the glass out in front of her, she did not stir.

"Here you go, honey," I said.

She looked up, then grabbed the glass with both hands and drank deeply. In under a minute, she drank half the water, took a breath, then drank the rest and sat back with the empty glass set in her lap.

"Wow," I said. "You must have been pretty thirsty, huh?"

She nodded.

"I'll get you some more here in a minute, but I'll get some medicine first."

After I'd poured out a serving of medicine, I searched the cabinets again for anything else to fend off her sickness or her fever. There was nothing else. When I returned with the dose, I stood in the doorless frame separating the hall from the living room.

I had hoped she would have found something to do by the time I came back. Maybe she would be fiddling with the TV remote, coloring, or doing cartwheels. Instead, she looked exactly as she had when I left to get the medicine. She sat slightly hunched on the edge of the couch and stared blankly at the television, the empty glass still grasped in her tiny hands.

My stomach churned as the feeling of dread returned. I stamped it down. There was no time for that. She was going to be fine. I walked to her, knelt, and held the tiny cup to her lips. She complied and drank the medicine in one gulp. She did not grimace; her face was blank.

"Did you sleep okay?" I asked.

She nodded.

"Are you still tired?"

She shook her head, and I looked around the room in search of something to help spur conversation.

"Do you want to watch a movie? Is there anything you want?"

She shook her head again.

"Okay," I said. "Let me know if you need anything."

Again, I put my hand on her forehead. Still hot, maybe hotter than before. I grabbed the glass from her hands, filled it in the kitchen, and set it down on the table in front of her.

"Wait a little bit to drink that—"

She lashed out a hand and knocked the glass off the table. Water splashed across the carpet as the glass bounced on the floor and came to a rest. I stared down at the result of her action, unable to look Kaylee in the eye but able to see in my peripheral vision that she was again just sitting there. Aside from knocking the glass off the table, she hadn't moved. I retrieved the glass and returned it to the kitchen.

"I'll get some more water for you later," I said. "Feel better, okay?"

She said nothing.

The electricity died partway through the afternoon. I spent the rest of the day watching her, giving her water and medicine, and peering outside with the hope that Alex would show. When night fell, I guided her back to bed and tucked her in. When I wished her sweet dreams, she only glared at me and said nothing.

I returned to my room, lay in bed, and stared at the ceiling as I listened. Screams, gunshots, and shattering glass—all were beyond the confines of my home, but for how long? I had already seen numerous murders from my front porch. Chaos was just off my front stoop, and it was only a matter of time before it made its way inside, to Kaylee and me.

I felt my stomach clench. With the way Kaylee had been acting, I could no longer deny the possibility that while the front windows had not yet been broken and foreign footsteps had not yet stomped up the stairs toward us, chaos might have already made its way inside, concealed in her bloodstream. But whether or not she had the South American flu, I knew I had to get her out of the house and out of the city while we still had at least a semblance of a chance to escape.

But Alex was still MIA, and the prospect of leaving before he arrived was not a hopeful one. As far as I knew, he had no weapons and was almost entirely dependent on me for supplies. With what was going on outside, I had no idea if he could catch up with me on his own. I couldn't stand the thought of abandoning him. We had been friends since kindergarten, and I trusted him as much as kin; as far as I was concerned, he was family. But there were no assurances that he would make it to my house at all. If he was trapped or lost with no way to contact me, it was unlikely that I would ever find him. And if he was hurt . . .

I sat up on the edge of the bed and tried to maintain focus. There was no use wondering about the unknowable. All I knew was that Alex was late and that our window for escaping the city was rapidly closing. Though I tried to think of any possible recourse aside from leaving, I knew that I couldn't wait much longer, not when I had Kaylee with me. As much as it hurt to think of leaving Alex behind, she had to take priority. At the most, I could wait another day. Beyond that, I would prepare a suitable pack for Alex and leave a note with instructions on how to catch up with me. I could only hope he made it to me intact.

Something thudded against the floor in Kaylee's room. As I waited for another noise to follow it, I realized that I was gritting my teeth. When a few minutes passed and I heard nothing more, I stood and opened the window facing the alleyway so that I could hear Alex or whatever else passed through it. Then I dragged my dresser across the floor until it blocked the open doorway. With that configuration, nothing would be able to get to me without me hearing it first. I turned my bed so that it faced the doorway, lay back down with my feet facing the door, and laid one hand on the gun beside me.

It gave me at least a small feeling of safety.

10

I awoke in darkness to the sounds of gunshots followed by a brief silence, then a scream from the street. I leaped out of my bedroom and down the stairway. With one hand on the banister and the other holding the pistol, I took the stairs in bounding leaps and by the time I reached the first floor, I had built up such speed that I lost control and stumbled into the wall. I regained my balance and ran down the hall, unlocked and opened the inner door and stepped on top of the bench. I had just looked out through the window above the outer door when a second scream let loose and was cut short by another gunshot. I scanned the street and surrounding houses but saw nothing. The same dead bodies and trash from before were scattered throughout the street.

Then something moved. Between two houses across the street, a head poked out from behind a trash can before disappearing again behind it. Immediately after, a man passed by in a dead sprint down the middle of the street. He was completely naked, and the front of his body was smeared with blood. The back of his legs were smeared with shit. I couldn't tell whether he was infected. Once he ran out of sight, I looked back to the alleyway across the street and noticed the toes of a bright-blue shoe poking out from behind the trash can. A few more people ran past as I remained at the window and waited.

Finally, after the area returned to relative quiet, the person behind the trash can peeked their head out and pushed laboriously to their feet. I swore as they stepped into the glare of the moonlight and I was finally able to recognize the face: it was Alex. Limping heavily and splotched with blood, he stepped to the edge of the sidewalk and looked tentatively in both directions as he moved slowly to the street. In one hand, he held a small revolver. The other hand hung limply at his side. Suddenly, he broke into a sprint.

I turned and leaped off of the bench, pulled it out from between the doors, and threw it into the hall. It landed precariously on its feet, then tumbled over as I raced to the outer door and unlocked it. A pair of screams sounded as I opened the door and ran outside. Alex was lying on his back on the porch steps. In front of him stood the naked, blood-and-shit-covered man. As he approached, I raised my pistol and fired. The bullet hit him in the shoulder, but his eyes remained on me as he took another step. Then, almost as an afterthought, he stopped and screamed at the hole in his shoulder as he clawed at it with both hands. I fired into his face and he collapsed in a heap. I rushed to Alex and slapped him hard on the shoulder.

"Let's go!" I yelled.

He didn't move. I leaned in closer and looked at his face. The dark substance covering the right side of his face confused me until I felt the moisture; blood was seeping from an unseen wound on his head. He had been knocked unconscious.

With my free hand, I grabbed him by the front of his shirt and sat him up, then moved around behind him and hooked my arms under his armpits. As I pulled him up the steps, feet slapped against pavement, accompanied by guttural breathing. It was growing closer. I looked toward the sound: a lean, growling man in a light-gray suit was running directly toward us. As the man came within fifteen feet, I dropped Alex and raised the pistol. I fired once, then a second time, missing on both shots before honing in on his center mass and firing twice more. The bullets hit home somewhere in his belly. He collapsed and smacked sickly into the sidewalk at Alex's feet.

As I grabbed Alex again, another man emerged from the alleyway across the street. He spotted me, stopped, and cocked his head, then emitted a high-pitched cry as he broke into a sprint toward me. He had nearly reached by the time I had dragged Alex up onto the porch. I dropped him, aimed, and fired at the sprinter as he reached the nearest sidewalk. I hit him twice in the abdomen, then once in the neck. He went down headfirst into the steps. Someone else let loose a loud, curt grunt. I looked left, then right and though I couldn't see anything, I knew the source of the noise was close. As I again lifted Alex's limp body, I glanced behind me at the doorway and froze. Kaylee was standing in the door.

"Kaylee, go upstairs!" I yelled.

She looked at me impassively and said nothing.

"Kaylee, go to your room!" I screamed.

She did not move. I returned my focus to Alex, then the street. Several runners were headed toward us from the street to my left. As the group passed in front of a neighbor's house, one of them, a thin man in torn sweats, noticed the newest bodies near my porch. His eyes scanned the scene, then shifted quickly to me.

I laid Alex down, took aim at the approaching group, and waited for a shot. I couldn't remember how many rounds I had already fired, but I knew I couldn't afford to miss. As the man in sweats came within a few feet of the porch, I fired. He fell and landed on the steps, then twisted and grabbed at his groin as I aimed and fired at the next monster, a towering brute in boxers and a sweater. The first bullet struck him in the arm, and he continued toward me unabated. I fired again, and a hole appeared just below his chin. He dropped, and I fired in rapid succession at the next three, who ran shoulder to shoulder. I aimed for the head and missed at first, then hit a neck and one of the attackers fell. I shot at the next person and missed, then struck her chest and she went down. As the last of them leaped up the steps, I fired wildly at his chest. He whimpered like a dog, then went silent and fell. He landed on top of Alex. I moved to push him off, then glanced and did a double take as I noticed another group of people approaching quickly from down the street. More footsteps came from the alleyway across the street as two more people ran at us. Another woman came from down the street to the right. I didn't know how many bullets I had left. Maybe a few, maybe just one. It wasn't enough.

I looked at Kaylee and felt the sum of the instant calculation of my odds. There was no way I could get both Alex and Kaylee inside with enough time left to replace the bench and defend the house. Even if I managed by some miracle to drag Alex inside and secure the door, I wouldn't be able to get both him and Kaylee upstairs.

We were out of time.

As sneakers slapped on the sidewalk across the street, I let go of Alex, scrambled through the outer door, and slammed it shut. Just as I secured the locks, the door was rocked in its frame. I stumbled backward, then fell to the floor beside Kaylee. A barrage of impacts struck the door, then ceased and the handle jiggled violently. Kaylee, who had been facing the door, turned to me with a scowl. For just a moment, there was a terrible silence.

Something slammed violently into the door. I pushed myself up and wrapped my arms around Kaylee, then carried her down the hall and set her down at the base of the stairwell. I ran back down the hall as something forcefully struck the outer door. I grabbed the bench and pushed it up against the outer door, slammed the inner door shut, and locked it as the impacts continued.

I ran to Kaylee, who was still standing where I had set her down. I knelt beside her.

"It's gonna be okay, honey. We need to go upstairs, okay?"

She said nothing at first. Then her features hardened again into a scowl.

"No," she said.

As she said that single word, a quavering cry rose from outside and was punctuated by multiple shorter, louder screams. Sounds of a struggle broke out on the porch and something thudded dully against the side of the house. Glass broke in the front room and was accompanied by the thunderous sound of the entertainment center as it toppled to the floor. Kaylee screamed and flailed wildly as I picked her up again and carried her up the stairs and back to the guest room. I set her down beside the bed and shoved the pistol into the back of my pants as I looked around the room.

My eyes settled on a double dresser against the wall. I moved to the end of the dresser that was farthest from the door, pushed it into the hallway, and kept going. More glass broke downstairs, followed closely by a loud bang. Footsteps thudded through the first floor as I reached the top of the stairwell. I lifted one end of the dresser until it stood vertically at the top of the stairs, then heaved my weight against it and let gravity do the rest as footsteps started up the stairs toward me. As it fell, an almost deafening roar reverberated throughout the hall. I tripped backward into the wall as the dresser slammed into the nearest attacker, slowed, and stopped. I aimed at a gap between the dresser and the wall, but before I could fire, the dresser continued downward. It thudded violently down the stairs and came to a stop with a sickening crack in the turn of the stairwell. At least one of the infected was pinned between the dresser and the wall.

As I stood up, a man behind the dresser reached over the turn of the banister toward me. I descended the stairs and stopped just outside of his reach. Many of the details of his face were muted in the dark, but from what I could see, he looked normal. There were no wounds, no splashes of blood, and no obvious discoloration, just an expression of hate and an obvious desire to kill me. When he looked me in the eyes and roared, I fired a bullet into his head. He fell back against the wall, slid down to the floor, and stopped moving.

Just as I lowered the pistol, someone else ran into view. Before I could raise the pistol to fire, she turned and stomped off through the house. Her footsteps were accompanied by the sounds of shattering glass and heavy thuds as she took her aggressions out on various furnishings and appliances. Someone else joined her after a few seconds, and they broke into a fight. The noises of their struggle—the grunts, the screams, the muffled impacts, and the sound of breaking glass—lasted only a few minutes. Eventually they fell silent, and the winner, whomever it was, stumbled through the house and disappeared.

I returned to my bedroom, pushed my double dresser out to the top of the stairs, tipped it up on its end, and pushed it over. It toppled down the flight. With some effort, I managed to maneuver it until it sat atop the first dresser. I then used the wooden bed frame from my room to as further reinforcement. It wasn't an impregnable barricade, but I would hear any intruders before they could weasel their way past it. I listened again for any stray sounds but heard nothing. No sirens, no movements, no voices. The silence included Alex.

I ran through the hall to the front of the house and opened one of the windows facing the street. With the porch roof in the way, I couldn't see Alex or any of the bodies on the porch. Slowly, carefully, I crawled through the window and onto the roof, then crouched and stopped moving. I looked around as much as I could without turning my head, and after I felt relatively sure that no one was watching, I leaned forward, lowered myself onto my stomach, and crawled forward to the edge of the roof. With my hands clamped onto the tarred shingle edges, I looked down at what remained below.

The expected scene in the street might not have been so bad if I hadn't been searching every body and face for Alex's features. Though I had looked at the bodies before, I hadn't had the time to take in the full details of the scene. The sheer number of corpses was by itself shocking, but it was something else entirely to know that every single one of those inanimate bodies had been neighbors less than a week ago. With all those bodies spread out over the street and already decaying in the moonlight, it didn't look like a movie or a game. It looked like a photograph of some distant war-torn country, the kind you see in a magazine or on the Internet, accompanied by a disclaimer to notify you of the graphic nature of the image. Every split skull, every contorted body, and every ominous, shadowy outline were the horrors of so many foreign lands brought to my doorstep and laid in a heap. Yet the human context of every single body was muted when I finally saw Alex. Even in the darkness, I could see the whites of his eyes; but he wasn't looking at me. He wasn't looking at anything.

He must have woken up after I'd closed and barricaded the front doors. Maybe he panicked and tried to run or was attacked and had no choice but to try to defend himself. Either way, the end result was the same. He was on his back, sprawled over the porch steps with his head on the sidewalk. His neck and limbs were bent at angles that didn't seem unnatural so much as uncomfortable had he still been alive. Though I couldn't be sure because of the shadows, it looked like his neck had been gouged, adding to the pool of blood that already covered most of the street and sidewalk in front of the porch.

I crawled back across the roof, sat against the wall, and cradled my head in my hands. He had looked tired and weak when he first appeared in the alleyway. The strike of his head against the steps must have left him concussed, confused. With the numbers of infected outside and the position he had been left in, there was no way that he could have survived. Not without me. But I wasn't strong enough. I left him there and ran. Alex, my friend, was dead. It was my fault.

I dug my nails into my scalp and held my tears in check. There was no time for crying. Kaylee was in the back room, and I had to take care of her. I had to get her out of the house and out of the city. There was no time for remorse or regret. There was no time for anything but survival.

I collected myself as best I could, then crawled back through the window and returned to Kaylee's room. When I saw her, I stopped in the doorway and leaned against the frame. She was still standing exactly where I had set her down, facing the door. Her expression was that of unfettered hatred. For a few minutes, neither of us said a word. She just stood there and stared at me, her little hands balled up into fists, as I tried to convince myself that she was going to be okay. Finally, I forced myself to speak.

"Kaylee," I said as gently as I could. "Are you okay?"

"Shut up!" she screamed.

It was the loudest I had ever heard her scream. I swallowed.

"Do you feel si—"

"Shut up!" she screamed again.

Suddenly, she turned and punched the metal bed frame beside her. Her fist impacted with a clank, and she swung again, then again.

"Shut up, shut up, shut up!"

I lurched, almost fell, then ran to her and wrapped my arms around her from behind to hold her arms and bloodied hands against her torso. She screamed so loud and at such a high pitch that it hurt my ears, and for a brief moment, I thought that maybe she was just scared after what she had seen, driven to mindless panic. But as much as I wanted to believe it, I knew that wasn't true. She had been sick, first with the sniffles, then with the fever . . . and then her mood had begun to darken, just like Shelly's.

She kicked her legs wildly, and I cried out at the sound of her shins hitting the underside of the frame. I fell backward with her, away from the bed, then turned onto my side and held her as tightly as I dared. Tears formed again in my eyes, but I sucked in my breath and held them in. Her teeth clicked as she tried to bite me. I held her and waited, hoping that she would calm, hoping that she would run out of energy and . . . I don't know. Anything.

Fall asleep? Surrender? Get better?

But she didn't. Five minutes passed, then ten.

Fifteen. Twenty.

She didn't calm, she didn't tire, she didn't even wane. Her rage became and remained as potent and fresh as I had ever seen in her for as long as I had known her. The muted fear I'd felt before quickly flamed into growing terror at what I knew had happened and what would have to be done. Some part of me hoped that somehow she would wake up and realize she wasn't herself, that she was hurting both of us more than even I could stand. But she didn't stop. She couldn't. And the longer I lay there, the more it felt like I was holding a feral, rabid animal and the harder it was to avoid the truth: Kaylee was gone.

Finally, I let her go. I pushed away from her and ran stumbling from the room, then slammed the door behind me and braced myself against it. She battered herself against the flimsy wood just a second behind me, and I could do no more than hold my ground and stare at the floor. I tried to shut off my mind, to pretend I was somewhere else, anywhere else, but I couldn't. I was stuck there with Kaylee in her frenzied self-destruction. There was no escaping it. There was no stopping it.

The pistol fell out of the back of my pants and thudded onto the carpet. From the stairway down the hall came a muffled banging from one of the creatures, either living or undead, trapped in the staircase. The door thudded behind me, and the husk of a human being who was once my niece screamed incoherently. The sound of whimpering came from somewhere very close.

I picked up the pistol and stepped away from the door, then turned and waited. It wasn't long before Kaylee, the little girl, stopped beating on the door and fell quiet. After a few seconds, the handle of the door turned and clicked, and the door opened. She stood there, the little creature, her face a grimace of rage and hate. Her hands and arms hung limply at her sides, covered in blood. One of the bones in her wrist had snapped and pierced through the skin. Her hand dangled beneath it. She stepped noiselessly toward me, her expression unchanged.

I couldn't bring myself to speak to her. I told myself it wasn't my niece, that my niece was already dead, and that I was only looking at the shell of a human being; nothing more, nothing less. But I couldn't believe that entirely. Despite the blood, the bruised, torn, and bleeding skin, the wild, furious eyes, and the raspy breathing, I couldn't bring myself to believe that Kaylee was gone. Not so long ago, I had chased her through the house while she squealed with the kind of unbridled joy that only an innocent child can have. Not so long ago, I had tucked her into bed.

"Bad!" she yelled.

She ran at me, and I swung my free hand. My open palm hit her in the side of the head and knocked her against the wall. She bounced off of the plaster and fell to the floor. As I backed away, she sprang toward me again. I extended a foot toward her and held it there until she ran into it, then I flexed my leg and shoved her back down the hall. She fell stiffly onto her back, then turned over and pushed herself to her feet. She left bloodstains where she touched the floor. Blood dripped from her arms, hands, face, and everywhere else she had been injured. Skin was scraped away from one of her shins to reveal bone.

I felt a kind of tiredness overtake me, not so much physical as mental, as if some part of my mind had finally given up on trying to deny the inescapable fact that I was doing no more than delaying the inevitable and extending unnecessary pain. I think I also felt, from somewhere within me, a deep hatred for what had taken my niece from me and turned her into a monster.

In all my daydreams, I had never brought myself to imagine this scenario. But it was right in front of me, tearing itself apart as it approached. It would destroy itself, me, and everything and everyone else that let it. I knew, and had known since I was a boy, that the infected were no longer who they once were. The infected were the zombies depicted in so many horror films. They were monsters, and they had to die for the sake of the rest of us. The zombie apocalypse had come, and there was no other recourse.

The pistol felt impossibly heavy in my hand. As she ran at me again, teeth bared and hands curled into claws, I raised the pistol and fired. The sight of her body collapsing to the floor reminded me of a time before, when she'd tripped over a tree root at the park. I'd heard her start to cry from where I'd stood, fifty yards away. This time, there was more than just a bump on her knee. This time, I could hear nothing over the sound of my own screams and the ringing in my ears.

I grabbed her limp body and was caught somewhere between the need to hug it close to me and the urge to let it fall, to run. So, stooped over and frozen, I held her at arm's length and just looked down at her. I couldn't bring myself to look away from what was left.

What had I done?

Her body spasmed, and I dropped her, then screamed at the dull thud of her body against the floor. I reached down to pick her back up, then stopped, watched, and waited for her to move.

When she had lain still for a while, I willed myself to carry her body back into the room and lay her on the bed. I started to adjust her pajamas before glancing at her head and struggling again to maintain control. I pulled the blankets up, laid them loosely over her, and tucked them in around her body. I stood at the foot of the bed, looked down at her form, and tried to imagine her as she had been. Not a corpse. Not a monster. My niece. Little Kaylee.

On the way out of the room, I stripped off my clothes. I left them where they dropped, then walked to my room and sat against the wall by the window. As my mind poured over everything that had already happened, I held the pistol against my head and squeezed. The trigger clicked. There were no bullets left.

I don't know how long I remained there, wordless and defenseless, and I couldn't say where my mind was, other than to say that as I sat there, some part of me also sat in hell. Eventually, the tears returned and grew into heaving sobs; I let them come.

I mourned myself into a shallow sleep that was interspersed with panic attacks and blind terror, and I woke several times half expecting to see Kaylee standing there, watching and waiting for me to wake up. I don't know if I woke up the same day or the next, but I stayed in the house until long after the sun had set. If any one of the things outside had managed to work its way past the blocked stairway in the meantime, I doubt I would have been able to defend myself.

I drifted from the disorientation of fatigue and numbly took note of my surroundings. Supplies were scattered around a nearly empty backpack in the middle of the floor. The pack I'd intended to use sat in a corner by the door, prepped and ready. The medical mask from work was still sitting on the floor by the mattress where I had tossed it a few days prior. I put it on, stood, and collected my things. I left behind everything I had set out for Alex, including one of the pistols; excess weight would only slow me down.

Someone was still moving in the stairwell, pinned in place by the dressers and unable to escape. I sat and listened for anything that might have been hiding elsewhere in the house, but aside from the scratching and muffled moans from beneath the barricade, I heard nothing. I shifted the dressers enough that I could ease my way past the infected and make my way down to the first floor.

I walked through the hall toward the rear of the house, my footsteps measured and my mind nearly empty aside from its necessary calculations. I waited for a scream or for a hand to shoot out from behind a corner, but nothing came. I watched for the body of the vanquished infected from the night before, but I never saw it. Moonlight glistened off of the framed portraits and landscapes on the walls and floors, the zombie figurines and memorabilia scattered liberally throughout the house like dull jewels of destruction, gore, and death. I thought for a moment how wonderful it was to have only imagined the horrible realities they depicted.

L. Marshall James

11

I left through the back door and made my way slowly and quietly toward the street. When I reached the front of the house, I knelt and eased my way around the toppled trash cans and scattered garbage until I was even with the front of the porch. I took my time and scanned as much as I could without being seen: the street, the sidewalks, and every porch within sight.

After a few minutes of seeing and hearing nothing aside from the faint sound of barking dogs, I laid down my shotgun, pulled my slingshot from the side of my bag, and loaded a piece of steel shot. I leaned out into the sidewalk area, pulled back the rubber bands, and let go. The shot flew down the street and traveled some fifty yards or so before hitting the side of a concrete stoop with a loud crack.

As I waited for something to investigate the sound, my eyes wandered to Marge's body. What was left of her head looked like nothing more than a pile of bony mush attached to her neck. Her arms and hands lay at their respective sides like sleeping snakes, the bones shattered by the pipe into segments and shards beneath the skin and flesh. I tore my gaze away from her corpse as I loaded and fired another shot down the street in the opposite direction of the first. Again, I waited for something to respond—a cannibalistic psychopath, a mutilated torso, a stray animal. Nothing appeared.

I moved tentatively out into the street, looked again in both directions, then sprinted over and around bodies and trash. I came to a stop just inside the alleyway from which Alex had emerged and looked back at the porch of my house. The body of the gray-suited man was gone. I shook off a new fear and peered into the shadows, but I couldn't make out any more than a silhouette of Alex's legs on the steps. That was all I was given to signify the end of a lifelong friendship and the death of a friend: just one shadow among many others, salted by a distant chorus of screams and the promise of more hardships to come. It was hard to let go and tear my eyes from the scene in the street, let alone the house and what remained inside. For a few minutes, I only crouched there in the darkness, my eyes focused on the house and my mind lost in thought. Eventually, I moved on through the alleyway and into the night.

I continued on to the backyard area behind the houses, then stopped, hunkered down beside a pile of tarps, and ran down the potential list of friends I could seek out. With razor-sharp determination, I wrote each of them off, one by one. Alex was dead. Terry had been sick. Zack's status was unknown, but he lived too far away. It was doubtful I would survive the journey there, and even if I did, there was no telling where he was or if he was even still alive. As for Erin, I wasn't even sure I remembered where she lived. What I did know was that the longer I stayed in the city, the worse my chances of survival became. Beyond that, all I could do was hope that my escape plan worked and that I would make it to my parents.

I fired a shot to my right, then another to my left. The first hit a wooden rail of a porch and the second crashed into a pile of gravel. Again, nothing investigated or reacted to the sounds. I continued through the backyard, then on through the next alleyway.

As I approached midway through the alley, something moved ahead of me. I moved as silently as I could to the side of a house and pressed myself against it as an obese woman in a muumuu sauntered past along the sidewalk. From what I could tell, she didn't appear to be infected. She had no blood on her, and she wasn't manic or trying to kill someone. I considered getting her attention, then decided against it. If she was infected, she would attack and probably attract attention; if she was uninfected, she would almost certainly hold me back. Either way, she was too much of a risk.

Once the woman had been gone for a few minutes and nothing else appeared, I broke out of my crouch and continued to Liberty Avenue. Aside from the faint image of the woman in the muumuu, I saw nothing. Assuming that she would have attracted any attackers if there had been any, I skipped the slingshot procedure and ran for the other side of the street. Once I reached the other side, I hurried along the sidewalk until I came to Sassafras Street, which ran perpendicular to Liberty. After a hasty glance around the corner, I proceeded down Sassafras.

The plan I had previously conceived was to move through an area that had once been owned and operated by a local beer brewing company and had since been all but abandoned. One of the buildings had suffered severe fire damage at some point, and either as a direct result of the fire or because it hadn't been repaired since then, it had partially collapsed. On the side facing the street, there was a massive hole covered loosely by chain-link fencing. The bottom edge of the fencing, which was at roughly the same level as the street, had no reinforcement and had been left unsecured, resulting in a large gap beneath it. I had discovered the gap while scouting the area for possible entry points. It was part of the plan.

I removed my pack and set it down by the gap, then leaned my shotgun on the bag and lowered myself partway down into the hole. Once I found stable footing, I brought the shotgun down to me. As I reached up to retrieve the pack, footsteps slapped on the pavement nearby. With the bag still partly lodged in the gap, I froze. The steps came closer, and I felt my heart rate skyrocket as a silhouette moved past the fence in the darkness, continued down the street, and disappeared around a bend.

I brought the pack down to me as quietly as I could, then sat down and removed the flashlight from the end of the shotgun. I used one hand to cover the end of the light, then turned it on and slowly opened my fingers until just a sliver of light was allowed to escape. Just below the ramp of dirt I was standing on was a metal desk with what looked like a wood-paneled top. Scattered around the room were similar desks, as well as chairs, tables, cabinets, and the like, all seemingly at least a decade old. I slid down to the desk, then lowered myself, the bag, and the gun to the concrete floor. Crouched beside the desk, I killed the light and listened.

After a few seconds of silence, I pulled on and secured the pack, then moved through the room toward a doorway in the opposite corner of the building. Though I had given my eyes time to adjust to the low light, I couldn't see much; the only sources of light I had were the windows, the gaps in the outer structure, and the hole in the front of the building. With the shotgun cradled in the crook of one arm, I turned on the flashlight again and used the sliver of light to pick out and avoid any potential obstacles. As I came within a few feet of the door, I froze and covered the flashlight entirely at the sound of movement near the street. Slowly, I craned my neck toward the noise.

A man stood at the edge of the street. Though it was dark, I could tell by the lightly colored pants that it was not the same creature I had seen a few minutes prior and while I couldn't discern the details of his face, it was clear from his position and the direction he was facing that he was peering into the darkness of the building. Was he searching for me? Had he seen me climb down into the hole between the fence and the road? I watched as he stood there, noiseless except for the sound of his breathing.

Abruptly, he belted out a yell, struck the fence with a hand, and fell silent. I couldn't tell if he was looking at me or only near me, but as he stepped closer, he began to growl, then raised both his hands to the fence and thrashed it back and forth. Even in the scant light of the moon, it became clear that he was facing me.

He knew I was there.

The quick and sudden sound of footsteps was accompanied by a roar, and the man turned from the fence only to be violently tackled into it. The fence flexed deeply but held and tossed both of the men back onto the street even as they rained blows upon each other. Though I couldn't tell for sure, it appeared to be the same person who had run past a few minutes before. I bolted to the door and pushed it open, then glanced behind me to see if either of the scrabblers in the street had noticed. As they continued fighting, I slipped outside and ran.

I reaffixed the flashlight to the shotgun as I moved through the area between the buildings, then worked my way around the end of the main building toward the train tracks. Though I had previously scouted the area from a distance, I had never had the opportunity to see it up close and had never been exactly sure how I was going to access the tracks leading north across the river.

At the corner of the next building, I stopped and peered around its edge. In the many times in the past that I had walked above the brewery grounds via the Herron Avenue Bridge, eighteen-wheelers had typically been parked out by the loading docks and music had often played from some unseen source. This time, they were empty and quiet. Part of me, for some reason I could not explain, wanted to stay there.

I looked up to the silhouette of the bridge and remembered walking over it with Shelly and Kaylee. I had told them about the collapse of one of the brewery buildings and the brewery grounds' abandonment, as well as my intention to someday sneak in to explore. I had tried to talk Alex and the guys into sneaking in with me for a long time; it felt bittersweet and empty to finally do so alone when it no longer mattered.

After I made my way across the open grounds and around another building, I came to the tracks, which stood atop a concrete wall at least ten feet high, well beyond my reach. I walked along the wall's edge until I came to a large pile of dirt and gravel that was nestled up against it. With furtive glances around me, I climbed the mound, lifted my things up to the tracks, and pulled myself up beside them. Once I was up, I lay down as flat as I could and remained absolutely still. After a few minutes passed and I was confident that nothing was tailing me, I got up and broke into a crouched jog.

The tracks remained relatively level, but because of the downward slope of the land, they rose gradually relative to the buildings below, like a catwalk over the city. Once I had reached a high-enough altitude and low-enough visibility that I could move without being seen, I broke into a more casual walk and scanned the land below me periodically. For the most part, it was quiet. Dogs and cats slunk through the shadows here and there, and birds slept silently on wires and in trees. Smoke wafted through the air, screams rang out from time to time, and I sometimes saw people running around in the streets. Otherwise, it seemed almost normal aside from the fact that I was walking where I had never been before and was equipped for a life-or-death hiking trip of indefinite length.

Normal. Yeah.

After I'd gone a couple hundred yards, I heard sounds of violent banging accompanied by cries and screams that sounded like a woman and child. I scanned the streets and sidewalks for the source and finally honed in on a pair of windows that faced the tracks. Though one window was open and the other was closed, I couldn't tell exactly where the noise was coming from, even after zooming in on both with my monocular. I used the slingshot to fire a ball bearing at the closed window.

The glass shattered in two, and as both halves slipped out and down to the earth below, the screams and the banging ceased. As I readied another shot, two hands emerged from the darkness of the inside of the building and rested on the windowsill, followed by the face of a man. His eyes settled almost instantly on me, and I could tell from the expression on his face that he was infected. I held up a hand and raised my middle finger. Fuck you, zombie.

At first, he only stared. Then he released a guttural roar so sudden and loud that I jumped. Faster than he had appeared, he withdrew from the window and was gone. When he didn't return, I diverted my eyes to the open window.

"Hello!" I whispered loudly.

There was no response.

"Hello!" I said again, louder.

A small boy appeared in the window. I raised my hand and waved, but he only stared back at me. A woman walked up behind him, knelt, and rested her chin on the child's shoulder as she wrapped her arms around him. I caught her attention with another wave, and she hesitantly raised a hand and waved back.

"Are you—"

Before I could finish my question, a loud bang came from below, and the man from the window emerged into the street. He came to a sudden stop and turned slowly, his chin raised. His eyes were tracing the tracks. His gaze settled again on me, and he broke into a run down the street and disappeared. When I looked back to the window, the mother and child were gone. With another tentative glance at the street, I continued down the tracks and fell into a measured jog.

A few hundred yards later, I stopped at the sight of a blond-haired woman in one of the backyards between two lines of houses. She paced silently back and forth within the limit of what I assumed was her backyard, then leaned over what must have been a corpse and stabbed it violently and repeatedly. I had no idea how long it had been dead or how many times she had stabbed it, but if I'd been told it was just a Halloween prop, I wouldn't have been able to argue otherwise. As best as I could tell, it was more or less just a lump of flesh.

When she stepped away from the body, she slashed wildly at the wooden fence between her yard and a neighbor's, then stumbled across the yard and sat down under a small, wooden arbor. I noticed then that she was holding something under one arm. When it moved, I realized it was a cat. Like the woman, it was covered in blood. It mewed loudly, and as it did, the woman raised her arm and shoved the cat into her face. Abruptly, the mewing stopped.

I turned away, removed my pack, and sat down against the railing. I had wondered many times before whether zombies would eat anything aside from humans; now I knew. It was just one curiosity among many that would finally be realized in the wake of this disaster.

Was the infection transmitted solely through saliva? No, Kaylee hadn't been bitten and neither had my sister. And Marge, my previously sweet-as-pie neighbor, had rarely even left the house before she developed a curiously strong propensity for violence. How she had been infected was a mystery. So how was it transmitted? By air? Water? It didn't seem to spread from person to person; really, the infected were too preoccupied with killing to even bother spreading the sickness. In fact, they didn't seem to express their violence only toward the uninfected; they hated everyone equally.

Eating seemed to be secondary, and even when they ate, they obviously didn't feast primarily on brains or seem to be hungry for anything in particular. In fact, aside from the one below me feasting on a cat, I hadn't seen any zombies eating; they were too busy trying to kill every living thing they saw. Maybe they would start to eat more often as things calmed down. In that case, maybe they'd even gain some weight, considering all the food and bodies scattered around. Perhaps in addition to the first zombie pandemic, we would see the first zombie obesity pandemic. They'd waddle around after each other, then resort to snarfing down a bag of stale chips instead.

Hopefully that would slow them down a bit, since the shambling zombies of yesteryear had been definitively superseded. There were no braindead rotters moaning and shuffling hopelessly toward me; some of them were capable of at least rudimentary speech, and they were fast.

As if on cue, there was a faint slapping down the tracks from where I had come. I stared into the darkness, and as the sound grew louder, the bobbing silhouette of a man came into view. I pushed quickly to my feet, readied the shotgun, and waited. The running figure drew steadily closer, and my stomach knotted as I recognized the man from the window. He had found a way to get to me.

So they were not only fast but also relatively smart. Not just smart enough to scan the tracks from the street until he saw me, but also smart enough to track me down. In that case, maybe a shotgun wasn't a good idea unless I wanted to risk catching the attention of every one of the bastards within a mile radius. I let go of the shotgun and let it hang from the shoulder strap, then pulled the kukri from its sheath as the zombie continued to approach in what wasn't quite a run and definitely wasn't a shuffle. It seemed to have adopted a light jog.

The question of whether zombies required oxygen was answered by his heavy and erratic breathing pattern; he was obviously out of breath. In fact, he seemed to be on the verge of exhaustion judging by his short footsteps and the way his hands dangled limply at his sides. I squinted at a glinting sliver in his hand. He had a knife.

Fuck.

I had long before adopted a policy of taking minimal, calculated risks. If someone brought claws and jaws to a fight, you brought at least a machete. If someone brought a knife or a machete, you brought a goddamn gun. You don't try to match the physical arsenal of a psychopath; if you do that, you might win a few times, but the odds will eventually weed you out. You must exceed their arsenal and defeat them with overwhelming force. Shock and awe weren't just for war; they were for survival in general.

That meant I couldn't use the kukri to take him down because I couldn't risk the bastard cutting me open. Even if he only landed a glancing blow, it would weaken me and slow me down. I had to use the shotgun. Hopefully, if I took him down with a single shot, it wouldn't be enough for the other zombies to hone in on where I was.

I slid the kukri back into its sheath and raised the butt of the shotgun to my shoulder. As he came close enough that I could see the whites of his eyes, I thumbed the safety off. Suddenly, he came to a stop and regarded me as his chest heaved. Without warning, he wound up like a baseball pitcher and grunted as he threw the knife. It flew wide left, clanked off the railing, and disappeared below the tracks. He then extended a hand toward me and raised a middle finger as if to say, "Fuck you too, human."

As he started toward me again, I aimed for his neck—low enough that I couldn't miss but high enough that his head would not survive—and let loose a round. The report of the weapon was met with silence, as far as I could tell with the ringing in my ears.

I turned around and broke into a jog down the tracks.

12

I maintained my pace until I had crossed the river to Herr's Island, a sliver of land in the middle of the Allegheny River. Aside from a few businesses, office buildings, and townhouses, the island was also home to several docks. The docks were part of Plan A, which was to steal a boat and follow the river past downtown Pittsburgh. Passing so close to the city was admittedly risky, but it was still far less daunting than trying to exit the city by land.

Just beyond the downtown area, the Allegheny and Monongahela Rivers met to form the Ohio River, which I would then follow as far north as I could. Depending on fuel and river levels, I figured I could at least make it past Ellwood City, then abandon the boat and proceed on foot. Though there were several towns nearby, the region overall was relatively rural, making potential unwanted altercations easy to avoid as long as I was careful. From my studies of the area via local maps, online satellite images, and my own experience, I was familiar enough with the area to get to my parents' home near McConnells Mill State Park.

Plan B, which I was hoping to avoid, was to skip Herr's Island and cross the entire Allegheny, then follow the tracks along the north side of the river until I came to the 40th Street Bridge. From there, I would sneak through the woods at a slightly northwestern course until—gods, maps, and compass willing—I made it to Interstate 279, which I would parallel until it joined with Interstate 79. It wasn't a straight shot, but it would avoid the areas with higher populations. From there, I would follow I-79 until I made it close enough to my parents' home that I could shadow the back roads that snaked their way to it. Plan B sucked, but it was a plan. More importantly, it was the only backup plan I had, aside from the generic plan of not dying; that was Plan C, until I thought of something better. My fingers were crossed for Plan A.

The tracks led to the northern tip of Herr's Island, which was where most of the businesses and office buildings were located. Chances were that the buildings would be empty or only sparsely populated. The southern tip of the island was where the townhouses were located and was potentially a haven for respectable, rich yuppie bastard zombies.

Midway across the island, I descended a heavily rusted set of stairs. I had to vault over a small gate at the bottom, which was somewhat of a pain in the ass with all the weight I was carrying. To avoid making any noise, I removed my pack and dropped it over the fence before making my way over. Once I was safely back on ground, I backtracked slightly and walked underneath the tracks until I came to a lightly graveled running trail. Though I tried to keep out of the moonlight, there wasn't really anything to hide from. Aside from a rabbit, nothing moved. There were no zombie joggers, no zombie bicyclists, and no elderly zombies walking their zombie dogs. Not only that, but the distance to the docks was so negligible that I almost walked right past the wooden steps leading to them.

Boats had never been my specialty, so I knew next to nothing about them. Aside from a boat with keys or a boat that I could try to hot-wire, I wasn't entirely sure what I was looking for. At the northernmost point of the docks, I stepped aboard the last boat and spotted a closed compartment near the steering wheel. I tried to open it but it didn't budge. I leaned the shotgun against a seat, then looked nervously around me, at the docks, at the railroad track bridge in the distance, and at the water. As far as I could tell, there was nothing but silence.

I pulled the kukri out of the sheath and slipped the tip of the blade into the small gap between the compartment door and the dash, then shoved it in hard and pried. It gave a little but not enough. I moved the blade closer to the locking mechanism and tried again. I kept prying until something snapped and the compartment fell open. I looked around. Satisfied that I was still alone, I resheathed the kukri and flashed a light in the compartment. I tossed a handful of papers on the floor and ferreted through the rest of the contents: a bottle opener, a cigar cutter, a lighter, and a whistle. No keys. I pocketed the lighter and moved on to the next boat.

Though I'd had high apple-pie-in-the-sky hopes of finding a set of keys, I feared that in the end, I would have to figure out how to hot-wire one of the boats. As I searched boat after boat, I discovered that my fear was only half-correct; as rich as the local yuppies might have been, not a single one of them had been dumb enough to leave the key to a boat unsecured. Unfortunately, I had no idea how to hot-wire a boat, and since most of them were high-end models, the majority had security systems to prevent tampering.

I shook my head begrudgingly at one of the boats I had already checked for keys. As far as I could tell, it was older than the others, so I figured it would be the one boat I would have the most luck in attempting to hot-wire. It also had a security sticker pasted on the side.

I looked across the river at the shore I had come from. It was around a thousand feet away, but very quiet, meaning that any sound I made could be audible. Disregarding the zombies that might have already been on the island, I already knew the infected were smart enough to track me down if they knew where to find me. Not only that, but aside from the bridge I had crossed, there were five or six other bridges connected to the island. If I made the mistake of attracting attention, I could end up quickly overrun.

My pet hypothesis had been that the neighborhood would be close to empty, its inhabitants well-to-do enough that they would have skipped town at the first sign of trouble. However, while I was curious about my hypothesis, I had no real interest in testing it firsthand. I couldn't afford to have an alarm go off. Even starting a boat could attract unwanted attention and potentially get me killed if I didn't get away fast enough.

I looked back toward the island shore. I couldn't see past the trees, but I remembered what was there. A single street, called Waterfront Drive, spanned almost the entire length of the island. The southernmost third of this street, which was provided a liberal allotment of cul-de-sacs (because who doesn't love a good cul-de-sac, am I right?) was flanked on each side by a row of townhouses. Given the close proximity of these townhouses to the docks, there was a damn good chance that more than a few would have keys to one or more of these boats. There also existed the possibility that I could stock up on supplies and give myself a better chance of surviving the trip, assuming I wasn't murdered before I made it back to the docks.

I walked back to land and alongside the gravel toward the houses. For whatever reason, be it the prospect of rousing the crazies or the feeling that I was pushing my luck, sinister shadows startled me and vague silhouettes jumped out at me with a maliciousness I had not experienced since grade school. It was a stressful, if uneventful, third of a mile.

When I finally caught sight of one of the first houses, I dropped into a low crouch and sidled up beside one of the trees between the path and a paved driveway. Nearby was a little row of townhouses that sat perpendicular to Waterfront Drive. It was all dark, but noises here and there ruled out the possibility of the neighborhood being empty.

I skimmed along the tree line until I was even with the edge of the first house, then moved up a slight incline to follow along the front wall and continued until I came to the side of a semi-enclosed stairway leading to the door. I peeked around the edge, then moved quickly up the steps. The upper portion of the door was made of clear glass but was covered on the inside by opaque curtains that restricted my view. It was locked, so I sneaked to the next house.

The next two doors, which stood right beside each other, were both locked. I started to move on, then swore under my breath. The steps of the last townhouse in the row led to an open porch area that faced Waterfront Drive. Directly across the street were the first few townhouses of another row. I honed in on the front windows of the other apartments with my monocular but couldn't see much of anything. The few muffled noises I heard seemed to come from farther down the street. For the time being, the area I was in seemed quiet.

I made my way to the last porch in the row, then proceeded up the steps. Since I didn't want to raise my head into view above the front wall of the porch, I ignored the first window. When I reached the door, I stopped and eyed it uncertainly. It was ajar. I pulled it open and duckwalked into the entryway, then pulled the outer door shut behind me and moved to the inner door, which was closed. As quietly as I could, I tried the handle. The latch clicked, and I pushed the door open, then listened for movement and stepped inside. As I closed the door behind me, I decided to move with as little light as possible, or at least avoid using the flashlight near the front of the house so I wouldn't be seen from the street.

With a finger on the flashlight switch, I scanned the darkness. To my right was a massive dining room table encircled by several tall chairs. Beyond that room in the far right corner of the house was a kitchen. Directly in front of me was a stairway leading left to the second story, and to my left was a living room with a couch and an exercise bike, both of which faced the front of the house. Behind them and standing against a wall was a large, wooden cabinet.

Even without the flashlight, I was able to see well enough that nothing could hide from me without effort. With the shotgun at the ready, I stepped into the living room. I gave the furniture a wide berth as I walked around the couch and through the room, then back to the front door. Once I'd checked under the table, I did a quick circuit of the dining room. I stopped outside the kitchen, covered the end of the flashlight, and flicked it on briefly once, twice, and a third time as I moved in and scouted it out. Aside from the normal appliances and utensils, it was empty.

I moved through the kitchen and briefly checked a bathroom at the bottom of the stairs, then flashed the light up through the stairwell. Picture frames lined the walls on both sides. Inset into the wall at the top of the stairwell was an open window. I made my way to the top of the flight and peered left into darkness. On the front wall facing Waterfront Drive was a large window, perhaps eight feet by seven feet and roughly fifteen feet above the floor. Below that, at roughly eye level, were two smaller windows. Despite the windows, I shaded the flashlight with one hand and toggled it on.

The second story was almost entirely one large, open area. Directly across from me in the nearest corner was a large wooden desk, on top of which were two monitors and several stacks of folders that were stuffed to capacity. When my light settled on the middle of the room, I saw what at first appeared to be a couch. When I moved closer, it turned out to be the largest bed I had ever laid eyes on. I wasn't sure of the dimensions, but it appeared to be the size of four queen-size beds pushed together to form one megabed. I made a mental note that if it came down to it, I would sleep there.

One corner of the room was sectioned off into another, smaller room. Opposite that corner was what appeared to be, in the same exaggerated style of the house, a massive L-shaped couch. Beyond the couch was a television that might as well have been used in the middle of an arena. I wondered briefly about the merits of watching a hockey game on that TV as opposed to seeing one in person. Cheaper beer, better seats, an arguably better view . . .

As I turned back toward the small room in the corner, I froze when the light hit the coffee table. Unlike the rest of the apartment, which had been clean and orderly, the table was littered with broken glass and blood. I backed up slowly as I panned to the left and the scene gradually came into full view. On the corner of the couch near me were huge splotches of blood that coalesced into a trail leading all the way to the bend in the middle section. There, on the edge of the cushion, sat a woman smeared with blood. I moved my hand from the flashlight and placed it on the pump of the shotgun. In the full brightness of the light, the woman began to stir. Something crackled in her right hand, and I realized with relief that it was a breakfast bar, still partially wrapped. I wasn't sure if that meant she wasn't infected, but she was disoriented and possibly badly hurt.

"Miss," I whispered.

Her head raised and turned slowly toward the light. I lowered it out of her eyes.

"Miss, it's okay," I said a little louder. "Are you okay?"

Her brow furrowed, and she nodded without turning to acknowledge me. I flipped the safety on as I stepped closer. As I did so, she turned her head and held the breakfast bar at arm's length, then slowly brought it to her mouth and took a bite. The chewing motion of her jaw seemed exaggerated and pained. Rather than grinding the piece of food in her mouth, she moved her jaw up and down as if to compact the food. She kept chewing like that, then took another bite and chewed it in much the same fashion without bothering to swallow. She took another bite, then another, until chunks spilled out of her mouth onto the floor.

With a surge of panic, I realized that I had not checked the entire room. I turned the light toward the room in the corner for just long enough to be sure it was clear, then turned immediately back to the woman as she continued to eat. Finally, she shoved the last of the breakfast bar into her mouth along with the wrapper, which crackled between her teeth as more crumbs spilled out onto the floor and settled among the bloodstains on the couch and carpet. Suddenly, her head jerked backward and her hand shot to her mouth. She gagged loudly, and her jaw distended as she forced her hand inside. I shone the light directly on her, and as her hand pulled away from her mouth, something emerged. With a shriek, she yanked violently at a mass in her mouth, then bit down hard. Blood began to pour out, and I realized then that the mass was her tongue.

"Oh God," I said. "No, no, no."

As she flung the remains of her tongue to the ground, I ran around the couch and started toward her, then stopped. From my new vantage point, the extent of her injuries became apparent. Her left hand was gone. The wrist ended in a ragged, bloody stump. The left side of her face was a mess of gore, the flesh gouged and pulled away to such an extent that I could see part of her cheekbone. One of her eyes hung from the socket by the optic nerve.

"Jesus Chri—"

Her good eye darted toward me, and she leaped to her feet. I backpedaled as she ran at me, her approach silent aside from the rapid thud of her feet on the floor. I raised the shotgun and pulled the trigger. The safety was still on. I screamed in panic, stepped farther backward, and tripped. I flipped off the safety as I began to fall, and with her face in full view, I pulled the trigger.

The shot increased my momentum, and I tumbled backward. My head slammed against the wall, and for an instant, my vision went black. I loaded another round and blinked wildly until I could see, then shoved myself up into a sitting position and aimed at where the woman had been. When the light settled on her feet, I pushed myself up and quickly approached her body. Once I saw her and verified that she was dead, I panned the light back and forth across the entire room two, then three times before settling on the other room's door. I strained to listen, but my ears were still ringing so much that I couldn't have heard something coming if it had run toward me at a full sprint. I circumvented the couch and moved toward the other room with a cautious slowness that grew increasingly unbearable to the point that I began to find it difficult to breathe. Finally, I sprinted to the door, pushed it open, and aimed the shotgun into the room with my finger on the trigger.

Everything in the bathroom was smeared with blood: the tub, the sink, the toilet, the walls, and the floor. Strewn across the floor were chunks of something resembling meat, each one as ragged and unrecognizable as the rest. I searched for movement, for life, and found myself relieved that neither was present. I pulled the door closed and leaned back against the wall, then closed my eyes and tried to slow my breathing.

The purpose of going to the second floor had been to make sure the house was clear before I looked for keys, since I didn't want to have something sneak up behind me while I was distracted with the search. I had hoped I could get in and out without confronting anything, and I figured that if I did, I could use the kukri to take them down silently. The shotgun was supposed to have been a last resort. So much for that.

I walked back to the top of the stairs, sank into the corner, and waited for the ringing in my ears to fade. Despite knowing the room was empty, I found myself glancing periodically over at the couch and while I knew it was best to wait until I was fully prepared before continuing on, I felt an urgent need to get out of the house. In addition to the ringing in my ears, there was a series of alarms going off in my mind that I couldn't seem to override.

There was a dead body forty feet away from me on the other side of the couch. One of its arms ended in a bloody nub, the hand likely gnawed off by its possessor. The tongue of the body was lying on the floor by the coffee table, and the head was only barely there. In the bathroom were various unidentifiable body parts. This was not normal. This was not right. I had to get out of there.

But I knew I had to wait, and as I continued to sit there, the alarms shut off one by one. Like a guard dog returning to bed after fending off an intruder, I felt my feelings abate as I stared through the darkness and waited for some tortured soul to peek around the corner. Gradually, a sort of calmness overtook me as I stared down the stairway.

It was a deadly silence.

13

I found a set of keys hanging on the wall between the stairs and the kitchen. Without knowing, I had walked past them on my way to the second story. Engraved into the head of one of the keys was the image of a sailboat, along with a name: *Empress*.

I raided the kitchen for food and supplies. When I left, I had two grocery bags in one hand and a pistol in the other. The shotgun hung loose from the shoulder strap so that I could get a grip on it without having to scramble, if it came to that. Despite the noise of the bags and the possibility of encountering more infected, the walk back to the docks was quiet and uneventful. I scanned and moved with a measured calm, and in a way, I was not there at all. My eyes saw, my legs carried me, and my brain calculated, but there was nothing going on in my head beyond what I needed to get to the boat and leave the city. There was no choice; if I had allowed myself think about what I had seen, maybe I would have made a mistake or failed to notice an approaching attacker. Instead, I shut down and carried on like a good soldier would, like I knew I had to if I wanted to survive. Even still, I felt a touch of relief when I set the bags of food on the dock and began what I assumed would be a short search for the *Empress*.

A half hour later, I found the boat. Or maybe it was a yacht. Or a schooner. I never knew the difference, but it didn't really matter. It might not have been a speedboat, but it would get me where I needed to go. I loaded the food, then searched the other boats one by one until I had scavenged four mostly full gas cans. Once I had secured the fuel, food, backpack, and weapons as well as I could, I untied the boat from the dock and started it up. The engine rumbled easily to life, and I eased the *Empress* slowly out into the open water. With a cursory glance back at the shore, I punched the throttle forward.

Apparently movies, television, or assumptions based on my minimal experience with boats had given me an extremely inaccurate expectation of average boat acceleration and speed. I had expected to be almost thrown backward with the force of my acceleration. Instead, I looked around as the engine revved up and the nose of the *Empress* tilted slightly upward. Slowly but surely, I left the docks behind.

Even in the darkness and relative quiet, the ride through the city was unsettling. Fires raged on bridges and on the shores, unaccompanied by the normally expected sounds of approaching sirens. Screams sounded out sporadically from all directions. Sometimes the screams were full of rage; sometimes they were full of fear. I searched for music to help drown out the surrounding chaos but found nothing aside from a disc in the CD player. The first track was Whitney Houston's "I Will Always Love You," and when I skipped it, the song played again. In fact, the same song was burned fifteen consecutive times. I surrendered, turned the volume up as loud as it would go, and let it play.

The music and the roar of the engine quickly attracted the attention of every infected within hearing range. Suddenly provided with something better to do than their newfound hobbies of murder, arson, money laundering, and whatever else they did in their free time, they tumbled toward me from the shores and bridges, then tromped or leaped into the water and paddled furiously toward me, finally answering the question of whether zombies could swim.

The swimmers didn't really concern me though; it was the bridge jumpers that had me on edge. Bodies plummeted from the sky in near darkness, screaming incoherently as they plunged into the water. Though there were more than a few close calls, I avoided the impact of all but one who landed headfirst on the bow of the boat, slipped helplessly into the water, and disappeared.

The *Empress* surged on. As the shadows of downtown faded from view, I felt a poignant sense of finality. Pittsburgh was the city of my birth, and I had lived in the reaches of that city for almost every day of my life, from infancy through childhood and far into adulthood. I had seen the city recover from the steel crisis and utterly redefine itself as a premier source of health care, science, and education. It seemed to have so much ahead of it, and then, in a matter of days, it was all but empty and dead. There had to be people still alive somewhere inside, clinging to survival amid the sea of violence and death, but Pittsburgh as I knew it was gone. It was no more than an empty husk, tinged with the memories of my entire life.

With Whitney singing in the background, it seemed even more tragic than it had to be. I ejected the CD and threw it into the water, then returned focus to the river ahead of me. I settled passively into the rhythm of the engine and tried to prepare for the long, watery journey that would take me most of the way to my parents' home. Barring some sort of mechanical failure, a bizarrely successful zombie attack, dysentery, or some other unforeseen event, I was well on my way to being home free. The worst was over . . .

Or not.

As I rounded a bend in the river partway along Neville Island, a slab of gray appeared out of the darkness. I slowed the boat to a crawl, then pulled the monocular from my pack and walked to the front of the boat. In the river ahead was a wall of concrete spanning almost the entire river. On the right side, where the wall appeared to stop, there were two solid, massive doors. I lowered the monocular and stared at the wall in all of its immense, ball-busting glory.

I had planned on what supplies I might have needed if the zombie apocalypse actually happened, as well as how to get out of the urban area I lived in, across the river, and beyond. I had even created custom devices to try and save life and limb in a world where my life was critically endangered. But in all my half-assed plans, I had overlooked the crippling fact that the Ohio River heading north out of Pittsburgh was locked and dammed.

Had I left a few days prior, the lock might have been irrelevant. I could have paid the toll and continued onward along the river toward my destination. But the lock was undoubtedly abandoned. With no crew capable of operating the necessary machinery and no electricity to run it, the dam might as well have been no more than solid concrete and rebar. If I were going any farther on the Ohio River, I wouldn't be doing so aboard the *Empress*. I brought the boat to a full stop, sat down against the side of the cabin with my laminated atlas, and flipped through to my location.

There it was. The Emsworth Dam and the Emsworth Lock. Four medium-blue lines whose existence had somehow completely escaped me. On the other side of Neville Island was the Emsworth Back Channel Dam. No passage there. So soon in her short journey, the *Empress* would have to be decommissioned. But . . .

I flipped through the pages and searched farther downriver until I spotted it: the Fifty States Marina, on the north side of the river, just below the train tracks. I flipped back through the pages, traced the train tracks back upriver and confirmed that they ran right past me. If I could get onto land, I could follow the tracks to the marina, then find another boat, and—

"Wait, shit."

It was over three miles to the other marina. That meant the gas and most of the food was gone; there was no way I could carry it that far. It was possible that I could get more food and gas in or around the marina, but doing all that without attracting attention was another matter entirely. I had been lucky at the docks of the *Empress*, but I didn't want to press my luck any further than I had to.

If I found a car, I could pick up the supplies, drive down to the marina, transfer the supplies to a new boat, and go from there. But if there had been any question about attracting attention while walking, there was no chance of a vehicle going unnoticed or ignored, and I would still need to find keys to one of the boats in the marina. If my journey had attracted attention, there was no way I would have the time. Beyond all that, even if I managed to get a new boat and continue up the river, the whole process would have to be repeated if I encountered another dam.

Almost as an afterthought, I traced a finger farther north along the river, past the towns of Emsworth, Glenfield, and Sewickley. My finger stopped. Again, not even eight miles downstream were the Dashields Dam and Locks. Farther north of that, no marina was even marked on the map. Granted, there were probably private docks somewhere, but while it was possible that I could find another boat, the notion that I could find a boat with keys and get to it with the gas and food in hand without being noticed was beyond wishful thinking. I unwrapped a protein bar and stared sullenly out over the water as I chewed.

Plan A was inarguably a bust. My other options, however, were limited. The most direct route might have been to find a vehicle on or near Interstate 79, which I could follow most of the way to my parents' home. Unfortunately, it would also likely be rife with zombies and even if it was mostly empty, there was plenty of road left for pileups and general blockage. If I could find a motorcycle or a dirt bike, I might be able to get around all that, but I wouldn't be able to bring much food or gas aside from what I already had in my pack. Further, I had ridden a motorcycle only once or twice in my life, so I had no idea how well I would be able to handle it while wearing a full pack and brandishing a shotgun. Plus, the sound of the engine would surely attract attention and if they came after me, I would be easy to locate and vulnerable to attack. If I was thrown from the bike, trapped between cars, or had to abandon the bike for whatever reason, I would have no recourse but to run and I already knew the infected were more than willing to participate in footraces. Even if I managed to eliminate the zombies who were chasing me, the sounds of gunshots would only attract more, so the river was out and the interstate was out, which left wandering back roads, forests, and . . .

Train tracks. It could be tricky driving, particularly if a train was blocking the way, and it would be slow, but there was little chance of infestation and since train tracks were generally a good distance from any homes, it would be unlikely that I would attract any rotters.

I traced the tracks again as they paralleled the edge of the river, never deviating more than half of a mile from the water's edge. I followed them as far as the atlas covered, then rummaged through the pack and retrieved a stack of paper maps. None of the maps showed the tracks, but from what I could tell in the atlas, they came to within about two and a half miles of Ellwood City. Any point after that and before Route 422, I could start heading east toward my parents' home by taking any number of back roads. It was risky, but it was the best I had. I couldn't stay where I was, and I sure as hell wasn't going back.

I stuffed the maps and atlas back into the pack and maneuvered the boat toward the shore. I floated along a concrete embankment until I came to its end, then steered the boat up to the land until the front scraped against the trunk of a tree and crunched into the rocky earth. Before the boat could drift back away from the shore, I killed the engine, wrapped a couple of ropes around a tree, and tied it as tightly as I could.

With the boat secured, I sat on the front of the *Empress* and listened. After a few minutes of silence, I heaved the gas and bags one by one up onto the concrete embankment. It was too high for me to climb up, so I collected the rest of my things and started up the bank. With the shotgun cradled in one hand, I scrambled up through the growth and rocky earth of the slope. Once I had reached the top, I slipped off my pack and looked around as I caught my breath.

On the other side of the train tracks, the ground rose sharply to form a hill that was hopefully as impassable to those above as it was to me. Atop the hill was the town of Ben Avon, a little touch of civilization that I hoped to avoid if at all possible. Down the tracks and not far beyond where I was, two streets came to a point almost exactly at the border of the town of Emsworth, which was the namesake of the river lock I had so recently grown to dislike.

I hid my pack and supplies under some bushes, then followed the tracks. I walked on top of the railroad ties to make as little noise as possible. Nothing really caught my attention; there were no sounds that seemed out of the ordinary, and there was nothing much to look at, aside from shadowy trees on one side and the glistening river on the other. When I came to a sagging fence that separated the tracks from the streets, I stepped onto and over it.

At first, the area seemed to be entirely deserted aside from an old sedan parked by the fence. Two brick buildings stood out, and as I strode along the street toward them, I noticed a cluster of large, white vans parked across the street. I ignored them and tried the front door of the first building.

Locked. I walked to the first window and peered in, then flashed the light tentatively through it. Aside from a couple of small tables, a tall counter in the rear of the room, and several desks scattered randomly throughout, it seemed empty. Beside one of the tables was a doorless frame that led to another room. I tried to focus the light on the doorway, but I couldn't see anything beyond it.

I walked past the other windows to the edge of the building and peeked around the corner. Behind the building and ten feet below street level was a dirt parking lot. In the middle and back of the lot were shapes that resembled vehicles and one camper. On any other road trip, the camper might have been an option but I doubted that it had the power to traverse the train tracks with all the extra weight of the bed, toilet, kitchenette, and whatever else was inside. Nearer to me and parked at the base of the building was a large pickup truck. I briefly flashed it with the light, and a Ford logo glinted back at me. I couldn't tell how old the truck was, though it appeared to be weathered.

A door slammed shut somewhere in the distance, followed by the sound of breaking glass and a brief scream. I couldn't tell where any of the sounds originated. With the hill to my back, it seemed possible that the sounds could have come from any direction. After nothing else happened, I continued down the street and past the second building, where I followed a driveway into the back lot, made my way to the truck, and inspected it. It had obviously seen some serious shit in its day, but it looked like it had the width, the ground clearance, and the tread to handle the tracks. If the rest of the vehicle could handle the trip, that was all I needed. I tried the handle of the driver-side door, but it was locked.

Beside the truck was the rear side of the building I had looked into. Built into it was an older wooden door with what looked like single glass panes inset into the upper portion. I tried the handle. Locked. It was too dark inside to see anything, and I didn't want to risk using a light. With a glance behind me, I brought an elbow to the lower right pane. Though I had hit it so lightly that the glass didn't break, the sound of the impact still made me cringe. With another look behind me, I hit the glass again and it cracked. After a few more strikes, the glass was broken enough that I was able to push it out with the barrel of the shotgun, then reach through and unlock the door. After I walked in, I closed the door behind me and shielded the flashlight as I looked around.

Lining the walls on either side were tool chests and bins overflowing with myriad metal parts. Against the back wall was a staircase leading upward, presumably to the back room I hadn't been able to see from the front window. I started toward them, then moved instead to a squat metal desk in the corner at the foot of the stairs. Papers lay scattered across its surface, and above that mess was a mug brimming with pens and various other odds and ends. A small stack of folders sat at the far end against the wall. I pulled open the center drawer of the desk and rustled through it. Pens, small change, and . . . I removed a large keyring and searched through it. After finding one generic key after another, one thick, metal key finally stood out. Though it was heavily scratched and worn, I could still make out the label: Ford.

I returned to the door I'd come in, scanned the parking lot, and made my way to the driver-side door of the truck. The key worked in the door, and I climbed in, then turned the key slightly in the ignition. The radio blared loudly, and I jumped, turned the key off, and looked around again at the lot behind me. While I didn't see or hear anything, the desire to leave had become much more powerful.

I turned the radio volume down, lodged the shotgun between my leg and the center console, took a deep breath, and turned the key again. The engine turned, turned, turned, and then finally rumbled to life. I fumbled around with various knobs and levers until I managed to turn on the headlights, then drove back up the driveway I had come from and moved slowly along the road. Once I passed the first building, I cut through a parking lot and onto the tracks.

The truck turned out to be just wide enough to straddle the rails. It was a slow, bumpy ride back to my pack and supplies. I loaded the gas and food as quickly as I could as I listened for any approaching attackers. Nothing came. Once I had finished loading, I turned the truck around and began the next leg of my trip.

As I neared the point where I had crossed over the fence, a man stepped out into the glare of the headlights. I slammed the brakes as he turned to face me and came to a stop in the middle of the tracks. He started toward me, and I pressed lightly on the gas. Although my lights were directly in his face, he didn't shield his eyes at all; he looked directly at me in the blinding glare with his eyes wide open. He broke into a run toward me, but as I bore down on him, he seemed to realize the error of his overconfidence. By then, it was too late. His body slammed against the front of the truck, then slipped beneath it. I jounced about in the seat as I drove over him and continued along the tracks.

L. Marshall James

14

It was very slow going. Caught between the fear of attracting zombies and the fear of losing control of the four-wheeled steel coffin I had commandeered, I maintained a speed of around twenty or twenty-five miles per hour. When possible, I kept the headlights off. I stopped every so often, partly to scour the maps and partly to give my legs and ass cheeks a reprieve from the rumbling of the tires over the railroad ties. Since the radio was essentially nonfunctional, the rumbling was my only semblance of entertainment and distraction. If I had been in a better or more casual mood, I might have sung to myself. Instead, I just rode with the windows down and hoped I wouldn't be overrun when I drove through the larger towns.

I came much, much closer to civilization than I had anticipated. Even outside of the towns, stretches of houses sat adjacent to the tracks, quiet, ominous, and uncomfortably close. Since I was too concerned with what lay ahead of me to take my eyes off the tracks, I only watched them out of the corners of my eyes. More than a few of the fuckers ran out at me, but I was able to avoid them. I watched for the inevitable impassable blockage or collapsed bridge that would corner me against a horde, but I never came to it.

When I reached the town of Rochester, I came across a train that had jumped the rails as they bent to conform to the river. Most of the cars had tumbled down the slope of the land and out of sight, leaving only a few remaining on or near the tracks. Luckily, I was left with plenty of space to slip past. The shapes and sounds around me weren't just my imagination.

Somewhere between that town and the next town of New Brighton, the front right tire of the truck went flat. I don't know how long it had been running low, since it didn't expire all at once, but due to the rough ride of the railroad ties, both the tire and the rim were destroyed by the time I stopped to inspect it.

Since I was on what seemed to be a quiet and empty stretch of track, I decided to remedy the situation and was deeply relieved to find both a jack and a full-size spare stored in a recess in the bed. After a somewhat awkward and extremely paranoid replacement effort, the truck was back in action.

However, since New Brighton was depicted in the atlas as being a residential clusterfuck and I wasn't sure when another comparable stretch of track would present itself, I decided to take a short reprieve from driving to refuel and rehydrate. Though I was still very much on edge, I was beginning to feel the mental and physical strain of the journey. I had left the apartment some six or seven hours prior and had been operating in fight-or-flight mode since then. In all the planning I had gone through, I had never thought to bring caffeine. After all, who needs any help paying attention to their surroundings when they're under the constant threats of death, dismemberment, and infection? Despite how tired I was, I decided to cut my break short and carry on toward my destination. After only a few minutes, I jumped back in the truck and rumbled along tracks.

Leading into New Brighton were three train tracks that ran parallel to each other. One of the tracks snaked under the other two, then conformed to a bend in the river and continued northward toward my destination. The other two tracks rose gradually in elevation and bridged across the river bend to continue directly through the town of Beaver Falls, which appeared to be a veritable death trap. As it turned out, the distinct differences and separations between the tracks were not as evident in the atlas as they were firsthand.

Fifty feet out on the bridge above the river, I stopped, got out, and walked to the front of the truck. I squinted toward Beaver Falls. With the power out in the entirety of Pittsburgh and the surrounding regions, the landscape was nothing but a mess of gray, each tree and building only barely discernible from the next. I wasn't sure what exactly I expected to see in that darkness. Even the zombies approaching from behind were detectable only by the slap of their feet against the railroad ties and the thud of their bodies against the rear end of the truck.

I whipped around and turned on the shotgun-mounted flashlight as I stepped carefully back toward the truck. A man in a torn windbreaker slipped around the end of the truck and ran at me. I fired. The shot struck him in the shoulder, and he fell. I loaded a shell as another zombie approached from the start of the bridge in a dead sprint. I ran to the door, then stopped, fired a second shell into the man on the ground and a third shell at the sprinter. As he fell, I jumped into the truck, slid the shotgun in beside me, and started the engine. In the glow of the taillights, I saw another runner closing in on my rear. I backed up slowly at first, and when he was almost to me, I accelerated. He tripped just before I reached him, and his face hit the tailgate with a resonant thud.

More biters appeared as I backed up. At the edge of the bridge, I hit two more who seemed to be running in tandem. As I returned to solid ground, one girl avoided being hit and reached an arm in through the driver-side window as I passed. I jerked the wheel hard to the left, but she held on and landed a few blows before tumbling out when I slammed the brakes. I rolled up the window as quickly as I could, then performed a haphazard three-point turn and continued back down the tracks. I ran over several more of the crazies before returning to the point where the three sets of tracks separated, then steered onto the middle set of tracks and punched the gas. I kept the lights on as I shifted into third and then fourth gear, dangers be damned.

I didn't hit any others on my way out of New Brighton, but that was only because I was moving too fast for them to get in front of me. I reached forty-five miles per hour on the stretch of tracks leading me out, and while at least one other tire went flat on the way, I kept my speed above thirty for at least a mile after I left the town, only returning to the usual twenty to twenty-five when the entire right side of the sky turned dark with cliffsides that blotted out the stars. My breathing steadied as I drove, and I found some relief in the knowledge that there were no more large towns lying directly ahead of me. Even if I'd had more spare tires, I wouldn't have stopped; as far as my journey along the tracks was concerned, I was almost home free. Even still, I checked the rearview mirror habitually and frequently, which was why I didn't see the biter that ran out in front of me until moments before impact.

Purely out of instinct, I jerked the wheel hard to the right. Either the tire or the rim struck the track rail, then ramped over it and the truck careened down and off the tracks. I bounced in the seat so hard that my head hit the roof of the cab as the truck slammed into the dirt. Tree branches slapped and scraped against the right side of the truck, and before I could try to regain control, I was thrown hard into the steering wheel amid a violent crash. I fell back into the seat as the engine stuttered, then abruptly fell silent.

I looked around, stunned, then grasped around on the floor of the passenger side until I found the shotgun. As I turned to open the door, the window shattered. I twisted away from the driver's side and pumped my legs against it to propel myself across the seat, away from the arms and screaming face that appeared. I raised the shotgun and fired. The head exploded.

With my ears ringing, I looked frantically around me. After a few minutes, I slowly slid back over to the driver's seat and tried the engine. It rumbled miraculously to life, but when I shifted into reverse and pushed the gas, nothing much happened aside from an awful grinding noise. I shifted into first gear, then realized the uselessness of driving forward into the tree I'd crashed into.

After trying again to back out, I got out of the truck, made my way around the hood, and looked underneath. The axle, or some part that connected to it, had snapped during the crash. I didn't have to be a mechanic to be certain that the truck was out of commission.

Not only that, but with no additional spare tires, even a fully functional vehicle would have been unable to navigate the gravel on and around the tracks. The truck had become little more than a shelter from the elements. I stepped over the dead body by the door and climbed back into the cab, then worked my way across the seat and pressed my back against the passenger-side door, which was blocked from opening by the steep rise of the cliffside.

I turned on the truck and checked the clock. While I had a good few hours until sunrise, I had no solid idea where I was, what path I was going to take to my parents' home, or how long it would take to get there. What I did know was that I would be continuing on foot until I found another means of transportation. If I wanted to heighten my chances of survival, I needed rest. Since I had put considerable distance between me and the last town, and was sandwiched between a cliff and the river, the area around me was probably some of the most barren land I would see in a long while. If I were going to rest, it would be best to sleep where I was.

I pulled an emergency blanket from my pack and wrapped it around me as I curled up against the door, then swore quietly to myself as I pulled the bags over to my side, cradled the shotgun in my arms, and tried to sleep.

15

They breathed heavily through decaying faces as they stumbled and ran along the tracks. I ran as fast as I could, but the sounds of their breaths and their footsteps only grew louder and closer. I could feel them reaching for me, but I couldn't keep going. My legs were losing strength, and I was running out of breath. There was no way I was going to make it. I turned and fell as I aimed the shotgun and pulled the trigger.

There was a deafening explosion. I jerked awake and flailed wildly as I tried to orient myself. My ears were ringing so loudly that I could barely hear anything else. My eyes took in the scene of the inside of the truck, then settled on a giant hole in the windshield. A wisp of smoke was rising from the shotgun barrel.

With a surge of panic, I checked myself over for injuries. Though I was covered in bits of glass, I saw no blood and felt no pain. Somehow, I was unharmed. My relief was blunted by movement out of the corner of my eye, and when I shifted to get a better view, I saw someone running toward the driver-side door.

I kicked and pushed myself back, then raised the shotgun and chambered a shell. When a screaming face appeared in the window, I fired a shell into it. I looked again out the rear window and spotted someone else approaching at a run. I slid across the seat, opened the door, and jumped out of the truck. My feet slipped in what was left of the first person's head, but I regained my footing and pointed the shotgun at the approaching runner.

"Get back!" I screamed.

He didn't even slow down. When he came to within ten feet, I loosed a shell at his face. As he fell, I noticed someone else perhaps a hundred yards behind him, followed by another. Though I couldn't tell for sure, it looked like there were several more behind them. With the monocular, I focused in on the runners in the distance. There were more than several; there were thirty or more coming for me. I threw on the pack, pocketed the monocular, aimed, and waited. Once the nearest zombie came within range, I shot him and ran in the opposite direction.

While I had done some endurance running in the past, I had always done so in a pair of old running shorts or, in the few times I'd convinced myself to run in the winter, I'd worn sweatpants. But I'd never worn a pack or weighed myself down. That lack of foresight in my training came back to haunt me in the form of a gasping fatigue that slowly closed the gap between me and my pursuers. I wheezed like an asthmatic under at least forty pounds of equipment as I struggled to maintain footing on the tracks and gravel. I pushed on, expecting to eventually come across a path that I could follow or a house in which I could barricade myself and hide or make a stand, but there was nothing. On my right, there was only the same sheer rise of dirt and trees. On my left was the river. There was no escape except for the stretch of tracks ahead.

I don't know how long I ran. It might have been five miles, or it might have been one. I was struggling before I'd gone far and was more or less shambling by the time I finally spotted the shadow of a building near the tracks ahead of me. As I stumbled nearer to the building, I realized that it was a house sitting on the edge of a small neighborhood. I stopped to catch my breath at the beginning of a street, then thought again, turned, and gasped for air as I searched the darkness from which I had come. The nearest of the runners was two hundred yards away, maybe less. There was not much time, and even if I managed to kill them all, my gunshots would only attract more.

I stepped gingerly down the gravel of the tracks and made my way through a series of backyards. From there, I proceeded up a slight hill toward the back porch of a white house. I stomped up the steps, ran to the back door, and tried the handle, but it was locked.

A scream sounded from far behind me. I ignored it as I slipped off my backpack and let it fall to the porch. I then raised a foot and delivered a kick into the door beside the handle. The glass panes of the door rattled in their insets, but it did not give. I kicked again, and I heard a faint crack, followed by the sound of growling behind me. When I turned, a girl leaped up the porch steps toward me. I raised the shotgun and fired wildly. The shot took her legs out from underneath her, and she face-planted into the floor of the porch. I loaded another round as she crawled toward me, her shredded legs kicking uselessly. I fired a round into her head.

I fell back against the door of the house, looked around, and tried to listen for footsteps or screams. After a moment, I spotted a man in tattered running shorts emerge from the tracks where I had come. I watched almost impassively, either because I was almost mindlessly tired or because I didn't think he would see me. A roar sounded from right beside me, and I jumped, then stepped quickly away from the sound and looked for the source. An arm reached for me through the porch railing. With a glance at the street, I saw the other zombie change course. He was headed toward me. I rushed to the door, started to raise a leg, then stopped. I felt around on my belt until I found a solid metal slug shell, then loaded and chambered it in the shotgun, aimed, and fired into the door handle. As the door fell open, I ran inside and moved as fast as I could up a flight of stairs.

"I'm safe. I'm not infected!" I yelled, hoping to dissuade any sane inhabitants from blowing my brains out.

When I topped the stairs, I yelled again. I turned a corner into a short hallway, then encountered another set of stairs and continued on up. I screamed yet again as I reached the very top, but there was no one there. I ran to the window and looked down at the backyard to see several dark shapes moving. More crazies were coming. At least four more had run into the backyard, and I knew there were going to be many more. Light caught my eye, and I looked to the right with a combination of confusion, fear, and hope at the sight of two sets of headlights in the distance.

I loaded another shell as I walked back to the head of the stairwell, then stood and waited. Someone stomped up the first flight of stairs and screamed wildly while running through what sounded like every room on that floor. As he started up the second flight, he spotted me and screamed incoherently. I fired into his neck, and he fell limp against the wall. I loaded another shell and waited. And waited.

And waited.

Hesitantly, I moved back to the window and looked outside. Two pickup trucks were parked in the middle of the street in a V formation, their back ends touching. Between the two vehicles were four men carrying rifles. Each of them facing away from the trucks, and a smattering of zombies lay dead all around them. As I watched, one of the men raised a rifle and fired at an approaching zombie. I saw the flash of the muzzle but didn't hear the report of the rifle; whether it was because my ears were still ringing or because they were using a suppressor, I could not tell.

A grunt sounded from behind me. I jerked around, raised the shotgun, and fired haphazardly into the chest of a chubby man in overalls. The force of the shot sent me stumbling backward, and I bumped into the window, then sank to the floor. I loaded another shell, settled into a comfortable aiming position, and waited. After a while, the rumble of vehicles came closer and stopped near the house before ceasing altogether. Footsteps clomped slowly onto the porch and then inside. I pulled the shotgun tight against my shoulder and couldn't help but squeeze the pistol grip harder as footsteps ascended the first staircase, then stopped.

"Hello, anybody here?" a man's voice called out. "We're here to help!"

I hesitated to answer. I didn't know them, and I didn't want to know them. All I wanted was to get home. Still, they had already saved my ass, and even if I remained silent, they would eventually find me if they kept looking. The voice called out again and insisted that they meant no harm, that they could take me somewhere safe. I struggled to get up, then gave up, took a deep breath, and announced my presence. He responded by skipping the first floor and continuing up part of the second flight of stairs. He stopped before he reached the top, and I realized suddenly that I was still aiming the shotgun with my finger on the trigger.

I laid the shotgun down on the floor beside me as the man crested the stairs, walked toward me, and stopped. He flashed a light over me, and from what I could tell through the glare, he was a heavyset man, clean-shaven, and clothed in what appeared to be military-grade camouflage fatigues.

"Are you bit?" he asked.

"No," I answered.

"Are you sick?"

"No."

"Are you hurt?"

I looked myself over and wiggled my extremities. No pain was apparent, only fatigue.

"I don't think so."

He nodded.

"Okay," he said. "There's a town just across the river, so we've probably already attracted some attention with all the gunfire and whatnot. If you want to stay here, you're free to, but I recommend you come with us. We can get you somewhere safe."

Somewhere safe? I didn't want to hole up and hide. I had to keep moving. But at the same time, I was beyond exhausted and I knew that if I stayed where I was, there were no assurances of my survival.

"Can I stay the night?" I asked.

He hesitated before answering.

"Yeah. You have somewhere you need to be?"

I nodded.

"I need to get to my parents," I said. "It's out by—"

"We probably shouldn't talk here," he said. "If you want to come with us, we're leaving now. You in?"

I started to push myself up in response. He stepped to me, extended a hand, and pulled me to my feet.

"Sam," he said.

"Paul," I replied. "Nice to meet you."

I bent down to grab the shotgun, and by the time I turned to follow him, he was already headed back down the stairs. I followed him down and out to the back porch. The same two pickups I had seen from the window sat silently in the backyard as the other three men stood watch. I stopped just outside the door and looked around the porch for my bag, but it was gone.

"We loaded your bag," Sam said. "Hop in. We're outta here."

I climbed into the bed of the nearest truck, lay back against the pack, and cradled the shotgun in both arms. As somewhat of an afterthought, I flipped the safety on, then closed my eyes. When I opened my eyes again, it was to the sound of a child's voice.

"Is he dead?"

"No, honey. He's sleeping."

My eyes were open, but with my face buried in the side of my pack, I saw nothing but blackness. I turned my head toward the voice and was instantly blinded by light. I squinted but couldn't make out the shapes in front of me.

"Don't shine the light in his eyes, Emily."

"Sorry."

The brightness abated, and I pushed myself up into a sitting position. Sam stood at the rear of the truck and a blond head peeked at me from just above the tailgate. Some twenty feet behind them was a house, lightly colored with dark trim.

"Welcome to the Ranch," Sam said. "How are you feeling?"

"Not bad. How long was I out?"

He paused.

"Well, what do you remember of the ride?"

"I remember crossing the bridge," I replied.

He barked a laugh.

"Maybe an hour or so then," he said. "I can't believe you slept through that ride. That's a riot."

The tailgate clanked open, and he lowered it as he continued to speak.

"Come on in. Shove your bag on over. I'll carry it for you. We've got you something warm to eat."

I nodded and tipped the pack up, over, and toward him. He grabbed it with both hands, hoisted it off the bed, and walked away with the child in tow. With the shotgun clutched in one hand, I followed them into the house. He sent Emily to bed, then led me through a hall and into a room in which a large, oval dinner table sat unattended. A single meal had been prepared at one end. Beside it, a candle flickered.

"We figured it would be best to let you rest a bit, but I wanted to get you a meal. And a bed that wasn't made of metal and plastic."

He laughed quietly.

I forced a chuckle as I made my way over and sat down. On the plate was a warm square of lasagna and a side of bread. A glass sat beside it, filled with either vodka or water.

I looked up at Sam.

"Thank you," I said.

"You're welcome," he said with a nod. "You look like you earned it."

He walked to the other side of the table and took a seat as I stabbed a fork into the lasagna.

"Sorry I interrupted you before, when you were trying to explain where you needed to go. There wasn't much time is all."

"Oh, no problem," I said. "It probably wasn't a good place to chat."

"No," he said. "We ran into quite a few more of them on the way back here. I honestly can't believe you slept through that. I thought you might have bounced out a couple of times."

"I'd been moving since around midnight," I said between bites. "I was more tired than I realized, I guess. Not in that good of shape."

He looked at me with an expression that might have been curiosity, skepticism, or a bit of both.

"Since midnight? Where were you coming from?"

"Around downtown."

"Downtown Ellwood?"

I shook my head. "Pittsburgh."

His eyebrows raised.

"You came from downtown Pittsburgh?"

I nodded as I chewed.

"How did you manage that?"

"Well . . ." I said. "I stole a boat, then I stole a truck . . . and then I crashed. Then you found me."

He smiled. "Well, I can't take credit. God pointed you out to our lookout and guided us to you."

Since I couldn't think of anything to say, I waited again for him to continue.

His smile abated somewhat, and he spoke again.

"No one came with you?" he asked.

I looked down at my plate. My sister had already been sick, my niece had turned, and my best friend was murdered on my porch. My other friends were probably dead too.

Instead of giving him a full answer, I shook my head.

"Nah."

He fiddled with a napkin that sat in front of him, folding it in half, then in half again. For a minute, he said nothing; I kept eating. I would answer questions if he wanted to ask them, but I wasn't in the mood to do the same. All I wanted was to eat, sleep, shake all hands, and leave.

"So," he said at last, "you said you're headed to your parents? Whereabouts are they?"

"They're close to McConnells Mill State Park. County Road 2022. I can't remember the address, but I can figure out how to get there."

"Mmm, okay," he said, nodding. "What are you going to do once you find them?"

I looked at him, then out one of the windows, then back at him, unsure of what he was trying to get at or quite how to respond.

"I'm not sure," I said. "I hadn't really thought that far ahead."

He nodded.

"I guess it should be John's place to ask you this, but . . . would you consider joining us?"

I stopped chewing for a second, then willed myself to continue. I swallowed somewhat prematurely and had to take a drink of water to help coerce the bite down my esophagus.

"Joining you?" I asked.

"Yes."

"What do you mean, exactly?"

"Well, you seem to have a pretty good head on your shoulders. You're equipped, and you're obviously capable if you managed to get here all the way from downtown Pittsburgh. We could use a guy like you."

"Use me for what?"

He pinched the napkin between two fingers and set it down, unable to fold it again.

"Well," he said. "With the state the world is in, we could use as many good men as we can to clean up and start over."

I stared at him, and it suddenly occurred to me that, far beyond just my life, the lives of everyone else in the world had been changed, perhaps irreparably so. Maybe there were some isolated island dwellers who were still oblivious to recent events, but nearly everyone would be affected by the outbreak in some way. Like Pittsburgh, the rest of the world's civilizations had been, or would be, all but obliterated. Most people were either sick or dead, and the rest . . . Well, we were part of what was left. That was the result of the South American flu. More or less, it was the apocalypse.

Sam started to talk again, and I realized that I had been staring silently at him.

"I don't know if you believe in God," he said. "But trust me, he believes in you. And I believe that he sent you to us for very specific reasons."

He stopped and waited, maybe to let his words sink in or maybe to wait for a response.

I said nothing.

"So . . . if you'd consider joining us, we'd love to have you."

I took a deep breath and struggled to keep from nodding or shaking my head. This guy had saved my life, but his reasons behind it were something I couldn't afford to confirm or deny. I didn't want to join up with this guy and his posse. While I appreciated what they had done for me, all I needed was to get back to the only family I had left.

"I'll consider it," I said as diplomatically as I could. "But I need to find my parents first. I'd have to decide what to do from there."

He nodded quickly.

"Excellent," he said. "We'll help you get there."

He left the folded napkin on the table and stood.

"For now, get as much rest as you need. You can sleep in the living room there"—he pointed through a doorframe to another room—"on one of the couches. I'll make sure no one disturbs you. And don't worry. You're safe here."

He started walking out the side of the room, then stopped.

"I meant to ask you," he said. "What's with the air horns tied to your pack?"

"For distractions," I replied. "Just tie a zip tie around the handle and toss them. Like sound grenades."

He stared at me for a second, his face blank, and then a smile slowly began to creep onto his face.

"Yep, God definitely sent you to us," he said. "Good night."

94

I wished him a good night as he walked out, then sat in silence, half a bite of soggy bread in my mouth. He stepped through the house and disappeared up a flight of stairs. Eventually, a door creaked shut and I heard no more. Once I finished the rest of the food, I carried my things into the living room and lay down on a couch in the corner, the shotgun cradled in my arms, and tried to sleep. Despite my fatigue, I couldn't help but regard every noise and shadow with fear and suspicion.

The transition from wakefulness to sleep was seamless.

16

Morning arrived with the sound of children laughing outside, and I found myself at once disoriented and somehow concerned, despite the giggles and sunshine that flowed in through the windows. Gradually, memories began to surface of how I had come to be on that particular couch in that particular house, around which children played tag despite living through the end of the world.

After a few minutes, I retrieved my pack and weapons and made my way outside. By then, the children had already migrated elsewhere. In their place were a few adults, who sat around a patio table on lawn chairs and sipped what appeared to be lemonade. None of them had weapons, and I felt oddly out of place as I toted around two firearms and a kukri, not to mention the spare pistol in my pack. I was also still wearing the clothes I had been in when Sam and the other three had saved me, so in addition to the bloodstains, there may have been chunks of various body parts still stuck to me. I wondered briefly if I had ruined their couch, but my thoughts were interrupted when Emily stopped and looked up at me, wide-eyed.

"Hi! You're Paul, right?"

I nodded.

"I'm Emily. Are you going to help us kill the demons?"

I opened my mouth to answer, closed it, then opened it again.

"I'm not sure," I managed.

"Oh. Well, you should!" she said, unfazed. "My dad says you're real tough."

I managed a chuckle. If the kid hadn't seemed so utterly sincere, I might have thought she was being a smart-ass.

"Well . . . maybe," I said. "I have to go save some people first. Then we'll see."

"Ooohhh," she said. "Who do you have to save?"

"My mom and dad."

"Are they fighting demons too?" she asked.

"Uh . . . no, they don't live where there are very many zombies. I don't think."

"Oh, okay. Will you live with them?"

"Yeah, maybe," I said. "Do you know where Sam is?"

"Sam? I don't know. He's probably killing demons!"

"Uh . . . oh, okay," I said. "Thank you."

She told me that I was welcome, then ran off as I looked around, somewhat at a loss as to how to proceed. I didn't know where I was, and I didn't know anyone except for Sam, who apparently was busy doing God's work on the war front.

I wandered back into the house and past the living room, where I found a small, horse-themed bathroom near the foot of a staircase. It may have been partly due to the sunroof built into the bathroom or the fact that I was still groggy, but it was only after I had locked the door, leaned the shotgun against the side of the sink, stripped down to nothing, and flipped the light switch that I remembered the untimely death of electricity. With a sigh, I realized the loss of another beautiful thing: hot, convenient showers.

I threw my boxers back on and started to put on the rest of my clothes, then thought twice and retrieved a spare set of clothes from my pack. Despite the blood, sweat, and dirt on my skin, I still felt better after I got dressed. I wasn't quite a new man, but I was ready for the last and hopefully easiest leg of my journey home.

I took my things back to the dining room and spread out what maps I had on the table beside my atlas. I cursed my limited selection of maps; none of them showed the location of my parents' house or the area between it and where I assumed myself to be. I was then struck with the obvious realization that in addition to most of the world's population, the Internet was a casualty of the zombie apocalypse. Even with all the lines and equipment in place, it was all useless without power and people. With nothing but board games and books, that meant staying with my parents was going to be unbearably boring. Maybe I would join Sam and his crew in their quest to kill "demons" just so that I could have something to do. I refolded the maps and stuffed them and any other loose items into the pack, then pulled it on and hesitantly walked back outside.

In contrast to ten minutes prior, the adults were gone from the patio, and the children were nowhere to be seen. My hackles raised at the sound of a faint murmur to my left, and I flipped the shotgun safety off as I walked toward it. As I passed an ATV and rounded the corner of the house, I saw what looked like one of the trucks from the night before. The entire front end was splattered with comic amounts of gore from the windshield to the bumper, as if someone had picked choice bits out of a pile of meat, bone, and organs, then superglued them to the truck and sprayed it with blood for maximum effect.

I walked past the vehicle, then stopped suddenly as I rounded another corner of the house and came upon a large group of people. Though some stood, most knelt in constitution of a circle around a tall, slender man in a suit who stood, eyes closed, and spoke aloud. He appeared to be the source of the murmur at first, but as I grew closer, the whispers of others became audible. I came to a stop ten or so feet away, and as I heard more of what was said, I realized they were praying. The man standing at the center of the circle continued to speak, and as he finally ended the prayer, I again felt very out of place; I was fully armed and standing directly beside a group of mostly unarmed people who were unaware of my presence. The prayer ended before I could slip away unseen, but as the group stood and began to disperse, no one seemed to notice or mind.

The children ran off at full speed, already laughing, and I made the assumption that whatever they were laughing about probably involved the death of the "demons" that used to be their neighbors. While most of the adults ambled away toward the house, Sam and the slender man in the suit walked toward me. The man reached me first and smiled as he extended a hand.

"Welcome to the Ranch," he said. "You must be Paul. I'm John. I believe you met Sam already."

I nodded.

"Yeah, he was part of my rescue party last night."

"Ah," Sam said. "I think you would have been fine on your own."

"I don't know about that," I replied. "How many did you guys end up taking down?"

"Not as many as you could have taken out, I see," John interjected, looking down.

I followed his gaze to the shotgun shells on my belt.

"Eh," I said. "Having the ammunition is one thing. Having the energy to use it is something else. Thank you. Both of you."

"Well, don't thank us. Thank the Lord. Or, I guess you can thank us," he said with a grin. "And we'll pass those thanks along."

I forced myself to chuckle, but I couldn't think of anything to say, so I waited for one of them to continue the conversation.

John accommodated me.

"So, Sam tells me you're looking to head to your parents over by McConnells Mill?"

"Yeah," I said. "They live out that way."

"Mmhmm."

"I was, uh . . . actually hoping to do some planning, but none of my maps cover that area."

"Planning?"

"Yeah."

His brow furrowed as he looked at me.

"What do you mean?" he asked.

"Well . . . on how to get there. I just wanted to plan a route."

"Oh, uh . . ." John looked over at Sam, then back to me. "Didn't Sam tell you? We're going to help you get there."

"Oh yeah, he did," I said. "I can't ask you to do that. You already saved me once. Taking me all the way there—"

"No, no, I insist," he interrupted. "It's only, what . . . ten, fifteen miles at most? It's all mostly rural. No problem for a good group of guys."

He looked to Sam, who shrugged and nodded as he spoke. "We could probably do some cleanup on the way too."

"Right, right," John agreed. "And anyway, it'd be a shame to lose you after already saving you once, right?"

He laughed.

I forced another halfhearted chuckle.

"Are you looking to leave soon then?" Sam asked.

"Uh . . . yeah," I said. "I mean, I don't mean to put you out or anything, I just—"

"No, no, of course not."

"I just need to get back to them. They're relatively remote, but I haven't talked to them since before the . . . well, the whole zombie apocalypse thing happened, so . . ."

"Heh heh," John chuckled. "Zombie apocalypse, I like that."

I blinked, then smiled as much as I could manage, which wasn't much. Of course he didn't call them zombies. They were demons. That made much more sense.

"Well," John said. "I'll let you two get to planning. You can figure out all the details amongst yourselves. And if you need anything, just let me know."

He shook my hand again, then walked away toward the house.

Sam slapped me on the shoulder, then led me around to the back of the house and into a large metal building that seemed at first to be either a garage, an equipment bunker, or some combination of the two. He then led me to a small room off to one side. In the center of the room was a table on which various papers and small maps were scattered around one large, photocopied map. Sam walked to the table and pulled the map toward him.

"All right," he said. "Now, where are your parents?"

17

During all my half-assed strategizing before the outbreak, I had made a lot of assumptions. Rather than being based on scientific, medical, or real-world experience, my assumptions had been based on Hollywood zombie fantasies that revolved entirely around the whims of writers and directors. The realities of the apocalypse were very different.

Sure, zombies were insane. Yes, zombies were severely lacking in common sense. Of course, zombies made terrible diplomats; everyone knew that. But the zombies I encountered had exhibited behaviors I never originally planned on or expected.

The zombies I had encountered were capable of tracking someone down not only by sight and sound but also by memory of where that person had been and even inference of where they might be. The zombie who pursued me in Pittsburgh and the others on the tracks had all seen me and given chase.

Many of them could even speak. They weren't masters of the English language, but they seemed to have speech capabilities beyond that of just moaning, grunting, and screaming incoherently. They seemed to be limited to furious utterances and name calling, but that took a measure of intelligence that was significantly greater than the zombie stereotype.

Another difference was that their diet wasn't limited to just brains or just humans or even just living things. One woman ate a cat, and the woman in the townhouse on Herr's Island ate—or at least tried to eat—a breakfast bar. That meant that they had not only the primal urge to attack but also the primal urge to consume actual food rather than just flesh. As I discovered on the trip to my parents' house, those weren't the only such urges they had retained.

Sam and the other three, Greg, Rick, and Robert, stood outside the picture window of a small brick home and talked quietly among themselves. Our two-truck convoy had stopped every so often to "clean up," as one of the men had put it, and I had stayed in the bed of the truck as backup, since I was the odd man out with a shotgun instead of a silenced weapon. On every other stop, they had returned to the truck with relative haste, but something unexpected had apparently caught their collective attention.

From my vantage my point on the road, they looked to be at a loss as to how to proceed. Robert, the youngest of the group, took a few rushed steps off into the yard and vomited onto a shrubbery.

"What is it?" I asked, whispering for some reason.

They didn't respond.

"Hey!" I yelled.

Excluding Robert, who was still spitting out residual chunks of breakfast, they all turned to face me, their eyes wide.

"What—" I had to stop myself from swearing. "What is it?"

Sam waved me over, and with a cursory glance around me, I jumped down from the truck and jogged over to them. Robert was just returning to the group as I stopped beside Sam to see what had everyone so worked up.

The house was a testament to better days. The garden in front of the house was still very easy on the eyes, despite the vomit that adorned part of it. The inside must have once been a nice place to relax and relieve oneself of the day's events. Landscapes and art pieces lined the walls in the kitchen near the back, as well as the living room in the front, which might have been the centerpiece of the home. The walls were painted a shade of mocha and were topped with an intricate leaf-imprint border near the ceiling, which appeared to have been made from cherrywood paneling. The coffee table, which was made entirely of translucent, greenish glass, sat perpendicular to us in front of a leather couch that faced a respectably sized television. Large, treelike plants decorated every corner of the room. As far as houses go, it had once been beautiful.

Now, the entire room was smeared with blood, guts, and what might have been feces. A respectable stack of corpses had been piled carelessly in front of the television, which had been smashed and somehow impaled with what looked like either a very small dog or a very large squirrel. The plants had been mangled, the table had been smashed, and right there on the couch, utterly oblivious to us, were two zombies fucking doggy-style. It might have been because I had expected something entirely different, because I was still feeling tense about wanting to get home, or because of the group's overall reaction, but I couldn't help but laugh.

I tried to stifle it at first, and as a result, it came out as a sort of congested sneeze. Sam looked over at me as if to sympathize, then looked confused and almost concerned when he realized I was smiling. As I looked between him and the scene in front of us, my restrained laugh grew steadily into a full-throated chortle and then finally, as Sam cracked a smile, I let out a deep and resounding belly laugh. As the group began to catch on, I couldn't stop laughing; it was too much.

In the middle of all the putrid chaos of that room, in a house on a back road in the middle of nowhere, in a world that had been met with unthinkable tragedy, these two zombies were already hoping to start the world anew with their own sets of ideas. I pictured zombies coming together and forging new friendships to replace the friends they had mercilessly slaughtered. Zombies repairing communication mediums to keep in touch with other zombies all over the world. Zombies voting in local, state, and national elections for the zombie politician they felt most comfortable about eating brains with. Zombies homeschooling their hideous zombie children until appropriate educational facilities could be established.

I laughed so hard it hurt, then laughed even harder when the top zombie lover noticed us, stopped mid-thrust, and gaped back at us through the picture window. If I had been given just one wish, it would have been for a camera or, at the very least, a pencil and sketchpad. The scene ended only a few seconds later when the zombie charged us, leaving us no choice but to reduce him to a quivering mass of flesh and bone. The zombie on the receiving end hadn't moved during the entire ordeal and had in fact already been dead. Whether the guys noticed, none of them mentioned it. I tried not to think about it.

Either despite or partly because of the brutal and inglorious love scene we had witnessed, the rest of the trip was interspersed with bursts of uncontrollable laughter. Without prompt, one of us would lose control of a chuckle and the rest would break again into guffaws with the recollection of the ridiculous scene we had witnessed. It was at once heartless and hilarious.

When we finally arrived at my parents' home, I had no choice but to quell the laughter altogether, since my mom would undoubtedly ask what was so funny and I didn't want to have to lie to her. I kept a residual smile though. That could be easily explained away as feelings of joy at having finished the trip home without serious injury and having arrived at their house, which, despite my fears, had been untouched by the madness that had so deeply afflicted much of the rest of the world. Littered over the front lawn and sprinkled on the front side of the house were early Halloween decorations, replete with ghosts, witches, and zombies that I didn't really appreciate like I used to.

As I walked up the driveway from the trucks parked nearer to the road, I found it somewhat difficult to reconcile previous memories of my parents' home with my newfound knowledge of what the world had become. It was as if their home existed in another dimension, entirely separate and untouched by the more recent past—a dimension in which zombies existed only in theory and, even in theory, were too occupied with brains and violence to bother with sex.

For whatever reason, I thought of my attempted suicide after Kaylee's death. Had a bullet remained in the pistol, it would have been more than just an attempt. What would my parents have done if neither their grandchild nor their two children had returned? How would they have coped? I tried to force the notion from my mind but decided instead to just try to ignore it as I neared the front door.

I was surprised to find the front door unlocked, but then I smiled. They had seen me arrive and had already unlocked it before I made it to the door. I pushed the door open, walked in, and closed it behind me. The pack slipped from my shoulders, the annoying burden that it was, and dropped loudly to the floor beside the coatrack.

I had made it.

"Hellooo!" I called out.

There was silence at first. I waited with a grin until I heard my mother's voice from the living room.

"Heeeoooo," she said.

My smile vanished.

I knew without a doubt that it was her voice, but I could tell that something was very wrong. I stood in silence, and when I heard nothing else, I wondered if I had imagined it. I opened my mouth, then shut it, too scared to call out again. I stepped numbly through the hall as she called out again with the same flat, dull, and meaningless utterance.

"Heeeoooo."

I stepped into the living room. Two kitchen chairs sat facing each other in the middle of the room. The nearest of the two was empty, but in the other chair, with her feet in a tray of water, was my mother, her hands bound behind her back and her ankles tied to the legs.

"Heeoo," she said.

I wanted to run to her and untie the ropes. I wanted to hug her and tell her I was sorry I had taken so long, that I was sorry I couldn't save Kaylee or Shelly. I wanted to break the awful, terrible news to her and Dad and just get it over with so that we could express our sorrow over empty graves for each of them and then never, ever speak of it again.

As she looked at me, her lips missing and a trail of dried blood staining her front, her eyes abruptly changed from dull to furious and her face contorted into something unfamiliar, something monstrous. She screamed at me and rocked violently in her chair as she strained against the ropes. I backed against the wall and dropped the shotgun. It clattered to the floor, and my mom followed suit as she tipped the chair and landed on her side. The tray of water flipped and spilled out on the carpet. I lurched toward her, then caught myself as she screamed again and gnashed her teeth. Again, I backed up to the wall, then jumped as the door on the other side of the room rocked in its frame. My father called out from the sunroom on the other side of the door.

"Debby!" he roared.

"Dad!" I screamed.

It was hard look away from my mom as I made my way past her to the door, then grabbed the handle and tried to turn it. The door was locked. In all the time I had spent in that house, it had never been locked. It couldn't be. To lock it from the sunroom would require a key, and there was no one in the living room who could have locked it. My mom was tied to a chair. Something slammed against the door, and I jumped back.

"Paul!" I heard my father yell.

"Dad!"

The front door creaked open, and Sam called my name. The sunroom door slammed again in its frame, and as I backed away from it, I felt something beneath my boot. It was an old skeleton key. The key to the sunroom.

"Dad," I said, but the word came out as a ragged whisper.

"Dad," I said, louder.

There was silence, then something slammed against the door again, and again, and again. I heard Sam step into the room behind me. I ran to the door and placed my hands against it to lessen the distance, to get as close as I could to my father.

"Dad!" I yelled.

He stepped closer to the door, so close that I could hear him breathing on the other side. He sounded like an animal, trapped and mad.

I laid my forehead on the door.

"Dad, answer me!"

"Let me out!" he screamed. "Let me out!"

"Why are you locked in there?"

"Get me out! Pull me out!"

"Dad," I said. "I can't let you out. Not until you tell me why you're locked in there."

For a moment, he fell silent. He even stopped breathing. I waited for him to say something, to explain why he was locked away, to tell me that he wasn't infected and that he hadn't lost his mind, not really. But his breathing only resumed, faster and harder than before, and then he screamed. It was the loudest I had ever heard a person scream, and I knew what the scream was. It was a simple, primeval expression of who he was. It was what he had become.

I stared at the door and said nothing. Sam said my name and told me that I knew what had to be done. When I didn't respond, he said it again and went on to tell me that my parents were gone, that what was in the house wasn't them. He told me that I could leave and that he would take care of it, if I wanted. Instead, I drew my pistol.

From where my mother lay tied to the chair, she had to crane her head back to watch me. With the expression on her face and the tension in her body, she was like a ravaged, wild animal, backed into a corner and unable to escape. I searched her face for some sign that she was who I remembered her to be, that she recognized me, that there was something left of the woman who had birthed me and raised me. There was nothing in her eyes but hate. My mother was gone; in her place were the most violent and primitive urges of the human species laid bare and raw. All I could see, all that remained, was a monster. She growled as I stepped closer, then screamed and snapped her jaws shut with such force that one of her teeth chipped.

"I love you," I whispered.

I aimed the pistol at her head, but I couldn't pull the trigger. All I needed, all I hoped for, was a sign—a sudden calm, a flicker of recognition, a nod to tell me that she understood and knew that it had to be done. But if there was anything left of her, I couldn't see it. As with Kaylee, the choice was mine alone.

I pulled the trigger, and she slumped and ceased. The chipped tooth stuck to the flesh where her upper lip had been. My father broke into a frenzy on the other side of the door. I looked at my mom's body a little longer and blinked away the tears that had formed. I knew I couldn't cry yet. I wasn't done. I walked to the sunroom door where the noises were coming from.

Rattle, rattle, scream.

I unlocked the door, stood back, and waited for it to open. It just kept rattling, so I turned the handle, pushed the door open, and took a few steps back. From out of the room walked a man I knew, wearing a shirt I'd seen before. I had bought my father that same shirt. It was stained with blood. He stared at me and cocked his head to one side as he approached. He seemed disoriented, lost.

Sam said my name, but I ignored him as the man slowly approached, came within an arm's reach, and stopped. Sam told me to be careful as the man raised his hands, then placed them on my throat and started to squeeze. I shoved him hard in the chest. He stumbled backward and almost fell, then regained his balance and sprang back toward me. In one convulsive moment, I raised the pistol and fired twice. The first bullet struck him in the lower belly, and the second disappeared into his upper chest. His legs gave way beneath him. I backed away as he fell forward, and his eyes remained on me until the moment his head impacted the floor with a thud. He seemed stunned at first. Then, using his arms, he raised himself into the peak of a push-up position and froze, his legs askew and unmoving. I stepped nearer to him, knelt, and watched as he stared at the floor. Maybe he was all right. Maybe he was just confused. Maybe we could save him.

"Dad," I whispered.

For a while, no one said anything. Sam stood watch behind me as I waited for something, anything, from my father, whose haggard breath filled the silence like the wicked ambience of a horror film. A puddle of drool took form on the floor beneath his mouth.

At last he made a sound almost like choking, and his torso convulsed as he broke into a coughing fit. He spat out a phlegmy mass that clung to his lips with translucent threads that sagged and grew thinner as the liquid within them neared the floor. He spat weakly once, then again, seeming only to bring his lips together and release enough air to make a token effort at expelling the rest of the mucus. It was only when he spat a third time and extended the exhalation into a throaty, quavering moan that I realized he was trying to speak. My name, stretched to the capacity of his lungs, filled the house and emptied what was left of my resolve. I sat back on my haunches and finally broke into tears. There we remained as he screamed my name and I mumbled responses he could not comprehend: that I was sorry, that I should have got there sooner, that I loved him and Mom so much, and that I would never forget them.

After a while, the man who used to be my father lowered himself to the floor and fell silent. His body spasmed periodically, then fell limp after each iteration. I watched helplessly as his breathing grew quieter and his movements became less pronounced. Finally, he stopped moving altogether. I stared awhile longer, then rose and expended the last of my ammo to make sure he was dead.

Sam asked me if I was okay. When I did not answer, he asked me if I needed anything. I looked around at the room. On one side, a tattered couch faced a shitty old television that sat on an ancient, poorly stained table. Knickknacks and cheap zombie figurines littered shelves, and on the walls were myriad pictures of dogs, kids, and parents who were probably all dead. On the floor near the chairs was a picture of the man and woman I had just shot. They were standing on either side of a young man in a graduation cap and gown. For some desperate moment, I tried to pretend that the young man in the picture was someone else, surrounded by people I did not know; but I knew the truth. The house had seen what had transpired, and it screamed details with horrifying clarity.

On the floor in front of my mother's face was an empty ice tray speckled with spittle and blood. There were more like it scattered around the room, including one floating upside down in the remaining tray of water. Against the wall near my mom's head was an open bottle of pills, its contents spilled out onto the carpet. I knew from the color that they were ibuprofen. Good for fending off a fever. Ragged lengths of rope lay in a tangled heap at the far end of the room and in disorganized strips beside the empty chair in the middle of the room. Under that chair was an open utility knife.

Before she had lost her mind, Shelly had mentioned that Mom was sick. Dad must have returned from his business trip to see her, sick and increasingly hostile. Maybe he knew what was happening at the time or maybe the news reports clued him in, but eventually he knew that he had no choice but to restrain my mother to keep her from hurting him or herself. He must have tried to treat her with ibuprofen and ice water, but nothing worked.

I glanced again at the skeleton key.

Before long, he must have begun to experience the same symptoms as my mother: fever, ache, and mood swings. Knowing what would happen but unable to bring himself to end it before he succumbed, he locked himself in the sunroom and slipped the key under the door. While my mother lost her mind in the living room, he did the same in the sunroom.

I walked past Sam to make my way outside. I passed the group without a word, climbed into the truck, and scanned the empty road as Sam stopped by the other guys. After a while, he called me over. I joined them as they knelt in prayer, and at Sam's gentle behest, I knelt with them. I kept lookout as they prayed. I only looked back at the house as we finally drove away.

Whatever the infected were, they were not supernatural. Neither their strength, their intelligence, nor their compulsions were beyond the realm of human possibility. Nothing about them was inhuman; just insane. They were still nothing more than compromised mammals somehow driven into unsustainable violence. They were men, women, and children whose minds had become black holes, and who would pull each and every other human being down with them, deep into madness, if they could just reach them.

18

Sam sat with me in the back of the truck and did his best to console me during the trip back to the Ranch. Most of what he said revolved around God's mercy and the claim that I would see my parents again in the afterlife; I couldn't allow myself to believe it, no matter how good it might have felt. My parents were dead, my sister and her daughter were dead, and my friends were all probably dead. Nothing was going to change that, no matter how desperately or firmly I believed otherwise. But I didn't fight his claims. I at least knew he meant well, so I gleaned what comfort I could from his company and the sound of his voice, if not from his words.

One of the other guys must have radioed ahead to inform the Ranch of what had happened because there were a few people waiting outside for us when we finally returned. They approached as I dismounted the truck, and a kind-faced woman spoke soothingly as she took my hand. Part of me wanted to drop my things and wander off into the forest to disappear among the flora and fauna. Had they not gently shepherded me into the house, I might have done so. Though I made no conscious decision, I followed the woman and a few others through the house to a back room, where they prayed for me as I stared at the ceiling.

There were no mental calculations to be run and nothing to keep my mind from turning on itself, so it turned off instead. I had persisted after the deaths of Alex and Kaylee, but with my parents dead, there was nothing to aspire to and no one left to save. I had numbly returned to the truck and allowed myself to be guided into the Ranch, where I eventually fell asleep with the vague whisper of a hope that something, some sliver of meaning, would carry me onward.

When I woke, I found myself submerged in a world that was very different from that in which I thought I had fallen asleep. The Ranch was saturated with people who, like me, had been preparing for something extraordinary even before the outbreak. But while I had been preparing for an impossible and ridiculous zombie disaster, they had been preparing for an endgame in which Jesus Christ would return to smite evil once and for all. In more than a few alarmingly sincere discussions, I overheard rants and debates about the true identity of the Antichrist, the details of precisely how the world would end, and the true source of the zombie plague. Rather than smelling of death and loss, the air of the Ranch smelled like inevitable revolution over the armies of Satan.

As friendly as the residents were and as much as they tried to include me in their delusion, I had nothing of substance to say to any of them. I was only really there because I had nowhere else to go. For weeks, I drifted about the Ranch like a ghost, passing wordlessly through the buildings, grounds, and surrounding forest as I watched and listened to a world that carried on all around me. Kids chattered excitedly, adults carried on their typically inane conversations, and sometimes it was almost like the outbreak never happened. I was the harmless, friendly zombie of the Ranch, living in a state less conscious than subconscious until I heard faint screams in the chill of the night. As I moved closer to the source, I realized that the voices were coming from a radio in the map room. It was Sam's voice, and his urgent, panicked tone awoke me as if from a deep slumber.

"We need help! Now!"

From my meandering path, I broke into a run across the yard and burst into the room, where an older man, Tom, jotted down notes as he listened to the distress call.

"We have an injured man, and we're cornered!" Sam yelled.

"Where are you?" Tom inquired. "Give me a location!"

"On Route 18! The hotel on the left, past the industrial buildings!"

I strode up to the map.

"Show me where they are," I said.

My voice cracked as I said it, but Tom looked in my direction, wide-eyed with either surprise or adrenaline. Likely torn between showing me Sam's location and first alerting the backup, he stuttered a few words, then stood and looked over the map momentarily before laying a finger down just a few inches southeast of our position. I knew immediately that the backup wouldn't get there in time. They'd have to take the trucks out of the Ranch, then follow the road northeast, almost all the way to the town of Wampum before they met Route 18. It was more or less a straight shot to the hotel from there, but they would have to go at least two more miles to where Sam and the guys were holed up. With grim determination, I decided that I would get there first.

As Tom radioed for backup, I grabbed a spare radio and clipped it onto my belt as I ran into the house. The door thundered against the wall in the silence of the night, and I sprinted through the halls to my equipment where it had remained untouched since my return. I found my shotgun, shell belt, and a box of shells on the top shelf of a cabinet. I donned the belt, emptied the box of shells into a cargo pocket of my pants, and made my way back through the house with the shotgun in hand. Lights had just begun to turn on upstairs as I exited the front door and made a beeline for the garage. The backup trucks would have to follow the long driveway and then the road to the hotel, making their route unfortunately circuitous. My route would take me along the trails through the forest, a route that was more direct and, more importantly, might get me there before Sam and the guys were slaughtered. I slipped the shotgun sling around my shoulder, climbed onto one of the ATVs and started it up. As the backup crew began to emerge from the house, I sped past them, to the trees and along the trail.

In the headlight of the ATV, the trail was a blurred tunnel of branches, stones, and dirt as I sped along in a single-minded haze. Yells, gunshots, and predatory roars erupted from the radio, and it was clear that the window for rescue was quickly closing. The engine screamed as I held the throttle open on the straightaway leading deeper into the woods. I felt a surge of adrenaline as I turned onto the second, more treacherous leg of the trail, and though it had been years since I had ridden, I felt as if I had never stopped. I leaned into every turn and rode with as much speed as I could without losing control. In brief flashes of memory, it was almost like I was a teenager again, riding through my parents' woods and pretending to be chased by hordes of undead. This time, I didn't need to imagine the danger, and instead of fleeing from it, I was racing toward it.

I emerged from the woods into a parking lot and sped to the road, which ran parallel to Route 18. I turned onto the pavement and again held down the throttle as far as it would go. I heard yells and saw shapes in the shadows, and as I passed house after house, I knew the sound of the engine would attract even more unwanted attention. I don't know whether I was unafraid or if my fear was simply annulled by other emotions, but as I rounded the last corner and approached what was surely my goal, reality weighed down on me.

The number of infected was huge. When I ramped up the slope of the driveway, I was greeted by the sight of what must have been a hundred zombies swarming over the property, illuminated only by my headlight and the flashes of the muffled rifle shots coming from inside the hotel. I sped into the front yard, veered left, then back to the right, where I brought the ATV to a stop, shifted into neutral, and dismounted. As I brought the shotgun to my shoulder, I hesitated for a second at the realization of just how much of the horde's attention I had attracted in my noisy approach. Perhaps a third of the horde had started toward me by the time I fired my first shot.

My first target, a priest who was naked from the waist down, flew backward with the impact of a slug and fell into the legs of those behind him. I pumped and fired another round that struck a teenager in the top of the skull. A man's gut exploded on my next shot, and I fired the rest of the shells in rapid succession as the infected surged toward me. Though I couldn't hear any friendly sounds from the hotel aside from sporadic weapon discharges, voices yelled out over the radio, sounding equally urgent and jubilant, owing to what must have sounded to them like the arrival of a rescue party.

I jumped back onto the four-wheeler and raced across the yard, then paralleled the road until I had put sixty yards or so between the biters and me. I then stopped, turned to face the screams, and reloaded as quickly as I could. By the time I had filled the shotgun to capacity, the fastest of the zombies were already within range. I put them down with a few well-placed shots, then replaced the expended shells and drove the ATV back toward the hotel in a wide arc. As I rounded the edge of a swimming pool, I realized that the shots I had heard before had gone all but silent. I thumbed the safety on the shotgun, directed the four-wheeler toward the middle of the mob near the hotel, and gunned the throttle. As I blazed toward the infected, my fear faded and was replaced by suicidal fury.

I had nearly attained full speed by the time I reached the hotel, and it seemed that, all at once, the attention of the horde turned toward me in its entirety. In the gravel of the parking lot, I gripped the shotgun in both hands, stood, turned, and stepped from the ATV as it careened into the throng. I might have remained upright for an eighth of a second before I lost my footing and balance.

I flew and landed hard on my right shoulder, then tumbled and slid through the gravel before I finally came to a stop. I leaped to my feet, screamed, and swung the butt of the shotgun into an elderly woman's face. As she fell, I swung again, then again, striking several more of the infected that swarmed around me. I then backed up a few steps, aimed, and fired. The man in front of me flew backward into those directly behind him as I fired again, then again. Tunnels through the crowd appeared with each shot, and after firing all but one or two shells, I buckled down and barreled through the largest gap. The four-wheeler had left a swath of prone bodies behind, and I followed it with large, unsteady steps on and over bodies as I dodged outstretched hands and feet. The ATV had come to a rest to the left of the door around which the zombies had collected. A few of them still stood in front of the door. As they turned to face me, I raised the shotgun and fired once, twice, and a third time. The third shot was only an impotent click. I gripped the shotgun and ran as fast as I could.

"I'm coming in the door!"

My announcement, which was equal parts bellow and screech, was met with loud voices from inside. I gave a yell that grew in volume and pitch as I lowered my left shoulder and prepared to crash the door. My entry attempt was neither as dramatic nor as successful as I had assumed. I impacted the door with a thud, then sank to the concrete. Despite the shock of pain in my shoulder, I forced myself to my feet and turned to face the rage of the mob. I raised a foot to hold off a chubby girl in a bathrobe, and her impact with the bottom of my boot shoved me hard into the door. At the same time, sounds of movement came from inside.

"Let me in!" I screamed. "Let me in the door!"

I heard no acknowledgment amid the deafening roars in front of me, and as the girl wildly clawed at me, the rest of the crowd began to close in. I raised the other leg to try and hold them off, but I was too slow, and a soccer mom's pelvis slammed into my foot. As she tripped forward into me, I swung the shotgun as hard as I could and hit her in the side of the head with the stock. She collapsed into me, and I sank to the ground beneath her.

The shotgun was torn from my hands as claws, fists, and feet scratched and struck, and there was nothing I could do but scream and weather the storm into which I had plunged myself, using the body of the soccer mom as a shield. Even as the door behind me budged and Sam's haggard voice called out to me, I had every expectation that I was going to die. I reached out a hand, and two pairs grasped it, then pulled. I closed my eyes and was dragged through the open door into the relative calm of the hotel room.

"Get him up!" Sam screamed. "Up! Go! Into the bathroom!"

I struggled to my feet and was half-dragged by Robert and Greg into the room, past a bed and into a small bathroom. For a second, I thought it was only my imagination that the din from outside seemed to grow louder. Then, I heard the shots and roar of trucks. Our cavalry had arrived. Robert and Greg let go of me, and I half-fell, half-lowered myself to the floor by the shower beside Rick, who was applying pressure to a bloody wound on his leg.

"Dogpile!" Sam yelled through the door as he fired toward the front of the room. "The calvary's about to start shooting!"

The guys piled on top of me, and the noise quieted slightly when Sam stormed into the room slammed the door behind him. Beneath the weight and the pain, I tried at first to count the seconds and minutes, but eventually I gave up on time and let myself sink into the endless present. When the weight of the men finally eased off and I was pulled to my feet, I met the relief and calm of our rescue with wide-eyed bewilderment and awe.

I walked gingerly through the room, through a shocking sea of bodies and blood, and out to the waiting trucks, where I stood and regarded the fate I had thought would overcome and end me. As I stood there, covered in blood and flesh, I felt no small bit of schadenfreude at the fates of the infected. For what they had done and continued to do, they deserved what they got. They deserved to die.

"Fuck you all," I whispered.

The cavalry celebrated on the trip back, but the rest of us were too tired or traumatized to join them in their exultation. I spent most of the ride looking myself over for bite marks and injuries that might have indicated imminent and inevitable death. To my surprise, the miraculousness of my initial survival was compounded by the miracle that, aside from serious road rash, deep bruises, and some relatively minor cuts, I was unharmed. I allowed myself a single glance toward the heavens, and I shook my head in disbelief at the clouds.

After the rescue, life returned to roughly what it had been before, though the pity I'd detected in the Ranch residents seemed to have been replaced with hushed respect and wonder. I shook it off and continued to wander the Ranch, where I became something of a roaming watchman until a week or so later, when Sam asked me to accompany him to the map room. As I walked in, I noticed Greg and Robert standing about, waiting wordlessly. On the table in front of them was a shiny, silenced M4 assault rifle. Sam picked it up and handed it to me.

"This is for you," he said. "If you want it."

The rifle looked and felt divine. Before I could think of a response, he continued.

"We've talked a bit," he said, "and we've decided that we'd like you to join us on missions."

For some reason, I couldn't help but wonder if he was serious.

"If you want," he added. "But it's up to you. If you'd want to—"

"Yes," I interjected.

I looked around at each of the guys in turn before my eyes settled again on Sam.

"Please," I said.

Sam smiled.

"See?" he said. "I told ya God has a plan."

19

There is nothing as important to the human mind as having a purpose. Take what you will from people; if they can find purpose, you have not yet broken them, even if their only purpose is to enjoy your torture and to smile in defiance or to search until they find a more meaningful purpose. With no family or friends left, I searched for purpose in fighting with the Crusaders, as Sam and the group came to call themselves. At the very least, it kept my mind too busy to turn on itself; for that, I reveled in the environment that John and Sam provided.

We planned and strategized our every move from the safety and seclusion of the Ranch. Surrounded by a few square miles of forest and with only a sparse population on the few roads nearby, it served as a perfect home base for us. Despite the almost casual air of the Ranch, it was something of a fortress, with sentry points and heavily defensible positions in addition to heavily fortified housing. We departed on our missions like knights leaving a castle, our hearts and minds set on grim glory and the death of our enemies.

Our primary goals, as John had explained to us, were to save the innocent, eliminate the "demons," and clean out the buildings so that they could be repurposed for God's use. The running joke was that John was God's real estate agent and was trying to take advantage of rock-bottom housing prices. With the way he seemed to focus more on buildings and property, I wondered if the joke had more truth in it than anyone was willing to admit. Regardless, working with the Crusaders gave me at least a sense of meaning in a world that seemed more empty and meaningless every day. I felt more alive and more present with a weapon in my hands and a finger on the trigger than anywhere else. That's not to say I didn't have to make some concessions for the company . . .

"Brad, would you like to lead in prayer?"

Brad, our newest recruit, lowered himself to a knee before Sam had finished his question. The rest of us knelt around him, and I stared at the backs of my eyelids as I lowered my head.

"Lord," Brad said. "Thank you for carrying us to this blessed day. Thank you for your guidance in this dangerous world. Please continue to guide us, Lord, and protect us from the evils which seek to infect us and bring our ruin. We seek to honor your everlasting glory. Amen."

"Amen," said the group, and we double-checked our weapons.

"All right, guys," Sam said. "Keep on your toes. We've had it easy so far, taking out houses on back roads and that, but there are a lot of houses in this next area and a lot of infected people in them. Stay focused, stay systematic. And remember, if you get separated and all else fails, hole up in a house somewhere and radio us to let us know where you're at. We can get backup from the Ranch if we really need it. Nema?"

"Nema!" the rest agreed.

Nema. It was their version of "Hooah," the battle cry of the US Army. It meant anything from "Yes" to "Praise Jesus" to "Let's eat breakfast. I hope there's bacon." It was also a palindrome for "Amen." Go figure.

We walked to the trucks, and I hopped in the back of my designated ride. I could have sat in the cab, but I preferred the bed. God spoke through the wind, or at least that was my answer when asked about it. In reality, God said nothing to me through the wind or any other medium. It was just that I preferred the peace and temporary solitude of the bed to Rick, who mostly talked only about Jesus and his dead wife and kids as he drove. Even in silence, God held much less depressing conversation.

As I settled in against the cab of the truck and waited for everyone to get ready, I noticed that we were being watched. Sitting in the yard was the boy-and-dog pair we had found while clearing a small neighborhood just outside of Wampum. I use the word "found" because we sure as hell didn't save them; they had managed well enough on their own, and if we had never found them, they most likely would have prospered and set up their own strike force with which to wipe out the local zombie population. Instead, we managed to convince them to return with us to live peaceful lives on the Ranch. The boy watched us curiously and massaged the ears of the dog, which eyed us with a stoicism that I might have expected of a lion. He often reminded me of a lion, actually, in no small part because of the state in which we had found him with the boy.

It had been an unnervingly quiet day. After finding no resistance whatsoever in the first fifteen houses we had cleared, we had all been at least a little tense. We half-expected a rush of zombies or an ambush of some kind.

While I had my doubts as to how a group of semi-retarded zombies could effectively cooperate, I couldn't help but expect some surge of violence to balance out the day. I was almost relieved by the sound of sporadic screams coming from one of the last houses on the block. As we approached the front of the house, my relief was quickly replaced by nausea. The stench struck at about the same time that I saw the first rotting body, and as I stepped through the smashed-in front window of the house, I found myself wondering at the sheer numbers of the dead that were inside. There were more zombies in that house than in any house we had encountered up to that point and more than I had ever seen all at once, except for the rescue mission at the hotel. Every single one of them was dead. Bodies littered the floors from wall to wall in every room throughout the house.

Despite the body count, there were no apparent bullet holes, exploded heads, or detached limbs. Inert bodies lay piled in the main room, soaking in puddles of their own blood and frozen in their last expressions of rage. It was as if they had all had a group meeting and unanimously decided that instead of establishing the first democratic zombie society, they would just rip out each other's throats and call it a day.

As we moved through the house toward the sporadic screams, we heard a low and menacing growl. Down the hallway, the death count continued. Bodies slumped against walls, jutted out from doorways, and lay in piles on top of one another. A single zombie remained alive; it was the source of the screams. Beyond it and hidden in the darkness of a doorway at the end of the hall was the source of the savage growling. Whatever the zombies might have voted on during their town hall meeting, their decision had been contemptuously vetoed. Whatever lobbying they might have attempted to support their cause, the beast in the back room had apparently not been swayed.

In the glow of our flashlights, two pale green dots appeared beyond the doorframe, shrouded by darkness. Greg's breathing quickened beside me, and when I glanced over at him, I noticed that he was sweating heavily.

"You all right, Greg?"

He glanced over at me, then back down the hall, his eyes wide.

"Are you seeing this?" he asked. "It's a frigging beast of Satan!"

I looked back at the eyes. Gradually, the face of a creature appeared in the doorway and stopped just beyond the threshold. Most of its fur was caked with blood, though I could see patches of yellow fur here and there. It growled menacingly, its teeth bared, and its eyes flicked back and forth between our group and the zombie that crawled closer toward it.

"No, I think it's a dog," I said. "Or a wolf, maybe. Either way, I doubt it has anything to do with Satan. Canines don't have any religious affiliation, to my knowledge."

Suddenly, the beast lunged forward, grabbed the approaching zombie by the face, and shook it violently back and forth. The zombie screamed and attempted feebly to escape, and we watched in silent awe as the dog released its grip, then moved in and clamped down on the zombie's throat. The sight and sound of the biter's throat being ripped out was unnerving, especially because it didn't happen all at once. It took a minute or so of tugging, twisting, and shaking before the devil dog triumphed and the zombie finally ceased to struggle. The dog then retreated to the doorframe, stood, and regarded us silently as its mouth dripped with blood.

Hanging from the dog's collar and partially obscured was a blue, bone-shaped tag. I could barely take my eyes off the dog, and though I couldn't read the tag from where I stood, I assumed it said something to the effect of "Cerberus, Dog of Hades," "Badass Canine," or simply "He Who Kills." As we would eventually find out, his name was deceptively unassuming: Kotie.

As we all stood there, I noticed movement in the corner of my eye. Greg had raised his rifle.

I reached over and pushed it back down.

"You're not going to shoot that dog," I said.

"That's no dog, Paul. That thing—"

"It's a dog," I interrupted. "And that dog has killed an entire fucking army of crazies."

I noticed a hint of shock enter Greg's face. I silently cursed myself for swearing in front of him.

"Paul," Sam said in his best diplomatic voice, "that thing does look like it could be rabid."

I took a deep breath and lowered my tone. "Calm" and "Cool" were my two middle names.

"Look," I said, "there's no point in shooting a good dog. Right now, he's cornered and he doesn't know if we're friendly or just another group of demons. Maybe he's infected; maybe he's not. But if he's not, we could use a dog like that."

I looked back and forth between them and the dog.

"He'd be a hell of an asset, Sam," I insisted. "I'll stay here and try to calm him down—"

"Guys, look," Robert whispered.

I looked again to the shadowy doorway. Standing beside the canine of hell and with a hand resting on the top of its head was a small boy dressed in footie pajamas. He was covered in as much blood as the dog. He, too, regarded us silently, his eyes wide.

Sam cleared his throat. "Uh, hello there, son."

The boy said nothing. He just stood there.

Sam waited, then tried again.

"Are you okay?"

The boy nodded.

"Do you . . . uh . . . do you want to come with us?"

He seemed to think it over, then shook his head.

Sam stared agape at the boy, apparently unsure of how to proceed. As the boy lazily wiped sleep out of his eyes with the back of a clean hand, I wondered how the world had changed to such an extent that dogs and children alike could unsettle heavily armed men.

We all introduced ourselves in turn, and it took us at least a half an hour of pleading and coaxing before we finally convinced the boy to join us. Even as he walked toward us, Kotie held his ground and continued to growl. It was only when the child stopped in front of us and signaled for the canine to follow that the dog stopped growling and gladly tagged along, blood still dripping from his jowls as he grinned up at us. After that day, he never growled at anyone else on the Ranch. He just watched and listened, and no matter what, he stayed with the boy.

"You ready to send some demons back to Hell, Paul?"

I nodded at Brad as he walked past, then back at the duo as the engine roared to life. As we rumbled down the driveway to fight and kill, I was certain that some part of the dog wanted to jump up beside me and join our efforts. Domesticated or not, the killer instinct was ingrained into him and always would be. When the world came crashing down, he became what he had to be to survive. Still, I knew that there was no way he would leave the kid. Whatever the boy did for the rest of his life, the dog would follow. The boy might leave the dog, but Kotie would never leave him, so long as he lived. In a way, I envied that boy. As we pulled out onto the road, I averted my gaze to the surrounding landscape and cradled my M4. In absence of a good dog, a good weapon would have to do.

We stopped on Newcastle Road, a short distance north of Wampum and just shy of the first of the houses we had marked as targets. The main goal was to clear out Wampum itself, but we intended to sanitize the outskirts before we did that. One by one, we had already cleared out a bevy of houses scattered about on various back roads. Newcastle Road, which led straight south into Wampum from our position and was bordered on both sides by houses, was the last and most difficult of our aspirations before moving on to clear the town itself.

We encountered no resistance at all in the first few houses, but even after all the houses I had been through, I found myself routinely unsettled. Every zombie I encountered drove me to hate and fear them more, and the act of creeping around at night with no illumination other than the lights on our weapons was something out of a survival-horror game. Even still, we made steady progress down the street, systematically clearing each house before moving on to the next. So it went for probably a half a mile, before we hit a snag.

When we entered the house, I figured it was empty. Everything was in order; nothing was broken. It wasn't exactly perfect, but it was spotless by zombie standards, which meant to me that there were no zombies inside. It turned out that I was only half-right, and that fact became apparent as the sound of sobbing drifted audibly through the house. I noticed it first and motioned to Rick, who was closest to me. We moved slowly through the house toward the source of the noise and checked bedrooms and bathrooms along the way until we came to an open door. I pushed the door the rest of the way open and saw a man sitting alone at a desk, sobbing into his hands. Rick got Sam's attention as I walked into the room. I had come within a few feet of the man before he realized I was there.

He jerked away from the desk. As he did so, his hand wrapped around a pistol and he brought the barrel around toward me. I started to raise my rifle in response, then realized that I was too late. As he fired, I dove to my right and collided with the side of the bed. Once I hit the floor, I shifted quickly onto my back and tried to maneuver the rifle to shoot him before he realized that he could probably shoot me through the mattress.

"Get back!" the man screamed. "I'm infected! Get back!"

"Put the gun down!" I bellowed. "Put it down!"

Rick and Sam echoed my command from the hall.

"No!" the man screamed again, somewhat quieter. "Get out!"

I glanced at the door and saw Sam's face poke into the doorway, disappear, then tentatively reappear.

"Sir," he said. "Please put down the gun."

"I'm infected," the man repeated.

"I understand that. Please put the gun down."

I heard a silence, then a clatter, and Sam nodded at me as he walked into the room. I pushed up to a standing position, removed my earplugs, and brushed myself off.

"I'm sorry," the man said. "I'm sorry."

I could tell without looking at him that he was sincere, but I was still pissed at him for shooting at me, so I said nothing.

"It's all right," Sam said, filling the silence. "What's your name?"

"Will."

"Okay, Will. Are you sure you're infected?"

"Yeah," Will responded. "I'm sure."

Sam nodded slowly.

"Okay," he said. "We'll make sure that when you turn, you go quickly."

I looked at Sam, whose face showed somber concern, then looked to Will, who was wide-eyed with fear.

"You . . . you're not going to kill me?"

"No. Not yet," Sam said. "Not until you've turned."

Sam had meant what he said to be comforting, as in "We won't kill you; we'll kill zombie-you."

Will, decidedly uncomforted, stared at Sam, then looked at each of the rest of us in turn.

"But . . . no, you have to kill me," he said, his voice shaking. "I can't . . . I can't become one of them. I can't become that."

He shook his head as he pushed to his feet.

Sam stepped forward and laid a hand on his shoulder.

"Will . . ." he said. "Are you saved?"

"What? No, what . . . what are you talking about?"

"Do you know our Lord and Savior, Jesus Christ?"

Will's expression changed from confusion to indignation.

"I am not here to be baptized," he said. "I'm infected! I know what's going to happen to me. I've seen . . . the neighbors. I've been watching them. I can't become that. I can't . . . I can't lose my mind like they have. Please."

He looked beseechingly at Sam, then to me.

I don't know what my face said, but his eyes remained locked on mine. I had already felt bad for the guy, and despite the facade of faith I had maintained with the Crusaders, I couldn't help but speak out for him.

"Sam," I said, "he's dying."

Sam turned to me.

"I know, Paul. But his soul is still intact. He can still be saved."

"Maybe he doesn't want to be saved."

Sam raised his chin and took a breath. "We have to try," he said.

I glanced at Will, but I couldn't maintain eye contact. His eyes were begging me to end it for him, but I couldn't—not with the Crusaders there. There was nothing I could say to convince Sam to let the guy die peacefully. With Sam still facing me, Will reached for the gun lying on the desk. I knew he was reaching for it before I even looked, but my eyes shot to him nonetheless. I deeply regret that my eyes gave it away. Sam saw my gaze shift, then turned to see what Will was doing.

"No!" he thundered, and slapped the gun out of Will's hand.

It clattered against the wall, then fell back onto the desk. Will shot a hand out again, and Sam shoved him backward. He caught his leg on the chair, teetered, then toppled, and I winced as his back slammed against the floor. He rolled over to his stomach, then pushed to his feet with some effort. Sam, his hands held out with palms facing Will, stood between him and the desk. Will lunged for the gun but Sam shoved him backward again. He bounced off the wall and sprang for it again with the same result.

"Please!" Will screamed. "Don't do this! Don't let me turn into one of them! Please!"

"Sam," I said.

He didn't respond.

"Sam!" I yelled.

"What!" he yelled back. His eyes remained on Will.

"He's going to die, Sam," I pleaded. "Whether we kill him or not, he's going to die. We can at least make it painless."

Sam turned to me, his face red and sweaty. A vein on his forehead bulged and threatened to explode.

"Paul, we are not going to kill this man!"

Will took advantage of my distraction and tried again for the gun but stumbled. Sam dove for him, tackled him to the floor, and held him there.

"Kill me!" Will cried out. "Kill me!"

He struggled to free himself, but he was too weak and Sam was too strong. I looked to Rick and Greg, who had come into the room while Brad and Robert kept watch in the hallway. I searched their faces for validation in the form of a pained look or a regretful glance, but they both looked blank. Neither of them met my gaze. I left the scene and walked out to a corner of the front porch, where I stood and scanned the surrounding area with furious precision. Will's screams continued as the night dragged on. I put my earplugs back in; despite the danger of doing so, I couldn't bear the alternative to the quiet they provided.

20

Sam radioed John and requested permission to bring Will back with us so that he could wait out the process of going insane. After talking it over, they decided that bringing an infected person into the Ranch was too much of a risk, and that it was best to wait it out right there in Will's house. What had started out as a one-night eradication expedition became a hostile sleepover of indefinite length behind enemy lines. Robert suggested that a few of us continue to clear houses farther down the road, but Sam quickly shot it down.

"No, we're not going to split our group," he said. "We don't want to risk people getting lost or surrounded. We'll wait it out here."

"Why don't we all go?" I suggested. "That way, we can make good use of our time and then come back to Will. He's not going anywhere."

"No," Sam said. "At least one of us needs to stay and pray with Will. He's not saved. We have to convince him of Christ's love."

Of course, Sam. I wanted to say. I'm sure he is as receptive to God as any other infected person being held against his will solely for the purpose of a slow and terrifying descent into madness.

I nodded slightly and looked away. I knew there would be no convincing them. I stayed out on the front porch for a long while, hoping to wait out Will's deterioration without having to see or hear it. It was a futile hope. As the wait stretched on, it took us through night to the next day, then on again to night. At several points throughout, each of the guys came out and tried to convince me of the merits of letting Will lose his mind before putting a bullet in it. When that proved fruitless, they merely gave me regular appraisals of his status: Yes, he still seemed to have some measure of sanity left. No, he had not yet accepted Jesus as his Savior to secure his admittance into an eternal, zombie-free paradise in the afterlife. Yes, he was still begging to die.

Despite my desire to avoid the scene, I still wandered into the room from time to time. Maybe it was curiosity, maybe it was because I felt bad for him, or maybe I was hoping to find a way to help him. I don't know. I would stand just inside the doorway, watch, and listen as he pleaded for mercy. Each man of the group insisted in soft, hushed tones that mercy was what they were giving him. He wouldn't die alone, they said, and he wouldn't go to hell as long as he just accepted Jesus as his Savior and asked him into his heart. And, of course, suicide wasn't an option; suicides went to hell. All I could do was stand there and feel bad for the guy. Sometimes I just sat outside the door and listened, unable to risk the possibility of looking him in the eyes.

We stayed there for three nights and three days, during which the tone of Will's requests and conversations drastically changed. What had been a desperate, fearful, but lucid man became increasingly savage, hateful, and mindless as time went on. I couldn't bear to hear or see him on the third night as he neared his end, but I couldn't keep from thinking of him and my niece. Between scanning the surrounding neighborhood for threats, I gazed at the stars and thought about Kaylee, about my sister, about my parents. What I would have given just to spend a little more time with them, to tell them I loved them and always would. Or just to look at them one more time as they had been, as they should have been, before the flu finally reached them and broke them down.

I tried to imagine my family sitting beside me; my mom and dad on the left, drinking wine and beer, Shelly and Kaylee on the right, both of them drinking apple juice . . . It would have been a nice night for a campfire.

I thought again of Will and decided that I would have settled for being with my family before they finally turned, as long as I had the knowledge of what was going to happen to them. That would have been enough. It would have given me time to say goodbye, to tell them I would miss them and that I was sorry for what I would have to do.

Sam came out and sat beside me. He looked out at the sky, and for a minute or so, he was silent.

"Beautiful, isn't it?" he whispered at last.

Really bad timing, Sam, I thought. I said nothing, and he kept talking.

"You can see so much more without the lights of the towns and cities drowning out the sky. So much more of God's glory revealed."

He looked over at me as if expecting me to say something.

Perhaps he wanted me to agree that witnessing the vastness of the visible universe was a pretty awesome gift from God despite the fact that our planet was infected to such an extent that it could no longer sustain a human civilization.

Despite the fact that all my loved ones were dead. Despite the fact that we had been holding a man hostage as he lost his mind. I said nothing.

"We saved him," he said finally, looking again at the sky. "He accepted Jesus Christ as his personal Savior."

I took a deep breath and forced myself into what resembled a contemplative nod. I felt I had to say something.

"How far along is he?" I managed.

He took a deep breath, and I waited for an answer but was met with silence. I looked over to see that he was focused intently on something, and when I followed his gaze, I noticed a small, blinking light traveling across the night sky.

"Is that a plane?" I asked.

Sam nodded.

"I think so."

We both watched as it continued its course across the sky and eventually disappeared from view. We sat in silence for a while afterward. I didn't really have much to say, or at least not much to say to him.

He finally broke the silence.

"Paul, did you ever get vaccinations?" he asked.

"Flu vaccinations?" I asked without caring.

"Yeah."

"Not in a long time," I said. "Not since I was a kid, I guess."

I looked over again at him, somewhat confused by how random his question seemed, but he was still staring up at the sky. I considered the plane and tried to imagine his line of thinking. I thought back to playing Uno with Alex, Terry, and Zack, when Alex had mentioned claims that the vaccine was causing the virus.

"Do you think the vaccination did it?" I asked.

He shook his head.

"I don't know," he said. "But it damn sure came from somewhere, and I have a hard time believing it came about by itself. Evil doesn't just happen; it has to have a source and a cause. Someone is responsible for this."

He turned to me.

"Don't you think?"

I averted my gaze and looked back at the sky. The plane might have been irrelevant, since it was impossible to say who owned it, but it brought to light the question of whether some form of government still existed. It seemed unlikely that they had been wiped out entirely. While cities had succumbed to the infection, the government would have had contingencies in place for every conceivable disaster. They would have received greater forewarning and been given greater protections than the general populations. They would have been sequestered away at the first hint of a pandemic.

How could a disease have even grown to such a point despite the watchful eyes of the CDC and other similar organizations? How could something as sinister as the South American flu have come to be so widespread? Could someone have started the disease intentionally? Had the zombie infection actually been a biological attack?

"Why would they do it?" I asked.

"I don't know," Sam said. "Why does Satan do any of the things he does?"

I didn't respond to his question, partly because it seemed to be rhetorical and partly because bringing the devil into the conversation led to nowhere but the Bible. I didn't have the heart to tell Sam that the Bible wasn't real life and that whatever caused the pandemic wasn't supernatural. I had no idea what the source of the infection was, but the devil was a far cry from a real answer.

I closed my eyes and let my head sink into my hands. Discussing it with Sam or any of the Crusaders was pointless. Even privately theorizing about the potential cause was pointless. As far as I knew, most of the world's population was infected or dead and it didn't really matter what caused it. What was I going to do? Track down a government installation, break in, and find all their secrets conveniently located on an open, unlocked laptop in a dimly lit back room? Capture a government agent and interrogate him until he told me everything he knew, which conveniently turned out to be everything relevant to what had happened?

No, I wasn't going to do that. I was just some peon sitting on a porch outside of a town called Wampum with a guy who was blaming the devil for the world's ills. There wasn't a goddamn thing I could do about the breakout in the past, the present, or the future. There was no point in even discussing it. I remained silent. After a while, Sam stood and walked back inside. I let him go without a word. I stayed out on the porch until I grew too tired, then woke Greg and took a nap.

Near dawn, Will finally lost his mind sufficiently enough that Sam granted him the mercy he had begged for. While I couldn't say for sure because I wasn't in the room at the time, I don't think Will was able to fully appreciate the gesture.

We milled around in that house for the rest of the day and ate what was left of the canned goods. For a while, the group sat in a circle and talked while they played cards and sipped wine. They invited me to join them, but I chose to keep watch instead. Since I couldn't go outside in the light of day due to the risk of being seen, I wandered through the house and looked out each of the windows in turn, except for those in the bedroom where Will's corpse sat, tied to a chair. I couldn't help but look around as I made my way through the house. Though it hadn't been my intention, my perusal granted me an understanding of Will's life that was as interesting as it was painfully depressing. It was a bad end for a good person. Shitty luck.

An hour or so after dark had fallen, we left the house and began the short trip home. I lay in the back of the truck and searched the skies. Though I saw another plane, I could locate nothing inside or outside of my mind that could assuage the feeling of pointlessness that was again creeping up on me. Will's death had been made cruelly tragic. If that was the kind of thing the Crusaders did, how could I consider calling myself one of them?

I decided I was tired, so when we arrived back at the Ranch, I skipped the welcoming party and the group prayer, walked straight into the house, and dug into my bed. I slept more deeply than I had in a long time, probably since even before the zombie outbreak had reached Pittsburgh. Still, my dreams were vivid and memorable.

L. Marshall James

21

The next day, we returned to the job we had started four days prior. Rick and Brad grumbled about going out so quickly after our three-day stint, but I didn't really mind. I used any excuse I could to get away. Zombies, with their furious and often incoherent monologues, typically held better conversation than anyone at the Ranch. The fact that they always tried to kill me was overshadowed by the fact that they didn't hold constant prayer meetings and there was always the added bonus that I could shoot them when I got sick of them. It provided a much-needed catharsis.

That being said, the first few days back to clearing houses grew increasingly unbearable. For all his faith, Sam was careful to such an extent that I secretly suspected he might have OCD. He had developed a formation for the six of us, which consisted of two people in the front, two in the middle, and two in the rear, resulting in a columnar shape. Each person faced outward in the rectangle and covered their "respective perspectives," as Sam had explained it.

Our approach of each house was the same. We would scout the area ahead of us, then the two leading men would run to a safe place under the cover of the middle two. The middle two would then run up to positions behind the first two while the two rear men covered the flank. Finally, the last two would join up while the middle two covered them. That may sound fast on paper, but when I say "run," I really mean "jog slowly," since Sam had determined that it was safer to maintain a steady pace than to run at full speed.

Once we reached a house, we would engage in breach procedures. Five men would stand in a semicircle around the front door, facing away from the house in defensive posture while Rick picked the locks. If the door was unlocked, four men would cover the rear while the first two men entered. Once they had moved in and positioned themselves, the next two men would move in. Finally, the last two would enter the home and close the door behind them. Every room of every house was handled in the exact same fashion. I couldn't stand it.

"Paul. Paul!" Sam called out.

I stopped, sighed, and turned around.

"What?"

"What in the heck are you doing?"

"I'm gonna go kill some zombies, Sam."

"You're wandering off," he responded.

"Exactly," I retorted. "We've covered three houses in the last forty-five minutes. At this rate, we're all going to die of prostate cancer before we even clear Wampum. And Wampum—"

"Just get back in formation," he interrupted.

"—and Wampum isn't shit," I insisted. "Ellwood City is ten times as big. New Castle is even bigger than that. We need to pick up the pace."

The guys all looked between me and Sam, who only shook his head.

"We can't be walking around all willy-nilly like cowboys," he said. "It's too dangerous, and we'll end up getting killed. We don't have enough men to risk that."

"Then God will protect us."

I said it with the intention of being a smart-ass more than anything else, but I realized when I saw their faces that it passed as legitimate logic in their eyes.

With the exception of Sam, they all looked at me with wide-eyed acceptance of what they perceived as a noble truth. Even Greg bought it, and I vaguely suspected that he didn't even like me. Sam, for his part, looked at me with his head cocked. I wasn't sure if he knew I was full of shit or only suspected it, but in either case, he wasn't able to think of an effective retort to my faux-faithful claim.

"Okay, we'll speed it up," he said finally. "Two men to a house. Rick, go with Paul. Greg, you're with me. Robert and Brad, are you two comfortable with just yourselves?"

They each nodded their assent.

"Definitely," they answered in concert.

Sam's smile was strained but obviously genuine.

"Welcome to the Crusaders, Brad" Sam replied.

As Rick started toward me, I noticed that the others were standing idly, awaiting further instruction from Sam. I motioned to Rick, who was unaware of their hesitation, and he sped up out of his casual saunter. As he neared me, I turned and headed to the nearest house. He could follow me, and the others could follow Sam, but I was done holding hands in hell. Even without the promise of heaven, I wasn't scared of dying. There are worse things than death; endless monotony is one of them.

I scanned the area around me as I moved to the front door of the house, then tried the handle. Locked. I saw Rick reach for his lock-picking kit. I ignored him as I backed up, raised a foot, and kicked at the door beside the handle. It didn't give. I kicked again, and again, and again before the door crashed open. I stood at the open doorway, my rifle raised. If something was in there, it would have probably come to the door by then, but there was only silence from inside. Still, Rick and I stormed in and searched the place, room by room.

We found nothing in the first few houses we checked. As we continued, Rick and I worked out and perfected our own general method of searching:

1. If the door was locked, crash it open. If the door was unlocked, open it and yell.
2. Wait for the crazies, and shoot them as they approach.
3. Clear the rooms one at a time until the house could be declared empty.
4. Move on.

It was simple, and more importantly to me, it was faster than Sam's systematic, mind-numbingly slow method of clearance. The guy was trying to play chess with zombies, but zombies don't play chess. Shit, zombies don't even play checkers. Whatever they played, they didn't have any consistent set of rules, which is something that we had all seen hints at here and there. Some stood dumbly in their rooms and seemed to almost wait to be shot, whereas others attacked at the slightest sound. Some came at you with bare hands, whereas others wielded knives and clubs. Some attacked each other, whereas some teamed up with other zombies. Some ran at any loud sound they heard, like junkies looking for their next fix, whereas . . .

"Get back!" I screamed.

What I had assumed to be an empty house suddenly seethed with biters. They popped up from behind the couch, crawled out from under the coffee table, and ran in from the next room. I backpedaled and fired wildly as they came from all directions. I slammed into the wall beside the front door and kept firing. One collapsed with a bullet lodged in its chest. Another fell, its spinal cord severed at the neck. Rick, who had only just entered the house, stood in the doorway and fired from beside me. A tall, potbellied man stumbled into him, and Rick brought the butt of his rifle into the side of the man's head. The man fell at my feet, then grabbed one of my legs and tried to bite through my boot. I shot him in the ass and back, then raised my foot and stomped his head into the floor. He kept moving, so I kept blindly stomping as I fired at other approaching biters. I kept pumping my foot into his head even after the last of the zombies had fallen and the house had settled into a comparative silence.

"Paul, he's dead," Rick said.

I stopped and looked down. The head was a gooey mess. I backed up and aimed at it, then looked up at Rick and waited for him to move away. He stepped to the other side of the doorway, then stepped back across once I had lodged an insurance bullet into what was left of the brain. After we checked the rest of the house, we returned to the front porch for a breather. My heart was still racing. Whether or not I thought I was scared of dying, it was clear that my body certainly was; my apathy wasn't going to annul the result of millions of years of evolution. Sam and Greg looked over at us as they walked past to the next house.

"You boys all right?" Greg said, a smirk plastered on his face.

"Oh yeah," Rick responded with a cheerful chuckle. "Got a little excitement there, but nothin' we can't handle."

Greg's smirk widened, and they continued on. I pondered whether punching him in the face would feel better than shooting a zombie in the head at point-blank range, and I mulled that over as we continued on through the neighborhood. Though my adrenaline rush was fading, I felt fantastic, as if I was turning a corner in the race against the newly arisen zombie empire. We approached the west side of the town of Wampum shortly before dawn.

22

We turned back before we reached the main area of Wampum, but the impending mission remained on my mind and I kept thinking about it as I tried to fall asleep. It would be the biggest test yet of our collective capabilities as exterminators, but I couldn't think of an effective way to clear the place out. We couldn't go house to house like we had been. With the houses so numerous and close together, we'd quickly be surrounded and slaughtered, which was something I wanted to avoid. Sure, I hated boredom more than death, but it would be optimal to get my adrenaline fix and stay alive, if at all possible. I spoke with Sam and was relieved to find that he agreed with me, at least on the point that we could not continue through the main areas of town as we had in the outskirts. Still, we had no solid idea of how to proceed.

Bringing all the infected to one point seemed to be the best first step. That could be done easily enough, either by driving around town in a normal vehicle while blaring the horn or in a police car with the sirens on. What to do once the crazies were attracted was something else altogether. It stood to reason that they would do a significant amount of damage to each other when we brought them together, but we needed to wipe them out entirely. No one knew anything about how to make bombs, so unless we managed to slap together some propane tanks or other propellants into an IED, that wasn't an option. Simply closing in on them in the middle of town while they were otherwise distracted seemed like the best idea, but it left the gunners vulnerable to any flanking stragglers. We eventually settled, though somewhat begrudgingly, on using the bridge between the east and west halves of Wampum as our ambush point.

The plan as we devised it was to commandeer a police car and have one person drive it through the streets with the siren on. Once the driver had sufficiently incited and attracted the horde, he would drive to the bridge, where the rest of the group would be waiting. There was a good bit of distance and elevation separating the bridge from the east side of Wampum, which meant that our flank would be more or less secure, aside from whatever remained inside of a few nearby houses. It was decided that one person would probably do a sufficient job of covering our backs, but we placed both Greg and Sam on that duty. That left four men aiming at the horde once the driver joined the other three. Driving the vehicle was arguably the most dangerous part of the mission, so I volunteered.

As it turned out, we couldn't find any working police cars or ambulances, so we were forced to make due with an ice cream truck that had been ditched on a back road. Just two days after we finally cleared the roads surrounding Wampum, I found myself driving through the streets and singing my own custom lyrics to the tunes of the ice cream truck. It was only at the sight of the first zombie of the night that the surreality of the situation really struck home.

An obese man in overalls stood in the front doorway of what may have been his home. He looked confused at first, almost as if torn between rage and the alluring promise of cold, sugary treats. Settling on rage, he screamed and ran after me. As more biters approached, I sped up and passed them by. As I toured the town, I was surprised to see that other than one or two troublemakers, they weren't fighting among themselves. Apparently, they were all too focused on me to bother with each other.

The gaggle behind me steadily grew, and as I turned onto the main street for my last run through town, it looked like I had close to a hundred of them trailing me. A few ran out in front of me, and I swerved slightly to avoid them. One of them, a girl in a jogging outfit that I found disturbingly attractive, stood ahead of me in the middle of the road and engaged me in a comically stupid game of chicken. It ended in a draw, but she did not survive the contest. When I came to the last turn before the bridge, I slowed and waited for the mob to catch up. Finally, as some of the fastest among my pursuers drew too close for comfort, I sped down the bridge.

I reached the crest of the bridge and came within view of the Crusaders. As intimidating a sight as the horde was, my knowledge of the Crusaders' capabilities made them far scarier. Greg and Robert turned on the lights of the trucks as I passed them, and I heard the muffled reports of rifles as I came to a stop, shut off the truck, and jumped out to join the blockade. I found myself whistling the tune of the ice cream truck as I got into position on the firing line, though I only noticed I was doing so when Rick started to laugh. Brad and Robert soon joined him in laughter, and I soon followed, no longer able to keep the tune.

We kept laughing as the zombies continued their approach in the headlights of the trucks. It was going to be a bloody, raucous good time.

They came in a steady wave. Many of the foremost attackers might as well have been normal human beings, aside from obvious anger management issues. They came at us in dead sprints and determined jogs, often swearing and screaming as they approached. As the horde continued to pour in, their overall condition steadily worsened. Minor cuts and broken hands gave way to deep lacerations and broken feet, which gave way to shattered legs and discolored, gaping wounds. It seemed to drag on forever, ending with the agonized efforts of bodies that barely retained even a fraction of their previous functionalities. Biters shambled and crawled toward us, moaning as if begging to be freed from their organic prisons. As I fired off rounds into heads and chests, I felt almost as if I was fulfilling a sacred and solemn duty to end the tortuous suffering of what had once been good people.

That feeling temporarily faded when we called it a night and tried to cross the bridge back toward the Ranch only to find ourselves trapped by the mountain of corpses. As we set to the task of moving the bodies out of the way, I realized two facts that had previously escaped me, the first being that headshots were not required to kill the infected, and the second being that once the infected were dead, they stayed that way.

Both revelations were equally obvious, partly because we had already killed infected by other means and partly because the concept of a human body persevering without a head, heart, or at least one functioning lung was ridiculous. How could the trillions of cells of the human body continue to work without oxygen, blood, or an intact nervous system? That had been part of the zombie lore, but those had all been fairy tales. What we were killing were not zombies at all, in the traditional sense; they were just people who were hopelessly, irrecoverably insane.

They also smelled terrible, and we all dry heaved uncontrollably during the hour it took to clear a path for the trucks. Robert, who had puked at the sight of the necrophiliac zombie, vomited yet again during our ghastly task. I was going to tease him, but I also forfeited my dinner before I could. Not long after we made it back to the Ranch, we outfitted the trucks with plows.

We took the following night off and returned to Wampum in daylight to officially clear the town. We overrode our unwritten "nighttime only" rule, since the town was mostly empty, and since we would need to be able to see whatever infected remained. Our objective at that point was to neutralize the town of any remaining threats so that it could be deemed safe for our scavenging crew, or at least as safe as an abandoned town could be in the nightmarish world we lived in. Cleanup was minimal, aside from numerous rotting corpses and a few leftover zombies that had been all but incapacitated.

We also found a few people who had managed to remain uninfected and alive. Four teenagers had hidden away in a church basement while subsisting on the Lord's considerable stock of canned goods, and one older man had barricaded himself inside his home with an army of cats. In his haste to defend his cats, he had almost taken Robert's head off with a World War II–era Russian rifle before Brad managed to talk him down. After that near-disaster, we established new procedures for drawing out survivors. Rather than smashing in front doors and waving guns around, we walked through the streets and loudly proclaimed that we didn't want to hurt anyone and had ample access to coffee. It worked surprisingly well. Sometimes it's the smallest details that make the biggest difference.

23

Emboldened by our success on the bridge, we soon moved on to the east side of Wampum where I repeated my role as the ice cream truck driver. It took a single night to wipe out the majority of the area's zombie population, and we managed to clear it utterly over the course of the following few days. It was one beautiful massacre out of many to come, and I began to feel increasingly positive about our efforts to clear out the land. My enthusiasm and my sense of purpose were returning.

Every town we cleared was a notch on my belt, and I took pride in each of them. In the new, terrible place that the world had become, I was part of the crew that would slowly but surely eradicate the infected and protect those who wished to live on and start anew. In spite of myself, I felt not just a tolerance but a deep and growing fondness for John, the Crusaders, and the other people of the Ranch. I still resented what they had done to Will, and while I could never fully buy into what they believed, I found myself harboring at least a modicum of respect for their religion if for no other reason than that it served to preserve the innocence of the children. The children laughed and played, joyfully oblivious to the vulnerability of their safety and blind to the horrific realities that lived and died beyond the confines of the Ranch.

It was as I peered down at our cleanup crew in Wampum from an overlook on the other side of the river that I decided my search was finally over. I had found my purpose with the Crusaders and was driven by it. Whether or not their beliefs had been truly valid in the civilized world before, they certainly seemed to bear some credence in the wake of its collapse. It was up to us to protect the innocent from the monsters that roamed.

Then again, not all the demons roamed. There were many who simply remained in their homes and subsisted on beef jerky, family pets, their own hands, or whatever they could find until they ran out of food, died, or were disturbed from their god-awful rut. Why they stayed in their homes, none of us could figure out. For a while, I pondered whether it was the result of some differences in how the infection affected certain people, whether it was more a matter of chance or just habits left over from their previous sedentary lives. After a while, I let the mystery die; I just called them lazy.

There were other differences among the zombies that seemed more profound. While most of the infected raged and attacked either on their own whims or when disturbed, there were some who seemed only to stagger about in ambivalent states of confusion, often seeming to settle on violence accidentally, à la *Of Mice and Men*. This was the presumed cause of death for an old woman whom Rick identified as Gretta, a family friend of his, whose body had been torn apart by her infected husband. When we had forced our way into their two-room cabin, the husband had moved toward us with small steps, seemingly unsure of what to make of our raised rifles and warnings. We might have made the same mistake as his wife, but we quickly realized that he bore no injury, which meant the blood he was covered in was not his. Once that fact had been established, I no longer felt bad about splitting his skull.

As I had noticed on our first bridge ambush, the overall state of the zombie population deteriorated over time. When the outbreak had first hit Pittsburgh, the majority of the infected could all have been easily mistaken for normal people who had made the mistake of doing PCP or "bath salts." But as the days and weeks went by, the infected were more and more often plagued with broken and missing limbs, gnawed flesh, and wounds that seethed with maggots and pus.

In our experience, the worse they looked, the worse they functioned and the less of a threat they posed. Some of the worst of them ambled stupidly toward sights and sounds and could be almost casually ended with a kukri or a club. Still, even the most decayed were threats to be taken seriously. Whether they killed directly or served as unwitting distractions for better-equipped zombies, they always bore the threat of death. Every day, there was death all around the Ranch. In the face of that threat, there developed what seemed to be an ever-stronger bond among the Christians, especially within our band of Crusaders.

At first, Rick had made me uncomfortable. When he wasn't talking about his slaughtered family, I would often catch him looking off into the distance, his scraggly face blank aside from the expression of sadness that seemed to be irremovably ingrained into him. Eventually, my discomfort waned, and he began to strike me as more tragic than anything else. Sometimes I would sit and talk with him, partly out of pity and partly to try and get him to lighten up for once.

From time to time, it paid off with a smile, a chuckle, or a belly laugh. It didn't always work, but when it did, it seemed to affect everyone in the group. As my dad used to say, "A powerful smile is rare, and a rare smile is powerful." Rick took a liking to the unnamed boy we had rescued and would often sit with him as they each petted Kotie. After weeks of attempted conversation, Rick was the first person the boy spoke a word to. After that, if you looked closely, you could sometimes detect a hint of a smile on his face.

Robert, who had a weak stomach and was a subpar marksman, seemed to excel as a husband and father. When we weren't out lodging bullets into flesh and bone, he could be found with his family, either cuddling with the wife or swinging his kids around in circles until they couldn't walk straight. It was rare to see him and his kids together without the accompanying sounds of laughter.

Brad, who had essentially joined us as an intern after the hotel fiasco and before becoming a permanent Crusader, was the Christian version of the zombie fanatic I had been prior to the outbreak. During neighborhood cleanups, he would pray and quote Bible verses aloud. One verse in particular tied well into the feeling that we were all doing some good for what was left of the world:

"And in those days shall men seek death, and shall not find it; and shall desire to die, and death shall flee from them."

With that verse in mind, I relished every bullet I unleashed as I did my part to help the infected find the death they so desired. Brad annoyed me at times, but he also tended to set a hell of a mood for killing; he became my go-to guy for inspirational Bible quotes. Though I walk through the valley of the shadow of death, I will fear no zombies.

Even Greg began to come across as more of an endearing character, and his smirks changed over time into what seemed to be genuine smiles. I never found out why he seemed to dislike me so much at first. My initial guesses were that he saw through my feigned faith or that my occasional disdain for Sam's authority struck a raw chord in him, but no one I asked could give me a straight answer. In the end, we got along pretty well, so it didn't even matter. He usually stuck with Sam, whether we were on the Ranch or on the move. I imagine he looked to Sam as something of a father figure.

In a way, I think that was true of all of us, to some extent. Sam was a determined and sometimes overbearing leader, but there was no denying that his obsessive attention to detail, strategy, and consistency was a primary reason we were all still alive despite the risks we took on an almost daily basis. His straightforward approach to extermination kept the entire group in check, except me, on occasion. According to the others, Sam's strategy had been simple almost to the point of being cavalier when they first started their missions, but he had buckled down after the incident at the hotel. Since then, there had been no situation even remotely close to what had happened, despite my rocking the boat. Sometimes I thought he tolerated me only because I hated the demons as much as he did and had become exceedingly good at killing them.

In a rare moment of casual curiosity, I once asked Sam how he kept going, how he kept believing despite the world we were living in. He told me that he felt more faith than he ever had before and that it wasn't despite the world we lived in but because of it. What had been an unexpected, traumatic, and tragic outbreak to me had been nothing more to Sam than the fulfillment of the prophecies of the Bible. He and John had been expecting and planning for the end of days, stocking up on weapons and supplies and forging what had come to be called the Ranch. Their preparations, which spanned over several years, made mine look like a child's indulgent scribbles.

We all rallied behind Sam. Despite all our differences, we agreed where it mattered. We fought together to protect those who couldn't fight for themselves. I began to count myself among the Crusaders, and in a way, it felt like we were kin, not by our own blood, but instead by the blood of our common enemy. Over the stinking bodies of the dead, we found our stride.

As we continued to clear the surrounding land and towns, our ranks swelled with survivors to such an extent that the Ranch was no longer sufficient to contain us. As a result, we expanded steadily beyond the confines of the Ranch and into the many houses nearby. We also significantly increased the number of lookout posts directly surrounding the Ranch and beyond, on various strategic points in and around other towns. In every town we conquered, we fortified building after building, focusing primarily on churches, government buildings, and other sturdy, easily defensible structures. We grew stronger every day.

With our extended reach, we grew even without clearing new areas. While a majority of the survivors who joined us had merely lived in or around the towns we cleared, many others wandered or fled into our territory. We were growing exponentially, and if John-the-preacher-man had decided it, we could have amassed a considerable fighting force with the people and munitions we had managed to collect.

John was insistent, however, that we would not attain victory with weapons but with the power of prayer. He was steadfast in his belief, and no matter how much Sam or I tried to dissuade him from it, he would not allow us to train others to be Crusaders. Somehow, prayer still held more sway with him than the multitude of bullets we had fired to clear the land. As much as I resented his reasoning, part of me understood it: to John, it was prayer that made all the difference because he wasn't the one who came home smelling like blood and gunpowder every day. He never had to deal with the harshest realities of what he ordered us to do, and until the day he finally did, it would be just the six of us clearing house by house, road by road, and town by town. Until something happened to change John's mind, Brad was the last recruit of the Crusaders.

In the end, I didn't really mind the end result of his decision. It meant I didn't have to train any new recruits, which left me with ample time for the considerable task of extermination, a task at which I had become increasingly proficient. Robert had coined me the "King of Headshots" after one particular night when I had been inexplicably ambushed by a group of seven or so biters in the middle of an office building. While I might have panicked in the same situation a few months or even weeks prior, I stood my ground and faced them as they came at me from all sides. In a span of no more than a few seconds, I had put a bullet in each of their heads in turn.

In truth, the accomplishment was not all that impressive, since I had dedicated all my time to zombie eradication, focusing largely on marksmanship as a matter of course. Still, the Crusaders had been spellbound by it. While the hotel rescue attempt had clearly caused them to reconsider me, it was that series of headshots that made me a veritable gunfighter in their eyes, a Wyatt Earp of the apocalypse. I took it in stride as best as I could, but I couldn't help but take pride in it. After all, it was part of what I strove for. It was what I wanted to be.

Still, it became clear to me that the dominance of the Crusaders would not last if we remained where we were. A wild-eyed refugee by the name of Jack told tales of the government descending on downtown Pittsburgh "like Normandy from the sky," quarantining entire neighborhoods and taking any and all people into custody, regardless of whether they were infected or consented to be taken in. He said the government had sealed off all of downtown and was using the buildings there as bases of operations, which were supplied by helicopters and trucks from God only knew where, though it was "probably the airport." He insisted that the government was using the infected and healthy alike as test subjects for an even more malevolent version of the virus that had already annihilated half of the world's population, and he went on to claim that what was left of the US government had declared war on all other nations, with the goal of wiping out what was left of its rivals and attaining hegemony over the entire planet. When I asked where he thought the virus came from, his eyes grew wide.

"Where do you think, man?" he said. "Haven't you ever heard of the Rockefeller Commission? The Tuskegee Experiments?"

I shook my head and prepared for an onslaught of conspiracy theories.

He blinked once, then twice and seemed to freeze in place, as if trying to retrieve an encyclopedia of knowledge from memory.

"Okay, uh . . ." he began. "So, long story short, the Tuskegee Experiments were clinical studies performed by the US Public Health Service, in which they not only intentionally infected two hundred people with syphilis but also intentionally failed to treat them, as well as four hundred others who already had it."

He took a breath, then continued,

"This went on for forty years before someone blew the whistle. By that time, most of the test subjects were dead. This was all investigated and documented. This led to new laws, and the creation of . . . uh, some new regulatory body. I forget the name of it."

"Now," he continued, "the Rockefeller Commission isn't directly related to that. That was . . . that was an investigation into the actions of the CIA. They had apparently done a lot of things, including performing 'experiments'"—he held up both hands and made quotation marks—"like experimenting on American citizens with diseases like whooping cough, yellow fever, dengue fever, and chemicals and drugs, all without their consent. And the Rockefeller Commission was only the beginning of the investigations into the CIA."

"When was this?" I asked.

"The Rockefeller Commission? That all came to a head in the late seventies. Think Nixon."

"Ah. Okay, but what makes you think they made this virus?"

"Okay, so, like I said, this investigation was just one of many, and this all led to new regulations, right? Regulations for everyone. Regulations that banned unethical experiments, among other things. One of those regulations said that researchers had to let people know exactly what they were getting into when they got involved in these experiments."

He stopped to light a cigarette.

"So one of the things they did was . . . they found ways around the regulations. They started running 'clinical trials'"—he made quotation marks again—"of drugs here in the US, but they also did them, and still do them, abroad. Especially abroad, where they can find poor people. Uneducated people. These people, they sign the contracts with an X or a thumbprint because they can't read. And they have no idea, no idea at all what's going to be done to them."

"That's all legal though," I said. "And it's clinical trials. It doesn't necessarily have anything to do with the South American flu."

"Think of it like this," he said, nodding. "Like you said, what they're doing in these clinics is all legal. As far as the law is concerned, it's all good. But it's wrong, clearly and undeniably. You don't need to look twice to see that. And what this shows you is that the people in charge, they don't give a fuck about ethics. And if this shit, these clinical trials, are what they're doing in the open . . . just imagine what they're doing in the shadows."

He continued before I could interject.

"Think swine flu. Think avian flu. Those are household names, but the media doesn't come close to covering every outbreak that happens in the world. You just take a look at what's listed on the WHO website, and you'll see—"

"Who?"

"The World Health Organization."

"Oh."

"Just . . ." He paused, then blinked a few times. "Just take a look at their . . ."

He stopped and took a short hit, then a long one.

"Well," he said. "I guess you won't be checking their website anytime soon, huh."

I laughed, then shook my head and quietly swore. We sat for a few minutes in silence before he continued. When he did, his energy seemed to have evaporated.

"Well, anyway. There are—or were—other breakouts all over the world. Yellow fever, polio, Ebola . . . Most of the legal experiments were done overseas. I'm sure the illegal ones were too. After all, if you're experimenting with pandemic-level diseases, you don't want to do it in your backyard, right? And where did the South American flu break out first?"

I waited for him to provide me with the answer to his question.

"India," he said with a sigh. "One of the most unequal countries in the world, with the poorest and least-educated bottom class. The people who couldn't fight back, even if they knew they should have. It didn't join the swine and bird flu in the big news until it hit Brazil and Venezuela. But by then, it didn't matter."

He took another drag, then held up his cigarette and stared at it as if for the first time. Then he flicked it into the dirt and lit another.

"Maybe it never did."

I tried to excerpt as much truth as I could from the tangled web he wove in order to estimate the more likely facts of what he said he had seen and discern how they affected me. For me, that meant what he had actually seen. He said that he had literally seen choppers, planes, ground troops, tanks, armored personnel carriers, quarantines, and forceful captures of uninfected subjects. I was more than a little concerned, and I couldn't help but believe that even if the government's intentions weren't as dark as Jack insisted, it sounded as if they were regaining control over an area not forty miles from us. While Jack was the most outspoken refugee, he was far from the only one with stories of the government's presence.

Not only that, but we had recently received word from our southeast lookout that a helicopter had come as far north as the town of Koppel, less than five miles from the Ranch. It had hovered for some time over the only bridge there, which had been littered with the bodies of zombies we had lured to their final destinations. After that, we went to greater efforts to hide the bodies of the dead.

What concerned me the most about the government was how it would affect our sovereignty. Without the government's control, we were free to act as we saw fit, living together in peace and eradicating the rotting pests that infested the landscape. The potential threat lay with what would happen if and when the boot of the government came down. I found myself confused and upset that no one seemed to share my concern. In fact, I was unable to find a single person on the Ranch who endorsed or supported what was left of the government, yet almost everyone I asked seemed supremely confident that our ragtag group of Christians would somehow overcome and defeat them. Many cited biblical passages and quoted likely deceased radio personalities in support of their beliefs that the end-time was at hand and that Satan would soon be defeated in "the final battle."

Unfortunately, I couldn't pursue the argument beyond the bounds of their beliefs without potentially outing myself as an atheist and risking my place in the Crusaders. Despite the fact that I could have had an almost constant supply of personable company, I sometimes found myself feeling strangely alone. But while my company's views didn't always match mine and I wasn't always killing time by killing the infected, I was able to find sufficient reprieve elsewhere.

Often while on lookout duty, I would just lie back and stare out at the sky. Sometimes I would daydream about my family and friends, walk through old memories of better times, and imagine conversations we might have had if they were still alive. We would discuss recent events and politics or sit and drink tea while my dad regaled us with stories of his youth. Sometimes I tried to pretend that my parents, my sister, and my niece had forgiven me.

When those thoughts proved too much for me, I searched for solace in context. I willed myself to imagine our planet, which was just one of eight planets in the solar system, which was just one of hundreds of billions within the Milky Way, which was just one of hundreds of billions of galaxies within the incomprehensibly vast universe, which was forever expanding. Light came from stars and worlds I would never see, reaching through space for billions of years before finally reaching my eyes. Now and then, meteors would distract me as they streaked past, but it was with increasing frequency that a plane or helicopter would pass within range of my sight and I would be drawn back to the troublesome realities that faced us in the present.

For a while, I wondered if Jack had been right about the government being behind the virus. Maybe he seemed like the standard conspiracy theorist, but there was enough truth in his story to make it seem solid. I knew, too, that to some people, the boundaries drawn by ethical guidelines were mere impediments to scientific advancement, to knowledge, to just doing their jobs as they saw fit. Really, every government in the world probably had blood on their hands in similar ways, the US government being nowhere near an exception.

After a lot of contemplation, I again came to the conclusion that it didn't really matter. Maybe the crazy-eyed refugee was right about what the government had done and what they were planning to do; maybe he was wrong. In the end, it wasn't my concern. Even if everyone on the Ranch took up arms against them, we would accomplish nothing but a tragic truncation of our lives. Whatever the government's goals, there wasn't a damn thing any of us could do to stop them. If I had learned anything from the apocalypse, it was that there was no room for worrying about things that were beyond my control. I intended to continue my dual roles as protector and killer or die in the effort. For every life, there should be a purpose for living; I had found mine, and I didn't intend to abandon it, even in the face of certain death. Still, I tried to have some fun with it.

"Bullets! Get your bullets here! Zombies eat free. Come and get 'em before they're all gone!"

I strode casually along Montgomery Avenue, through a neighborhood we had all but cleared out two nights prior. While it was not an insignificant size, it was just a small part of the city of New Castle, which we intended to sanitize over the following weeks. It promised not be an easy or simple endeavor, but after the ten or so towns we had already cleared and the renewed safety precautions I begrudgingly complied with, we were more than capable. Still, since I wasn't getting the same adrenaline fix from demon extermination, I was forced to find entertainment in other avenues of my everyday life.

"Extra, extra! Zombies are declared to be buttholes by local Crusaders! Read all about it!"

Rick had at first protested my asinine taunts, but I persisted. Eventually, he resigned himself to quietly scanning the neighborhood and smirking from time to time at my increasingly desperate attempts to humor the dead. The one thing I really grew to hate about the infected was that no matter how funny you thought you were, they never laughed. The bastards never even cracked a smile.

"Here's one," Rick said.

What had once probably been a pretty girl stumbled toward us in the middle of the street. I only say she had probably been pretty based on what was left of her face, body, and tattered clothes that remained attached to her as much by threads as by the fact that they had melded into the deeply infected wounds covering most of her flesh. Her ankles seemed to have taken a particularly brutal turn for the worse, as she was wearing high heels and was no longer able to walk correctly in them. I winced with her every step as she repeatedly rolled her ankles. I averted my gaze and looked around to make sure no one else was closing in on us.

"Just shoot her, man," I said. "She's giving me the creeps, the way she's walking."

Rick raised his rifle, aimed, and fired.

I turned to see her lying in the street.

"Thank you."

"You're welcome."

We continued our course down the street. Meanwhile, the rest of the Crusaders cleared the streets adjacent to ours. Somehow, I had managed to get stuck with the least eventful route and while I normally would have resented it, I welcomed it with all the gusto of a man who was secretly nursing a hangover. Against my better judgment, I had chosen to partake in some plundered wine on the previous night. I figured I was doing pretty well considering how much I had consumed, but I was definitely not in prime condition. I tried to find painkillers in a few of the houses we'd gone through but had no luck.

"You feeling okay?" Rick asked.

I nodded as nonchalantly as I could manage, and though I could feel his eyes on me, I knew his concern was sincere.

"Yup," I said. "Not too terrible."

He nodded, and we continued on.

"Brains for sale!" I yelled. "One easy payment of death!"

The radio on my belt crackled, and a voice burst out. It was Sam.

"Paul, Rick. You guys cleared?"

"Yeah," I responded. "We're a little past where you'll be coming out."

"Okay," he said.

I furrowed my brow at the odd tone of Sam's voice. He sounded . . . different, almost worried, which was unusual. Judging from Rick's expression, he shared my befuddlement.

"Uh . . . ." Sam said. "Can you guys come back to us? We have a situation."

I wondered what that could possibly have meant. Had a man had been injured? Was an infected mob en route? My mind wandered over possible situations as I replied, "Sure, we're on our way."

"Okay. I'll send Brad and Robert out to meet you at the intersection and bring you to us."

"Roger that. Out."

"Out."

We made our way back along the street until we spotted Brad standing conspicuously in some bushes at the corner of a house. Robert was standing behind him. Had the situation been different, I might have laughed at how awkward they seemed while they stood there, looking around and fingering their rifles. As it was, their nervosity only increased the sudden tension that I felt. I had come to know each of them well enough to see that something had them spooked.

"What's up, guys?" I asked as we grew close enough to speak at a normal volume.

"Hey," Brad greeted us. "You see much ahead?"

"Not much," Rick answered. "A couple here and there. No survivors yet. What's going on?"

Brad looked down the street, then back at us.

"Uh . . . I'll just let Sam explain."

Rick and I exchanged a glance, then followed the pair down the street. We all kept an eye out, since the area had not yet been cleared, but we encountered no problems. I kept looking for Sam, then finally spotted him with Greg, inside of the front entryway of a tall, aluminum-sided house. They seemed to be in deep discussion.

"What's up, guys?" Rick asked.

Sam looked to us, opened his mouth, then shut it. Hesitantly, he opened it again and spoke.

"It's a baby," he said. "And a mother."

I looked back and forth between Sam and Greg, then Brad and Robert.

"What the f—" I caught myself. "What do you mean, exactly?"

"An infected baby and an infected mother," Greg responded.

I cringed and felt a flash of animosity toward the group. As much as they professed to believe in their God, they still couldn't bring themselves to do certain things. While the Crusaders had vowed never to harm innocents as a fundamental tenet of their faith, they were certainly not averse to violence. They killed the infected without hesitation or second thought until something like an infected child, preacher, or nun somehow caught them off guard and they froze up, unable to continue, like a robot forced to divide by zero. It inevitably fell to me, the secret atheist, to do their dirtiest work.

As I followed Sam and Rick into the house, I was more angry than apprehensive. But even as the door closed behind me, I was immediately disquieted by a strange, muffled noise from deeper inside. Some alien, quavering sound resonated through the house as it rose, fell, and paused with no discernible pattern. I tried at first to place the noise and almost asked aloud what the source of it was. Instead, I resigned myself to finding out soon enough.

Still, I felt a distinct kindling of fear as if my subconscious had already identified the sound. I eyed each corner and open doorway with suspicion, though I knew the house had already been scoured of all other threats. The sound grew louder as we proceeded through the house. Rick slowed and fell behind me, and I followed Sam until we stopped in front of the door behind which the sound was clearly emanating.

I suddenly knew without a doubt that what we heard behind that door were the cries of an infant, though they were not quite like anything I had ever heard or imagined. They called forth within me some unknown or forgotten emotion, as if there was some terrible connection between the sound and some point in my past. For the first time in I don't know how long, I felt lost, as if I had wandered off and no longer knew the way home. The crying continued. I felt my breath quicken, but I knew what had to be done and I knew it was better to get it over with instead of dwelling on it.

"All right," I said. "The mother is in there too?"

"Yes. She's sitting in the—"

"Go. Go ahead and wait outside. I'll take care of it."

Sam looked at me for a moment and then, hesitantly, headed back out the way we had come. Rick remained.

"Do you want me to pray with you?" he asked.

I shook my head.

"Go, man. You don't want to see this, and no one should see it who doesn't have to."

When he still didn't move, I looked him hard in the eyes.

"Go."

He turned to leave. With a quick backward glance, he followed Sam out. I silently listened to his footsteps as the crying continued. When the front door finally opened, then clicked shut, I opened the door to the room and stepped inside.

There are certain things, in my experience, that society deems too contrary and too incompatible to willingly juxtapose. Things that for the stark reality of their existence are hushed and shooed from conscious thought for the sheer, unthinkable horror they represent to us. These things often change over time and vary from culture to culture, but despite all the differences between races and creeds, there are things that seem to be immutably shunned. The reality of what was in that room struck me, and I knew I had made a mistake. I should never have gone there.

Something that had once been a mother sat idle in a rocking chair, a squirming mass held tightly in her arms. A heavily stained blanket was draped over her legs and feet. Most of her torso was hidden from view, but her uncovered face had grown bulbous almost to the point of bursting open. The skin was shiny, red, and appeared firm even as her head shook in what must have been impotent rage at my unwelcome presence. She leaned toward me, and the chair rocked forward, then backward as she emitted a strained, guttural growl, spraying flecks of discolored liquid from her mouth. I noticed then that her body was bloated and swollen to such an extent that she was trapped between the arms of the chair, unable to escape from it. The baby began to scream louder than before, disturbed by its mother's sudden outburst and angry because it was hungry and there was nothing left to eat; no more milk and no more breast, both gone and replaced with a crusty, ragged mess of a chest.

I tried to calm myself, to focus on the task at hand. I knew what had to be done, and I knew that it wouldn't be accomplished if I didn't do it quickly. I strode toward them and raised the rifle, my finger on the trigger, but I glanced, just once, down at the mess in her arms.

I was lost.

From a pile of what must have been the shredded, rotting remains of the mother's chest, two little arms reached out. Some of the fingers were swollen, some were broken, and some were missing altogether, as if the mother's hunger had won over her residual maternal instincts, if only briefly. Framed by flesh, blood, and a layer of writhing maggots, the baby's face was swollen like the mother's but was also eyeless. And yet I saw the infant ghost of Kaylee, my only niece. I saw her there, dead because of me, because I couldn't help her, because I had failed her and everyone I loved.

My eyes shifted away on their own, back to the quaking, bloated face of the mother, and there I saw Shelly's face instead, somehow hidden inside the monster in front of me. I stood there, and more than disgust, more than horror, more than fear, I felt guilt. My eyes started to well up with tears. I squeezed the rifle tighter. Without meaning to, I pulled the trigger.

I jumped as a round exploded into the mother's chest. The baby's cries grew even louder, and the mother's growls grew angrier but more ragged; one of her lungs had been pierced.

"I'm sorry," I heard myself say.

With frenzied focus, I adjusted my aim, fired another shot into her head, then fired another into the face of the screaming creature in the mother's arms.

I had hoped to hear silence or, if anything, just the peaceful gurgle of breath emptying from the woman's pierced lung. I might have been able to handle that. Instead, I heard the voice of my sister, and there in the shadows, I saw her holding baby Kaylee. Both of them were bleeding out because of what I had done, dying without knowing why.

I said something else as I fired another round, then adjusted the fire rate with shaking fingers, squeezed the trigger, and held it. I braced myself and adjusted my aim until the mother's shadowy face exploded into a bloody mess, flinging blood and chunks of infected flesh in every direction. The clip emptied. I released it, let it fall to the floor, and loaded another. I chambered a round and squeezed the trigger again. Someone started screaming. I realized after a moment that it was me, and I took control enough to scream even louder as I loaded another clip and kept firing. Yells sounded from behind me, so I knew I was no longer alone, but I couldn't bring myself to stop. Each bullet only made it worse, but I couldn't bring myself to turn away or Shelly and my beautiful niece would come for me and there would be nothing anyone could do or any reason to fight them; I killed them, and I deserved to die. The clip emptied. I dropped it and tried to load another, but someone grabbed me from behind. Arms reached around my torso, and I struggled to free myself, but more arms circled around me while others disarmed me. I was dragged out of the room, through the house, and to the street.

I cursed and threatened them, but two of them held me down as two others ran back to the trucks. I forced myself to stop struggling, to seem calm. I said I was fine, but they didn't believe me, so I cursed them again and promised they would not live to see their families. The trucks came back and stopped beside us. As they pulled me up, I realized that they had zip-tied my hands and feet together. I hurled every insult I could at them during the entirety of the trip back, then continued to do so as I was loaded into one of the still-empty houses near the Ranch, where the children wouldn't be able to hear me. They left the zip ties on and used paracord to tie me down onto a bed, then knelt together at the foot of the bed and quietly prayed. I screamed so loud they couldn't possibly have heard their own prayers. Eventually, they left me in the room. I fell asleep after a long while, but when I woke up throughout the night, I was screaming and couldn't shut up.

My nightmares consisted of the obvious.

24

I slept through the night and through the following day. When I finally woke around nightfall, the zip ties and paracord were gone. I got up, then wandered out of the bedroom and past the living room to the kitchen. A group of people was huddled in prayer in the living room, and I was fairly certain that none of them realized I was awake until after I had gulped down three glasses of water, returned to the bedroom, and shut the door behind me. I immediately went back to sleep.

I remained in the house for several days, during which time I was sleeping, trying to sleep, or pouring over thoughts and memories that had been suddenly dredged up from the silt of my mind. From time to time, someone from the prayer circle would knock on the door and try to convince me to let him or her in, but I never bothered to answer. They meant well, but I knew that their idea of "help" consisted primarily of prayer and advice to pray, followed by more prayer. I had no interest in talking or being talked to, praying or being prayed for. I had better things to do, like sleep and stare absently at the walls. My meditative silence proved to be a vastly superior form of recuperation.

Sometimes the trucks of the Crusaders would rumble past as they departed the Ranch, and I often found myself listening for their return. None of the Crusaders asked me to come out with them, and I had begun to assume I was no longer a part of the group until they returned early one night and stopped at the house. The prayer circle greeted them loudly as they came in, and Sam's voice reverberated in the door as footsteps approached my room. When Rick first opened the bedroom door and stepped in, his eyes widened in alarm at the sight of me sitting naked and cross-legged on the middle of the bed.

"Come on in," I said.

I watched him and wondered what exactly was on his mind as he walked over by a dresser and stood awkwardly in front of it. Silence was the norm for me, but Rick seemed unsure of what to say. We remained there for a few minutes as I regarded him and he looked with uncomfortable bafflement at the floor. Finally, he managed to look me in the eyes.

"So," he said at last. "How are you doing?"

My brow furrowed. After the prolonged lack of stimulation I had experienced over the course of the preceding several days, I was starved for entertainment. I stared steadily at him and pondered his question for an intentionally excessive length of time, during which he began to fidget.

"I'm well, thank you," I said finally. "How are you?"

"I'm good, I'm good," he said, nodding. "We've all been praying for you."

"Thanks," I said.

Another silence settled on us. It took another minute or so before I tired of my stupid little game and began to feel like an asshole.

"How are the guys?" I asked.

"Uh, they're doing good."

"Good," I responded. "You've got along well with just you five?"

"Uh, well . . ." He seemed to hesitate. "We got one of the younger guys to come out with us . . ."

I nodded.

"Good. Been making progress?"

He nodded.

"Yeah, been clearing out some more houses in some other spots to the west. Not quite the same pace as with you. Gotta be real careful with the new guy, he's pretty green."

I nodded again and wondered if he was getting at what I thought he was. Footsteps moved slowly down the hall toward us.

Rick opened his mouth to speak, then shut it and brought a hand to the back of his neck.

"I, uh . . ." he said. "Look, I'm real sorry about . . . what happened. That . . . we never should have made you go in there. That was a tough thing for anybody to do, and . . ."

He stopped, and the sentence hung.

I waited for a moment, then filled the silence.

"Rick, it wasn't your fault. I took that on. I made it my own responsibility, not you. It turned out I couldn't handle it. That was my mistake."

He stared at the floor and nodded as the door behind him opened. In stepped Sam, who did something of a double take when he noticed my nudity. I smiled at him.

"Well . . . irregardless, I . . . I'm sorry for what happened," Rick said.

I cringed inwardly and considered telling him that Jesus cried when people used "irregardless" in a sentence, but I abstained.

"I accept your apology," I said.

I left it at that and looked to Sam, who was standing somewhat awkwardly just inside the bedroom door.

"Hi, Sam," I said.

He nodded.

"Hey, Paul. How are you doin'?"

"I'm okay," I said. "I think I'm gonna be fine. A little recovery was warranted, but . . . I think I'm ready to get out of here."

"Do you think you're ready to come back?" Sam asked.

"If it's possible, I'd like to leave what happened behind and never speak of it again. Just go to work. If that's an option."

They both nodded.

"Of course, Paul," Sam said. "Of course."

I nodded, and for a second or two, we were all nodding; they were acknowledging me, I was acknowledging them, and we were acknowledging each other's acknowledgments. I found it hilarious, but I couldn't laugh or they'd think I was crazy.

"Okay," Sam said at last. "We'll head out tomorrow night. Or whenever you're ready."

I got up and started to walk out of the room, then thought better of it and put on a set of clothes that had been laid out for me a few days prior. They followed me out of the house, past the prayer group that had waited just outside the front door, and to the trucks. I hopped in the back just as I had a week prior and looked up at the overcast sky as they took me back to the Ranch.

No one mentioned anything about the reason I'd been out of action for a week, and I offered nothing. I'd hoped we would just go back to the usual killing, and at first that seemed to be the case. The new guy returned to whatever the hell he had been doing before, and we original Crusaders departed the Ranch to continue our work in New Castle.

As we prepped for our return, there seemed to be an underlying tension among the group that had not been there before, and I could imagine no possible way that I was not the sole cause. I could only remember bits and pieces of what I had said during my post-zombie-baby freak-out, but what I did remember was pretty heinous, even to me. Perhaps that explained why none of Crusaders had come to check on me prior to their visit to extract me and why, when they finally had come for me, they had dispensed with the awkward small talk with relative haste before pulling me back into the fray. Then again, maybe they had just assumed that since I wasn't screaming at the top of my lungs about raping and murdering their families, I was back to normal, good ol' Paul.

The group decided through halting, awkward suggestions to head back to the area we'd been clearing when I lost my mind. We determined that I would drive the ice cream truck and once we were more or less sure that the area was clear, we would move up to the bridge just beyond and perform the usual Pied Piper routine. I simply nodded in agreement; nothing about the plan could possibly trouble me. I was out of the house and back in action; that was all I really cared about.

I was driving in the middle of our three-vehicle convoy when the truck ahead of me came to a slow but unexpected halt. Since I had been daydreaming, I was slow to realize they'd stopped, and had almost rear-ended them. No one seemed to notice. At first, I thought they must have spotted a group of zombies or some other random obstruction, since we hadn't been driving quite long enough to have made it to New Castle, but when I picked up my radio to call them, a flash of light caught my eye.

When I climbed out of the truck, I was met with a very different and terrifying sight. New Castle was no longer in possession of the zombies, nor was it a potential quarry for the Crusaders. It was firmly in the grasp of what was left of the awesome might of the US military.

The city looked alive with light, and if I hadn't known better, I might have thought that the apocalypse had somehow missed New Castle. I sighed, grabbed the radio, and held it up to my face, but I couldn't think of anything to say that wasn't a smart-ass remark, so I tossed it back in the cab and continued to watch. After a few minutes of hemming and hawing, we killed our headlights, turned around, and drove back to the Ranch in the dark.

When we got back, Sam called an "emergency meeting" that consisted of we six Crusaders and John.

"I radioed Joey at our west lookout," Sam said. "He said he saw a whole bunch of vehicles heading north on the turnpike. I bet they came from the airport and drove right past us."

"The good Lord had his eye on us, that's for sure," Brad said.

John nodded at Brad's entirely factual statement.

"What exactly did they have?" John asked. "What kind of vehicles?"

"A few choppers with searchlights," Sam replied. "Couldn't tell if they had guns and rockets on them, but I don't see why they wouldn't. We couldn't see what they had on the ground. Ground troops at the very least. Probably something larger. There was a lot of light coming from all around the city."

"Sounds just like what Jack described happening downtown," Robert said.

I almost asked who Jack was before I remembered the conspiracy theorist who had talked at length about the activities of the government in downtown Pittsburgh and elsewhere. After all the time John had spent ignoring that increasingly imminent threat, he finally had no choice but to confront it or flee.

"Do you think we should communicate with them?" Rick asked.

John was already shaking his head before Rick had finished asking the question. "They're not our people," he said firmly. "There never was and never will be any government but God's kingdom. We have no interest in dealing with them. It will only bring trouble."

I didn't entirely disagree with him; after all, we didn't know the government's intentions, nor did we know for sure whether they knew we existed. If we made them aware of our presence by attempting to communicate with them, we had no idea how they would respond. They were an unknown and potentially lethal threat.

"Okay," I said. "So we're planning on leaving?"

"No," John answered.

I looked back and forth between Sam and John and waited for further explanation but received none.

"Guys," I said. "They're right there. We know they're in Pittsburgh. They passed by just a few miles south of us, and New Castle is what, ten miles from here? Fifteen? We're almost surrounded. If we stay where we are, they will come after us."

"Paul," Sam said tiredly, "even if we run, we'll have to face them eventually. We'll stand our ground, and if they confront us, the Lord will decide the outcome."

"Sam," I responded, forcing myself not to adopt a mocking tone, "if we stand our ground, we'll all end up dead. If they cleared out Pittsburgh, we don't stand a chance of—"

"Then the Lord will protect us," he interrupted firmly.

I should have known that statement would come back to bite me in the ass. I tried to formulate a valid response but could think of nothing to convince them that the only way to survive was to abandon ship and get the fuck out of Dodge. They were prepared to face down the same government that may have designed the virus that wiped out nearly everyone on the planet, the same government that was taking over the infected cities around us, the same government with planes, helicopters, tanks, and troops.

Before, I might have argued. Instead, I only nodded.

"Okay," I said. "Tell me the plan."

"We're going to move on to Ellwood City and Ellport, and clear them out," Sam said.

Ellwood City and Ellport. I had pushed that exact idea on a prior occasion, but John had apparently spoken with God on his big red emergency phone and shot the idea down. Instead, he ordered us to clear New Castle, which was much larger and much more dangerous. I didn't bother asking what John had to say about God's decisions after the government had moved in and took over. Surely, God had been trying to tell us something. Maybe he had just been trying to give us a heads-up about the government troops. Yeah, that was probably it.

"They're awkward cities to take," Sam said, "so I think we should take them as Paul suggested before and move gradually from the railroad bridge to the west, just hook them in bit by bit with the ice cream truck and go from there."

I nodded and waited for further elaboration but no explanation was forthcoming.

With the government's increased presence and our obvious activities in New Castle and numerous other towns, there could be no doubt that they would notice us if they hadn't already. It was just a matter of time. How the government dealt with us depended on what they perceived us to be; an ally or a threat. While they had previously been too busy eradicating the infected to bother with us, they would suddenly have nothing but free time to spend on either befriending us or shutting us down. If John stood his ground on refusing to play nice, it was suicidal to stay where we were. But I had no other options; I was alone without the Crusaders. While I had managed to keep from cracking when I was left alone in a bedroom for a few days, I knew what extended solitude would do to me. As stupid as they could be, they were all I had left in what remained of the world. Come hell, high water, and government oppression, they were as close to family as I would ever have again. I couldn't abandon them. I would die with them, if it came to that.

But before we departed and marched bravely toward our collective doom, I had one final errand to carry out.

25

I asked to borrow one of the vehicles, some spare gas, and enough ammo to fight myself out of the middle of a third world war. Tactically, it was a waste of fuel and manpower, but Sam knew I intended to get there one way or another. To help ensure that I came back alive, he and the Crusaders accompanied me. They didn't even question my intentions. Maybe they knew.

The drive was much shorter than it seemed the first time. Before, the trip there and back had felt like an eternity. On the way there, I'd been brimming with the gamut of emotions. Leaving there, I was empty of emotion but filled beyond capacity with something else. Maybe it was a resolve to rid the world of what had hurt me. Maybe it was the knowledge that there was nothing sacred and there never had been.

I had spent much of my time alone after that, though a few people tried to bridge the distance. For instance, old man Tom from the radio room was always good for company and a few cups of coffee. There was also Sam's daughter Emily, a hyperactive ray of sunshine, who would often flit by to say hello and check on our progress on ridding the world of evil. There were even a few women who expressed interest beyond the usual banter. But any attempt at friendliness made me uncomfortable in a way, and as cold as it might have been, I just didn't have it in me to feel anything for them. I couldn't tolerate their well-meaning friendliness or intimate small talk; it wasn't who I was. Though I could fake it well enough, I wasn't really the man they wanted or needed.

What it came down to was that I had changed. I was no longer Paul the friendly zombie enthusiast; I was Paul the soldier, the killer, the god of headshots. I was a Crusader—nothing more, nothing less.

Sam, Rick, and the rest of the guys had beautiful, normal lives beyond their venerable jobs as exterminators of the dead. When they weren't out on duty, they could stow away their weapons, put on their casual clothes, and relax with family and friends. But when they put on their tactical gear, loaded their weapons, and readied for war, they became my brothers-in-arms in the war against horror. There were no unnecessary conversations, no questions about feelings, and no probes into the past. As the well-oiled machines that the Crusaders were, we dealt in violence: the language that superseded all others.

But while I was secure in my role on the Ranch, I was plagued by nightmares and memories. When I slept, the past was no longer the past; it was forever. It permeated every piece of me. And in my dreams and memories, every scream, every gunshot, and every speck or pool of blood was just as it had been when I was still too shocked and scared to really feel it. Somebody once said that you don't really have your memory, that it has you. I finally understood. In the tamest of my dreams, I wandered train tracks, streets, and alleys. More often, I found myself in my house in Pittsburgh or my parents' final resting place, and the pain and fear were always as potent as the first time. It felt like the recollections were eating away at me, like there would eventually be nothing left, and the only way I could think of to fight back, the only way that made sense to me, was to return to those places and erase what remained of them, to wipe them from the earth.

I stepped down from the truck and onto the lawn of what had been my parents' home. It was quiet to everyone but me. There were no screams, no gunshots, and no sobs, but I still heard them. The dull thud and muffled slosh of the gas cans promised relief. I hadn't been able to give my parents a proper burial before, but I would finally do what I could. Their home would be their funeral pyre. I broke open the windows by the front door and poured half a can of gas inside, then made my way along the edge of the house and did the same to the other windows, one by one.

As I neared the backside of the house, a familiar and forgotten face appeared. Champ, the family dog, peeked out at me from the cover of the shrubs, his hairy little face and muzzle caked with dirt and dried blood. I didn't need to guess what he had been eating. I kneeled, patted my leg, and called to him. He only stared, so I held out my hand and called him again. He remained completely still.

We continued our little showdown for a few minutes before I gave up and continued what I had gone there to do. He followed me mutely for a while before finally breaking his silence. At first, all I heard was a whisper of a growl, but it grew slowly in intensity as I neared the back door. Finally, his growling was replaced by barking, and he started snapping at my pant legs. I tried to ignore him at first, but when he began to find purchase with his tiny jaws, I carried him by the scruff of his neck and left him with Greg.

Once I had emptied all the gas cans into the house, I tossed in a few lit matches and returned to the road. The fire quickly took hold, and within a few minutes, the house was engulfed by flames. It took an hour or so before the house as I had known it was no more than sticks and ashes. At no point did Champ seem to acknowledge the blaze; he only growled, barked, and snapped. I tried to bring him with us when the time came to leave, but he had changed too much to regard us as anything but enemies. He had seen too much, had been alone too long, and had adapted to the world in which he found himself. Gone were the days of belly rubs, biscuits, and fetch. Like Kotie, he had resurrected the killer instinct. Like me, that killer instinct was all he had left. He had done what he had to do to survive, and there was no longer room for anything else. After he bit the hands that held him for the fifth time, I took him once again by the scruff of the neck and let him go by the side of the road. He gave chase as we drove away.

A few nights later, we drove to Ellwood City and Ellport, two cities so close on the map that I wasn't sure where one ended and the other began. It didn't really matter, since they combined to form a severe clusterfuck. Our usual method of drawing the infected to a bridge for easy elimination didn't have the same luster as it did before. With most of Ellwood City and Ellport divided by a river and most of the bridges located in the middle of the towns, we had little choice but to enter from the west via a railroad bridge. From that location, we would clear the towns gradually until we made it safely to the next bridge, then continue on from that point. It wouldn't be nearly as neat or efficient as most of our past missions. In fact, it would probably be ugly. But it would most likely work, given enough patience. It was the best possible plan for the location.

As we winded along the roads and tracks in our approach of the bridge, I couldn't help but expect that the government would have anticipated our decision and moved in to shut us down. Thankfully, the roads and the skies ahead of us remained dark.

Once we arrived at the bridge, I killed the engine and waited for the guys to get into position. Because we had limited space, they pulled the trucks off to the side of the tracks so that when I returned in the ice cream truck, I could simply drive past them, park, and join them on the firing line.

They jostled around and heckled each other as they got ready, and if I hadn't known them better, I might have thought they were nervous. With the talk in the air among the people on the Ranch, I knew that wasn't the case; in truth, they were excited. Despite the fact that we had run from the government in New Castle, they all thought we were headed toward an ultimate showdown, a final battle in which we would ultimately triumph and the forces of evil would "suffer the awful wrath of God," as one man put it. I wasn't sure how they expected that to happen. Considering the course of action they had decided to take, I didn't doubt that there would be a showdown of some sort, but I had no delusions about surviving it.

Once they finished getting ready, I fired up the engine and headed across the bridge. It wasn't exactly a pleasant ride, since I hadn't driven much on train tracks with the ice cream truck, but it was still nice to get back behind the wheel. I drove carefully and soberly when I first reached the streets, but after a few minutes, I was back to hollering bad puns and ice cream advertising slogans at every zombie that had ears to hear. It was a slow drive, but it felt damn good. I was back in action, and though I couldn't explain it, I felt oddly invincible.

The radio crackled to life, and a voice jumped out at me. The words were partially drowned out by my truck's scratchy rendition of "My Fair Lady," but I could tell from the tone that they were trying to get my attention. Apparently, they were feeling even more exuberant than I had realized. I killed the music and picked up the radio to answer back, but they called out again before I could speak.

"Paul, get back here. We have to move!"

I couldn't tell which of the guys it was, but there was panic in his voice. The engine rattled as I stomped the gas and steered around a corner back toward the tracks. Whoever was on the radio kept yelling before I could respond, and when I finally managed to get a word in to ask what was wrong, he didn't answer. I tossed the radio and put both hands on the wheel as I turned another corner and pulled onto the tracks. I looked for the trucks as I drew nearer to the bridge but couldn't see them. All their lights were off. I slowed to a stop, reached over, and grabbed the radio off the floor.

"What the hell are you guys doing over there?" I asked.

Shouts answered back.

"Kill the lights! Kill the lights!"

I swore, turned off my headlights, then swore again at what I finally saw. Lights. Not the truck headlights and not the guys' flashlights, but shafts of light above and beyond their position, reaching down from the sky.

Helicopters. Even from where I was, I could tell they were rapidly approaching.

"Guys," I said. "We have to move."

"We have to go back!" Rick screamed in response.

"There's nowhere to fucking go!" I yelled. "They're almost on us!"

I gripped my pistol and waited for a response.

Finally, Sam responded.

"Hold on," he said.

I started to count the seconds, then remembered that I was sitting in a three-ton zombie attractant. I grabbed my flashlight and peeked out the open door toward the back of the truck. With a flash of the light, I saw a biter headed toward me on the tracks from no more than thirty feet away. It grunted loudly and sped up, its legs pumping on the gravel. I grabbed the radio, but before I could say anything, the headlights of both the other trucks turned on.

"Hurry up," I said, and turned my headlights back on.

I peeked again around the side of the truck and saw the nearest zombie approaching the rear corner of the vehicle. Not far behind was the horde, and if it was anything like every other zombie bridge pull we had performed, it would number in the hundreds. Killing the nearest runner would only buy me a few more seconds at most, but it was moving too fast for me to wait.

I shifted into reverse, mashed the gas, and felt an almost immediate impact. An arm slammed against the driver-side window, then swung wildly and sheared off my side-view mirror. I glanced through the passenger-side window before remembering that the other side-view mirror had been torn off in much the same manner more than two weeks prior. Since the vehicle had no rearview mirror, I was driving blind.

Another body slammed into the back of the truck, followed by another, then three more in succession, and quite suddenly, the wheel jerked hard to the left. I bounced into the air, landed back in the seat, and scrambled to regain control, but I turned the wheel too far and overcompensated. I wrapped both arms around the wheel as the truck tipped, went airborne, and came to a violent stop on its side. I lost my grip and my back slammed hard into the roof. I struggled to my feet and stood on the driver-side door, then knelt and felt around for the flashlight. I felt the radio first and tried to reach the guys, but it didn't work. I tossed it without thinking and continued searching. In the darkness, I found the radio twice more before I finally found the flashlight.

I looked up at the passenger-side seat and was relieved to see that my M4 was still nestled in the grasp of the safety belt. I patted my torso to verify that I still had my M4 magazines, then climbed toward the passenger-side door as the metal body of the truck came alive with the chaotic impacts of hands, heads, and various other body parts. I tried to ignore them as I stood on the steering column and unbuckled the rifle but felt a surge of adrenaline when they started to attack the windshield. The glass held at first but quickly cracked and began to cave as I slid the door open above me. Unsure of whether the armrest would support my weight, I nonetheless used it as a stool and peeked my head out above the surrounding fray.

Screams and mindless roars sounded from all around me. The trucks were only a hundred feet away, but most of the crazies had not yet noticed them. I grunted inaudibly amid the noise, and with the flashlight in one hand and the rifle in the other, I pulled myself up onto what had become the top of the truck. By the time I made it up and pushed myself to a standing position, the trucks had nearly reached me. I noticed with a nervous glance that the choppers were getting closer. I stepped as close as I dared to the edge of the vehicle and tried to signal the trucks to drive past. The best I could hope for was that they could draw enough of the infected away from me that I could jump off and run away. I had no idea how I would meet up with them later, but I would cross that bridge when I came to it. Not being mauled to death in the immediate future was foremost on my mind.

The first truck came to a stop on the tracks, its front end even with me, and Rick poked his head out. Some of the zombies between us noticed and moved up the gravel toward them. Rick screamed something, but I couldn't hear him above the din. I waved him on, but he shook his head and screamed again as he held up a hand.

Stay. He was telling me to stay.

There wasn't even time to flip him a thumbs-up before the truck roared and accelerated past me, followed closely by the second truck. I looked helplessly around for a space and time to jump, then saw the first truck veer right and bound down off the tracks toward a small dirt area at the rear of a warehouse. Moments before slamming into the back of the building, it turned hard to the left and came to a sudden stop. The second truck skidded in the dirt but crashed into the building and stalled.

After two failed attempts to restart the engine, Robert, Greg, and Brad jumped out of the cab as Sam and Rick rushed up to join them. It was when they all climbed into the bed that I realized what they were doing: the crazy bastards were going to try to save me.

As they fired their first shots, I raised my rifle to contribute to my own rescue mission. Just as I had returned to my role as the ice cream driver, I would reprise my role as Paul, the King of Headshots. Screams and wordless roars were cut short as heads and faces exploded. Shot, kill. Shot, kill. Shot, shot, kill, kill. The rifle shots behind me suddenly and drastically increased in frequency, and I turned to see that the Crusaders were almost entirely surrounded. I fired a line into the crowd between us in a rapid staccato, aiming first for the few nearest me, then at those nearer to the other truck as the first several fell.

I dropped my clip and loaded another as a hand wrapped around my ankle. I wrestled free and put a bullet in the head of a biter that had managed to claw its way up to me. Then a flash of blinding light passed briefly over me. The chopper was almost on us. I swore, turned, and continued to fire. I emptied another clip and had already loaded the next when I saw that Robert was waving his arms at me, beckoning me toward him.

I moved to the edge of the vehicle closest to the guys, then jumped. I landed off balance and tumbled back into the rear doors of the truck, then leaned forward and broke into a sprint. I juked through the spattering of zombies that remained and made my way to the other trucks as the light hit me again. I didn't need to look back to know we had been spotted. Sam and the others, who had already realized the chopper's proximity and bailed out of the trucks, screamed for me to follow. I broke past the last few of the pursuers and joined the Crusaders as they rounded the corner of a warehouse, temporarily out of view of the chopper.

We fled on foot into the city.

L. Marshall James

26

The streets seethed. With Sam in the front and me in the rear, we fired wildly at sounds and silhouettes as we ran in single file between buildings. The infected poured from the shadows and were revealed with terrifying clarity by the mounted lights and flashes of our rifles. We met their rage with a stern resolve that threatened to fray into panic as we moved deeper into a city that wanted to eat us alive.

Light from the helicopter played over the upper stories of houses in front of us. We dashed through an alleyway into one of the many backyards separated only by low metal fencing. We moved along the rear edges of the buildings until we came to the street, then continued across it toward another row of houses. When we reached the other side, Sam broke right along the sidewalk and we followed.

He came to a stop at the front entrance of a church, then raised a foot and brought it hard into the doors. When they held firm, he tried again. Still no dice. Greg stopped him as he moved to try a third time, and they tried to crash the doors in tandem as the rest of us stood guard and picked off attackers. It was no use. The doors would not give. Sam swore loudly and continued on down the sidewalk with us in tow.

We turned down another alley and followed it. I wasn't sure if any of us knew what direction we were headed, but since the alley was less populated than the streets, I didn't think anyone cared. We stopped partway through and hunkered down by a loading dock to take stock of our ammo and check each other over. We all had ample ammunition, since we always erred on the side of having too much rather than too little, but we were already out of breath and heaving wildly to regain it. Since our missions were usually slow and deliberate, we rarely found ourselves in situations where we had to sprint, let alone sustain a sprint while almost constantly identifying and eliminating targets all around us.

I flashed my light briefly down the alley in both directions to see if anyone was in pursuit. When I saw nothing, I killed the light. The rest followed suit, and we all knelt together as we huffed desperately for air. When the sound of the helicopter grew deafening, we hid under a large metal awning. We stayed there for a while after it passed and sat in silence until we had all regained our breath.

"Do we have a map of this place?" I asked.

Something rustled for a few seconds and a light flicked on. Robert unfolded a map and laid it out on the concrete in the middle of our group. Unfortunately, since we had no real idea of where we were, all we could do was estimate that we should probably head east, then go either north or south until we hit a river. Without more information, we were still half-lost.

We moved the rest of the way through the alley until we came to a street, then I peeked around the edge of the building with my monocular and scanned for street signs. Once we had pinned down our location and determined a more specific route, we sprinted en masse across the street and headed east through myriad alleyways and backyards. The helicopter had wandered far away from us, and for the moment, the streets and alleyways were clear. Aside from the helicopter, the loudest sounds were the stamps of our boots and the huffing of our breath. It was during this lull in the action as we ran along the sidewalk that it happened. The attack came abruptly, violently, and without warning.

Sam, who had been in the lead, turned to his left and backed up suddenly as he fired into the recessed doorway of a small grocery store. At once, something slammed against the glass of the front windows of the store. We all moved out into the street to join Sam, suddenly wary of the grocer's patronage. Something moved behind us and Brad turned to face it.

"Guys," he said. "Check our flank."

As he said it, a guttural sound like choking came from down the street in the direction from which we had come. I turned to see that we had developed a significant following over our short tour of the town, the foremost of which were quickly approaching.

"We need to move!" I yelled.

As if on cue, each of the storefront windows shattered almost simultaneously to reveal a huge collection of obese, angry crazies. They screamed, and as they ran toward us, we opened fire. Five fell from my shots alone before I turned and ran behind each of the guys. As I passed, I tapped each of them on the shoulder and yelled.

"Run, run, run!"

I took the lead, and we sprinted again down the street with the biters in pursuit. I led us between a pair of houses, through their collective backyards, then past the next row of houses. As I neared the street, a body tumbled over the railing of a porch to my left and blindsided me. The collision knocked me off balance, and I careened to my right, slammed into the opposite porch, and then fell. Someone fired, and when I turned to face the body, it was dead on the ground beside me. Sam pulled me to my feet and ran out into the street. I jumped in line behind him and subsequently almost ran into him when he came to an unexpected stop. When I stepped up beside him, I saw what had brought him to a halt: there were many more infected ahead of us, and they were already headed our way. I looked down the street in the other direction and saw a moving wall of crazies plodding toward us. I heard Rick gasp beside me.

"What the fuck is this?" I said.

Rick joined Greg to cover our flank as the rear procession of zombies continued pursuit. I turned toward Sam to see that he was already looking for another route. After a moment, he motioned for me to follow him. I tapped Robert and Brad on their shoulders, then ran after Sam as he led us down the street to the left, toward the lesser of the two mobs.

Suddenly, someone sprung from an alley just to Sam's left and out of his line of sight. Before any of us could react, it was on him. Sam realized its presence in the last instant and with a raised elbow, he managed to fend off its snapping jaws for long enough that I was able to raise my rifle and put a bullet in its ribs. It yelped like a dog, reached for its side, and fell. As Sam threw it to the ground, something crashed into me from the left and a pair of arms wrapped around me. I stumbled, then regained my footing and twisted to get away, but its grip was too strong. I felt a flash of burning pain in my shoulder as a shot rang out, followed by another. The zombie went limp and fell to the ground. I stumbled back a few steps and reached a hand to my shoulder to feel wet, warm blood. Sam started back toward me as Rick shone a light on the wound, but I waved them off.

"No time!" I screamed. "Let's go!"

Sam nodded, turned, and continued down the street. Suddenly, light played over the upper stories of the buildings to our right.

"Chopper!" Robert screamed from behind me.

Sam broke left and ran up onto the front porch of one of the houses. With a swift and fierce kick, he crashed the front door inward. We followed him as he pushed open the inner screen door and ran inside, then continued through a hall that took us straight through the house. We passed through a kitchen, then through an outer door. As we stepped onto the back porch, my eyes settled on a large, square silhouette against the side of the house. It was an outdoor grill.

"Wait!" I screamed.

I screamed so loud and stopped so suddenly that Sam turned completely around in one step, his rifle raised, and Robert ran into me from behind.

"What is it?" Sam screamed.

"Propane!" I yelled. "We can set a bomb!"

"A bomb?"

"Just cover us from the porch!"

Greg joined Sam on the porch, and I directed Rick and Robert to go back into the house and cover the hallway we had come through. I called on Brad to shine his light on the grill as I tore the cover off. Shots rang out from inside the house as I closed the valve on the propane tank. Brad asked me what the plan was, but I ignored him. If it worked, he'd find out soon enough.

Once I removed the tank, I set it down beside the kitchen door and ran inside. I yelled for Brad to find flammables as I turned the knobs on the stove all the way up and made sure it lit. Though I heard only sporadic shots from the back porch, Rick and Robert's shots from the end of the hallway were becoming increasingly frequent. There wasn't much time.

I found a few rolls of paper towels and threw them on top of the stove, followed by cloth towels and a pizza box. As they began to catch flame, I yelled for Brad to stay in the kitchen as I made my way down another hallway. I moved quickly but with limited caution, my rifle raised as I ran down the hall, checking each door until I found a bathroom.

I didn't even bother to scan the room before throwing open cabinet doors at random in search of more flammables. I grabbed an armload of toilet paper, ran it back to the kitchen, and threw it in a heap onto the growing fire on the stove as Brad snapped the leg off of a wooden chair.

"Chemicals!" I yelled. "Propellants! Under the sink!"

As Brad threw an armload of wood onto the stove, I ran back to the bathroom. The gunshots in the hallway reached a frenzied pace as I searched through the cabinet and found the last piece to the puzzle: rubbing alcohol. I ran back to the kitchen, unscrewed the cap from the bottle, and tossed it a few feet down the hall in front of Rick and Robert. I couldn't help but smile at the body count. Bodies lay broken and dead as near as ten feet from the kitchen and as far as I could see down the hall in the flashes of the rifles. They were all pursuing us through the house.

It would be perfect.

Brad yelled from behind me with an armload of chemicals. I pointed to the fire on the stove, then grabbed the flaming corner of what was left of the pizza box and tossed it into the hall. The alcohol instantly caught flame. I pulled an air horn from my belt, then tapped Robert and Rick on the shoulders and motioned for them to join Sam. As they ran out the back door, I pulled a zip tie tight around the handle of the horn and threw it as hard as I could toward the bathroom. I could only hope it distracted the zombies for long enough.

I sprinted out the back door, set the propane tank in the middle of the doorway, and ran with Brad. The infected, drawn by the gunfire and the horn, were becoming more numerous. We fired at targets all around us as we made our way across the backyards and into an alley leading to the street. I ordered Sam and Greg to cover the street-side and for the other three to cover our asses as I took aim. One little white spot in a dark doorway.

I am Paul, god of marksmanship.

My first two shots either glanced off the tank or missed it entirely. My third shot was perfect, and the resulting explosion was beautiful. The windows of the house shattered, and flames shot out through every available exit. Screams came from farther in. They sounded equally pained and angry. A few smaller explosions sounded off, and as the house began to catch fire, we turned and ran.

We made our way to the street, then continued across it and through another alley. At the next street, we broke to the right, then ran perhaps a hundred feet before crossing the street toward another church. I was running with most of what I had left by the time we entered the parking lot and made our way to the back door. I watched our flank as the guys each took turns kicking the door, and after what might have been five minutes of impotent thuds and grunts, the door gave way and we flooded in.

We shoved a motley collection of furnishings against the door before proceeding farther inside, then moved as slowly as we could stand through the church. To avoid attracting any more attention, we used machetes and kukris on the few biters we encountered.

Once we found a suitable place to barricade ourselves in one of the upper stories, Sam tried to radio the Ranch. Meanwhile, Rick and Brad searched for medical supplies to treat my shoulder. After a few minutes, they managed to find some antibiotic ointment in a nearby cabinet. I found a bathroom and removed my tactical vest, then peeled the shirt off. The sweat and blood stuck to both the fabric and my skin, and I felt stinging pain with every touch of the wound. Rick flashed a light on it as I sat down, and Sam came over to get a better look.

"Is that a bite or a bullet wound?" Rick asked.

"Looks like a bullet might have just grazed," Sam said. "Paul, did you feel anything before the shot?"

I nodded, but couldn't meet his eyes.

"Yeah," I said.

Sam nodded in my peripheral vision.

"Okay, well keep an eye on it."

As Sam walked off, Rick stepped in with the ointment. I held out a hand to stop him.

"I got it," I said. "It'll hurt less if I do it."

He nodded as he handed me the tube.

"Let me know if you need anything, okay?" he said.

"No doubt," I replied.

I applied the ointment, but there was no gauze large enough to cover the wound, so I used my hand to try and cram it deeper into the flesh. Fear gripped me as tightly as the pain. I tried to place my mind over both.

So much zombie lore had been wrong. They were not all dumb, they were not undead, they didn't eat only brains, and as far as I knew, the infection was not spread by bite. Once I stopped fiddling with the wound, the pain was relatively easy to ignore but the fear persisted.

When I returned to the room where we all planned to sleep, I found that everyone was already out for the count. I locked the door and joined them. For the time being, a closed door would be a sufficient guard. I tried to tell myself that it didn't matter that I had been bitten, that if I had been susceptible, I would have already been dead, but I was too tired to really convince myself. Once I lay down, I fell asleep almost immediately.

At some point during the night, an explosion sounded in the distance.

27

"Paul," said a voice. "Paul, get up. We gotta get moving."

I jerked awake to near-total darkness. Though the contents of my dream had faded instantly from memory, I knew it had been a nightmare. I was damp with sweat. Rick knelt beside me, his one hand outstretched toward me.

"Not much time," he said. "There's some food beside you."

I winced at the pain in my shoulder as I sat up and pressed myself back against a wall. In the shadows beside me was a small plate holding an unidentifiable meal. I picked it up and felt around until I found an eating utensil, then tried the first few bites of the mystery food. Cold veggies, and . . . I worked my tongue into a square, salty chunk.

Mmm, butter: the breakfast of a true warrior.

As I ate and watched the guys check over their rifles and prep to move, I noticed a subtle flicker of light over the room that wasn't sunlight and didn't seem artificial. Once I moved to the window and realized the source of the light, I had to force myself to keep chewing. Starting just a few buildings away and spreading farther than I could discern, an almost unbroken field of flames reached up and licked at the sky.

Ellwood City was ablaze.

I shoveled the rest of the food into my mouth and chewed as I returned to my clothes and equipment. Once I had squeezed what was left of the ointment onto my shoulder, I clamped a hand over the mess and tried again to force it into the wound. By the time I had finished getting ready, Sam and the group were already waiting for me by the door. I hustled behind them through a maze of hallways and rooms that I didn't remember, then into the main congregation room and out the front doors of the church.

Once all of us were outside, Sam turned immediately to the right and followed the sidewalk. Rick kept an eye on our flank, and as I fell in line, I hoped they knew where we were headed. We stayed on the sidewalk until it tapered off to nothing, then moved up to straddle a set of train tracks that curved gently away from the residential areas of the city before burrowing into a hill.

It was when I saw the tunnel that I remembered the tentative plan we had laid out in the alley. I swore under my breath. Once we passed through the tunnel and crossed the bridge on the other side, we would move down to the river below the bridge and follow its winding course east until we made it out of town. We had originally wondered if we might be able to go west instead, but the possible presence of choppers and troops had rendered that option chancy at best. Add to that the swath of fire that was actively consuming much of the city, and the west became entirely untenable. East was our only option. Once we found a place to camp out, we could try to plan a further course of action and attempt to reestablish contact with the Ranch.

Reestablish contact. Those were the words Sam had used earlier. Somehow, it was only as we made our way through the tunnel that I was struck by the significance of what that meant. I tapped Brad on the shoulder.

"Hey," I yelled. "When was the last time we had contact with the Ranch?"

"The bridge," he responded.

The bridge. The railroad track bridge they'd been sitting at when we first spotted the helicopter. So Sam hadn't been able to reach them at all before we left the church. What did that mean? Had the government somehow managed to jam our communication?

"What did they say?" I asked.

Brad said something, but his words were drowned out by the sound of our footsteps.

"What?" I yelled.

"They were under attack!" he said again.

"Under attack from what?" I asked.

"What?" he asked.

"Who the fuck was attacking them?"

"Choppers!" he yelled back. "Government troops!"

Choppers. Troops. So they had hit the Ranch at the same time that they had tried to hit us. It had been an orchestrated attack. How long had they known we were there? Had they noticed us when we had approached New Castle during their takeover, or had they already known we were there? Had anyone at the Ranch been able to escape?

"What level of force did they use?" I yelled.

I saw him shake his head.

"Don't know."

"How many of our satellite towns are in contact?"

He shook his head again.

"We think they got hit too."

"What?" I said. "Who got hit too? Which towns?"

"All of 'em," he replied.

I stared at his back in the dark and asked nothing else. Though more questions flitted through my mind, I wasn't sure I wanted to know any of the answers. The rest of the tunnel was darkness and silence, interrupted only by our breathing and the crunch of gravel beneath our boots. I jogged in what felt like a haze; I was already tired.

I didn't know what to expect once we exited the tunnel and crossed the bridge, but it turned out to be devoid of any threats. No biters, no troops, no choppers. We came to a street and followed it east for a short while until we finally decided to move down to the water. From there, we rode the banks as much as we could and took to the water and the mud only when we had to.

We moved with no real urgency. Given that the government troops were probably occupied with the fire and the likely outpouring of zombies from the burning city, we expected to have a relatively clear escape route aside from any scattered infected we encountered. We came upon only two crazies on the way, which Sam dispatched quietly with a machete. Our path was a mostly quiet but miserable slog.

Despite moving almost constantly, I was tense and cold, a fact made worse by the few times I lost my footing and fell into the water. I shoved each hand into my pants alternately as we moved, and as I curled my toes in my boots, I thanked every god I could think of for the divine powers of wool socks. It was a long, awful trek, and while I had no idea of the exact length, I knew it was over as soon as I saw a house, because I had already determined that I would travel no farther. We stepped up the riverbank toward the house, and by the time we had cleared all the rooms, the sun had already begun to rise. Once we made sure the house was clear, I wasted no more time with security measures. I ransacked closets and cabinets for blankets and pillows, then stacked them all on a bed in one of the back rooms. Before I could lie down, Sam leaned in through the doorway.

"Hey, Paul. You gotta come out and see the sunrise," he said. "It's gorgeous."

I shook my head and wiped my running nose on the back of my sleeve.

"Nah," I said. "I'm gonna get some sleep. Wanna be well rested for when we start moving again."

He nodded and stepped off back through the house as I muttered to myself. Watch the sunrise? Everyone at the Ranch was probably captured or dead, and we had barely escaped the city with our lives. We had plodded through God knows how much water and sludge, had only just found an empty house with bedding, and he wanted to sit out and watch a sunrise? What, was it pretty? Was God speaking to him and the Crusaders through the myriad colors of the sky? Yeah, no thanks. They and their God could chat all day as Earth continued to orbit and rotate until the sun disappeared again from view. Maybe they could try again to contact John-the-preacher-man and concoct another idiotic plan to finally get us all killed. As for me, I was wet, cold, and tired. I laid my M4 on a chair in the corner, stripped off everything that wasn't made of wool, and slipped beneath the covers.

Even as I began to fall asleep, I couldn't help but dwell on the all too likely possibility that the Ranch and its satellites were gone and that we six Crusaders, the only ones who were even trained to fight, were all that was left. In what I had overheard Rick and Robert say to each other in hushed tones, they did not share my fear. They knew for a fact that even if the Ranch and all of its inhabitants were not secure, they could be made so with enough prayer, determination, and faith. Their confidence was supreme; mine was gone. Such fickleness is the curse of the faithless.

Once I finally managed to drift off, I found sleep to be dreamless but fitful. I struggled to get comfortable despite the warmth of the blankets, and I found myself waking again and again to the troublesome reality of a lonely, dark room in the apocalypse. On each occasion, I checked the far corner to see Sam keeping silent watch on the only door to the room. One time I awoke, I asked him if he really still believed in God, even after everything that had happened.

He nodded. "Always."

I rolled over and closed my eyes.

28

When I woke, the only dream I remembered was one of pressure and the inability to move or escape. It was unfortunately prescient.

The holster on my hip unsnapped, and my pistol began to slip out. I tried to reach for it, but my arm was stuck. Something was wrapped around my wrist. When I tried to tug free, the pressure on my wrist increased. I realized then that the pressure was all over: on my wrists, my ankles, my shoulders . . . I was suddenly wide-awake and aware of the fact that several hands and arms were holding me in place.

"No, no, no, you fuckers!" I screamed.

I fought to free myself, but with four of them holding me down, I was helpless. They slid the pistol out of the holster and finally released me. I ceased to struggle; they already had what they were after. As they backed away from the bed, I rolled hard to the left and onto the floor, then lurched over to the chair in the corner. My hands grasped the wood of the seat and came up with nothing; they had taken my M4 as well. I stood and backed into the corner, weary even after having slept. They were all standing in the room. Sam stood closest to me and held his hands out in an attempt at placation as I leaned my head back against the wall. I hopelessly felt around on my vest for the kukri, but it was gone too. They had covered all their bases. I knew what was going on, but I asked anyway.

"What are you doing?" I said.

I sniffled in response to my own question, but Sam still granted me an answer.

"You're sick," he said.

I sniffled again and sank down into a crouch.

"I can fight," I said.

"You can," he said, "but we don't know when you'll turn. We can't let you carry a weapon if you're sick—"

"Fuck you," I whispered.

He stopped talking for a moment, perhaps shocked that I would say that to him. Despite my anger, I felt bad for saying it. I liked Sam. I knew he meant well, and I knew his intentions were sincere. I also knew that he was right.

When he spoke again, it was slow and deliberate.

"You'd do the same thing, Paul. You know you would."

I nodded. "I know."

I didn't blame them. They were doing what they had to do. Life as a Crusader was nothing if not mercilessly pragmatic, and I had joined and remained with them partly because of that fact. But despite having resigned myself to death, I had secretly hoped to at least die honorably, perhaps by sacrificing myself to save someone else or by dying in a hail of gunfire. Instead, I'd been bitten by some crazy schmuck while trying to run from hundreds of brain-dead bastards just like him. I took some small consolation in the fact that I had set his neighborhood on fire in retaliation. Tit for tat.

"Are you going to leave me here?" I asked.

"No," Sam said. "We'll stay with you for as long as it takes."

I felt a flash of terror and the slow, creeping rot of dread in my stomach. If they left, I could have at least followed them and watched their backs from a distance while I slowly lost my mind. I could have protected them from afar and faded out as one of the Crusaders. Whether or not I believed in their religion, working with them and for them meant something to me. Even if that effort failed or I somehow lost their trail, I could have at least found a way to end my life in peace and, more importantly, on my own terms. It would have been a better way to go. It would have been a token of respect from a universe that had never cared.

But I was no longer a Crusader. I was just a man, and I was going to die slowly as I awaited the same mercy they had given to that poor bastard Will, who was denied the freedom to blow his own brains out in his own damn house.

"Go ahead," I said. "Don't worry about me. I'll take care of myself."

There was silence, then Rick spoke out.

"We're here with you, Paul. We're not going anywhere."

I burst into tears. Whether it was the purity of their intentions or the fact that I knew I was going to slowly go insane before I died and would have no control over it, I wept openly and didn't care. I let it all out. I squeezed my skull between both hands and screamed as loud as I could. I pounded the floor like a child and emptied myself until I felt tired, finished, and vacant.

When I finally fell silent, we all moved out to the living room and sat around the hearth where a fire had been built. Under Brad's watchful eye, I searched the kitchen and salvaged a mostly empty bottle of vodka. I offered it generously, but none partook, so I took periodic shots and sat on the floor with a blanket wrapped around me.

I stared blankly at each of them in turn as I tried to imagine what would happen when I turned into one of the insane. I would have a fever by then. I'd be delusional. Maybe I would be able to retain the fortitude to keep from trying to hurt or kill one of them, but that was an unlikely possibility. How long would they wait to kill me? Would they opt to tie me down before the end so that I wouldn't be able to lash out as my mind frayed? Would they shoot me from the front or the rear, and would I have to listen to them pray for me before they did it? Would I even remember what prayer was?

One of my eyelids twitched, followed by the other. For a while, I tried to think of nothing, an effort that I hoped would calm me down. It didn't work. I thought about pouring the remainder of the vodka on the wound but decided against it. If I was truly infected, then I was already doomed. There was no point in wasting good vodka. Besides, I was still nursing the faint hope that the alcohol would cancel out what felt like the growing symptoms of sickness.

"Why don't we go farther up the hill?" I said. "Maybe we can see the city."

I looked around the room at each of them as I said it. It hadn't really been a question. It was a statement. The vodka was almost gone, and if I was on house arrest until I died, then I wanted a better house with a better view. My eyes settled on Sam.

His jaw clenched, and he looked at me pensively, then nodded.

"Okay," he said. "Let's see what we can find."

We each collected our things and stepped carefully outside—or rather, they collected their things while I watched, then they stepped carefully outside while I walked with the casual air of a man half-drunk on holiday with a family he has reason to resent. We made our way to the road and followed it, each of them scanning the darkness as I meandered on. We passed by a dog kennel on the way, and Robert and Rick checked it out while the rest of us waited by the road. They came back after a very short time and said that all the dogs were dead. No one asked for elaboration.

We made our way over to a house that sat catty-corner to the kennel and went inside. It was a mess of a place, but the Crusaders found that it was utterly devoid of any sign of life, death, or anything in between. That was a welcome development to them. We scavenged some canned goods from the kitchen, made our way to the top story, and hunkered down.

For a long while, I just sat and stared out one of the windows as I finished the last of the vodka. In Ellwood, the fire we'd started had grown into an immense beast that threatened to level the entire city. Beyond the reach of the flames were helicopters that hovered over dark buildings and streets, their spotlights piercing the darkness. I had no solid idea what they were searching for. I thought at first that they were looking for us, but the prospect didn't make sense. While they couldn't possibly know how far outside of their reach we were, it seemed hugely impractical for them to go to such lengths for six men, unless we had actually been a larger thorn in their side than we had realized. But that seemed unlikely. If they were looking for biters, there were certainly plenty of those to be had, but the fire would consume them quickly enough without any intervention. They were wasting time and fuel, and I couldn't figure their aim.

Nearer to the west edge of the city and beyond the fires and helicopters, there was more light, though I couldn't discern one source from another. It was clear that the government had arrived in force. Perhaps they intended to finish the job we had started. What a shame that they had neglected to pack any firefighting equipment.

I wiped my nose and glanced around aimlessly, then noticed a pack of cigarettes on the floor beside me. I kicked it toward the wall and looked back at the guys. I realized then that none of them were sitting near me. In fact, other than when they had held me down to get my weapons, none of them had so much as patted me on the shoulder to express their condolences for my imminent death. Couldn't say I blamed them. In a way, I understood how they must have felt. As far as they were concerned, I had been their best marksman and therefore a premier Crusader. But I was no longer exempt from the punishments that had been doled out to the rest of the world; that scared them. If God had allowed me to fall sick, what would happen to them?

Despite my anger and resentment, I was struck by a wave of affection. It had taken a long time for me to truly warm up to the Crusaders, but I found myself troubled as much by my imminent death as by the fact that I would no longer be working with them. They were good soldiers and good men. I would miss them.

"Guys, before I go off the deep end . . ." I started. "I just want so say that it's been an honor . . ."

I stopped and took a breath. An honor? What the hell, I wasn't a US Marine.

"Fuck it," I said. "I love you guys. And I've really enjoyed working with you. I know I haven't always been . . ."

I trailed off and shook my head. What do you say to your family before they kill you? How do you tell them that it's not their fault, that you don't blame them? How do you release them of that burden?

"We love you too, Paul."

I looked with surprise at Rick as he said it. The others nodded their assent as Sam spoke.

"You're a good man," he said. "I have no doubt that we'll meet again. And it's certainly been an honor."

"Definitely," Brad said.

I nodded as Sam reached over and squeezed my good shoulder. In spite of the love I felt for the Crusaders and in spite of our mutual sentiments, the touch of his hand made me tense in a way I could not explain, as if I were sitting on the edge of a knife. I twitched, then lowered my head into my hands to hide my face. There was no stopping it. Gradually, I was slipping into the same madness that had taken my family, my friends, and those of countless others that we had killed. Now it would take me, and I would die just like Will.

I didn't want to think about it anymore. My eyes wandered the room and settled again on the pack of cigarettes. I leaned over and picked it up, then dumped its contents onto the floor in front of me. A grimy orange lighter clattered onto the wood amid a mess of paper and tobacco. I retrieved the sole respectable cigarette and examined it closely. I had never really enjoyed the taste of tobacco and had never smoked, aside from when I had been particularly drunk, but today was a special day because I was going to die. Whatever cancer came to life in the next few days would die with me.

I grabbed the lighter, stood, and made my way down the stairs. I heard whispers behind me, followed by footsteps. As I opened the back door, I turned to see Sam following me outside. I held the door open until he was close, then stepped out and made my way over to a patch of grass that looked comfortable in the dim moonlight. Sam hesitated, then sat down a few feet away from me as I lit the cigarette.

"You smoke?" he asked.

I took a hit, inhaled the smoke much deeper than I had intended, and immediately broke into a coughing fit. It took half a minute before I could answer his question.

"No," I said.

He kept watching as if he were waiting for me to say something else, so I obliged him.

"It gives me something to do," I said.

He nodded.

"How do you feel?"

I took a drag that was even heavier than the first, then fell into another coughing fit. God, I hated cigarettes. As I flicked what was left of it into the weeds, part of me hoped it would start another fire. With Sam still waiting for an answer, I tried to spit the taste out of my mouth but it didn't work. I took a deep breath and felt an unexplainable urge to punch someone in the face. Though Sam would have been a convenient choice, I knew I didn't want to punch him. It was just a feeling, though I knew it was more than that; Sam and the guys were right. I was too sick to trust, and it didn't matter if I lied to them or myself, because they intended to see it through until they were sure.

"It's coming," I said. "I can feel it."

For a while, he said nothing. He knew what I meant. We sat in silence and stared out into the darkness. In his mind, he might have been looking out at the demons that beset us on all sides. I looked out at nothing because there was nothing to see.

"We'll make sure it ends quickly for you, Paul," he said at last. "I promise you that."

Quickly. Sure, as quickly as it took for the infection to take full effect and turn me into a monster, not a second sooner. Only then, with a prayer in my ear and a gun to my head, would it pass quickly.

"Sam, just kill me," I said. "I can't become one of them. I don't want to end that way."

"Dammit . . ." he said. "I can't kill you. Not 'til you're gone. Not 'til you've turned."

There was exasperation in his voice, but there was something else too. There was sadness, maybe regret. I turned to face him, but he stared ahead.

"I can't turn into one of them," I said. "If you can't kill me, then just let me end it."

He looked over at me, then dropped his gaze and looked at the ground.

"Suicides end up in hell, Paul. You know that."

Without warning, without reason, the effects of the vodka and the symptoms of the sickness were gone and replaced by a powerful fury. I jumped to my feet and turned to face Sam. His eyes were wide and wary and though he might have tried to suppress it, I noticed the twitch in his arm that hinted toward his rifle. While he cared about my eternal soul and wanted me to go to his heaven, he knew that I was already a potential threat. He knew that I was capable of terrible things.

"Look around you, Sam!" I screamed. "Look at where we are. We're in hell! We've been in hell! This is it! Wandering towns, killing the people we knew and loved! Everyone we knew is captured or dead! This is where your god put us!"

"Paul, don't say that—"

I leaned toward him and swung a fist. He jerked back to avoid the strike, and I just grazed his chin. Stunned, he fell backward, and I shoved him hard in the chest before reaching for his pistol. He caught himself with his elbows as his back hit the ground, and he brought the butt of his rifle into my face. My vision went black, and I fell onto my side. I shook my head and pushed myself back up to see Sam on his knees facing me, his eyes as angry as they were pained.

"Dangit, Paul, don't be—"

I lunged at him with all my weight and tackled him onto his back. As I landed on top of him, I swung wildly at his face. It would be a lie to say it hurt me as much as it hurt him, but it still hurt me. I had grown to respect and love the man; he was a brother as much as anyone could be. But he was standing between me and a quick, easy way out. He had me cornered with my back to insanity and a long, slow end.

As he shielded his face with both hands, I tried again for the gun. He swung both fists in response, first the left, then the right. I ducked closer to him to avoid the first, but he caught me in the back of the head with the second. He swung again but missed as I pulled back and reached again, but not for the pistol. Instead, I grabbed the barrel of his rifle. He started to swing another fist, then stopped and held the other end of his rifle with both hands. The glare of the flashlight washed out my vision, and I fiddled blindly with the mechanism that fastened it to the barrel, working solely from memory. Sam released the magazine and cycled the remaining round out of the chamber, but my focus remained on the flashlight.

"What are you doing?" he yelled.

I pushed to my feet and ran as fast as I could. I looked back only once to see him standing there, facing me. In the dark, I couldn't make out the details of his face. But I knew I had hurt him far more than the punches I had landed. Rick and Greg emerged from the door and stopped beside Sam, their hands on their weapons.

"Paul, come back!" Rick yelled.

"I'm sorry!" I cried. "I'm sorry!"

With just the clothes I was wearing and the flashlight from Sam's rifle, I disappeared into the forest.

L. Marshall James

29

I tore through the brush and made my way down the steep angle of the land. The earth was rocky and loose, and aside from the beam of the flashlight, the forest was pitch-black. A branch hit me in the face, and I misstepped once, then twice before I collided with a tree, lost my balance, and tumbled into a patch of thorny undergrowth. I scrambled up and back into a run.

I broke out of the forest and fell onto the road. Route 488. Since I'd looked at the map, I knew where it led, but it didn't matter. There were countless houses and other buildings along the road's edge, and in at least one of those buildings was a means to a quick and painless end. I shut off the flashlight and ran along the road, glancing around me periodically at the insistence of imagined lights, shouts, and growls. I passed a cluster of houses and kept running. I didn't know if Sam and the guys could afford the danger of chasing me through demon-haunted lands, but I wasn't going to take any chances. If they were in pursuit, they would check those houses first.

A cluster of vehicles sat in a parking lot ahead of me. A short distance beyond them was a single tow truck, and beyond that was a small building. The front of the building was emblazoned with a large sign that advertised Jeff's Towing Services. I sprinted to the front door, mistakenly assumed it to be open, and smashed into it face-first when it didn't budge. I grabbed the handle and jiggled it. It was locked. I kicked it, then noticed an aluminum lawn chair a few feet away. I folded the chair, held it by the legs, and swung it into the window beside the door. After ten or fifteen swings, I tossed the chair, stepped through the window frame, and made my way to an area behind the front desk where various keyrings hung on a bevy of tiny hooks. The smell of rotting flesh wafted in from Jeff's office behind the desk, and I did my best to ignore it as I collected the keys. Once I had them all, I ran back outside to the tow truck.

The door was unlocked. I climbed in and dumped the keyrings in a pile on the seat, then locked the door and rummaged through the pile until I found one set of oversized, ancient-looking keys. In the light of the flashlight, one key stood out as being larger than the rest. When I tried to shove it into the ignition, however, it wouldn't fit, so I tried another. No dice. I glanced around me periodically as I continued searching through the keys. Finally, a key on the third set slid easily into the ignition. When I turned it, the engine tried to turn but failed. I pumped the gas and tried again.

"Come on, come on, you fuc—"

The engine roared to life.

"—king beautiful piece of shit! Yes!"

It rumbled mightily as I shifted into gear, accelerated out of the lot, and sped down the road. I glanced behind me and had expected to see Sam or one of the other Crusaders either pursuing on foot or on the backs of angels. No one was there. For the time being, it was just me, the road, and the thirty-foot vibrating monster I had stolen from poor Jeff, who was probably dead.

As I drove, I ignored the growing urge to pull over and search the first house I came to for a knife or gun or just jerk the steering wheel and speed into a telephone pole. No, I knew I couldn't risk being discovered and interrupted while searching for a suicide weapon, and a car crash was a risky way to attempt suicide; I could just end up maimed or paralyzed with no way to escape the inevitable madness that would befall me. I forced myself to drive at a reasonable speed past house after house and put crucial miles between me and the Crusaders.

A few barns came into view, and I let my foot off the gas. As far as I could tell, they were deserted. I pulled into the nearby driveway and followed it around the house, where I parked out of view of the road. I didn't know how far I had gone, but I felt confident that I would not be found. I turned off the engine and scanned the area around the truck as it settled into silence. After thirty seconds or so passed, I unlocked the door and got out. My head throbbed. I climbed back into the truck and scoured the giant front seat and the area behind it until I found what almost passed as a suitable weapon: a screwdriver.

I held it out in front of me like an old lady with a knife as I made my way to the back door of the house and kicked it open without bothering to see if it was locked. It flung open, impacted the wall, and bounced back with a clatter. I waited for something to rush at me, but nothing came. I flashed the light in and peered deeper inside. Nothing.

I stepped tentatively inside and made my way into the kitchen, where I exchanged the screwdriver for a large kitchen knife before continuing farther in. The house was not spotless but not messy, which meant that it had been lived in but it did not appear to have been died in. When I passed through the last room of the first floor without incident, I allowed myself to relax but only slightly. I knew better than to play it casual; death by mauling and mutilation was not my preferred way to die.

I started up the stairs and winced as the wood creaked loudly beneath me. I continued on up, each step as loud as the last, and breathed a sigh of relief when I reached the padded carpet of a hallway. With a glance in both directions, I went to the right. I did only a cursory check of each room as I made my way down the hall, and when I finally made it to the last door, I found it to be locked. I hesitated briefly, then shrugged and kicked the door open.

Before I saw anything, I had a rough idea of what was in the room. I tried to cover my nose with each hand in turn, then pulled the collar of my shirt over my nose and tried not to gag as I proceeded in. On the floor in the middle of the room was a series of bodies, all arranged neatly in a row and lying shoulder to shoulder except for one, which lay at the feet of the others but askew, its legs bent at the knees like an L. They might have been there a few weeks or a few months; I had never learned how to determine such things, so it was always a guessing game for me. What was obvious was that they had all died at roughly the same time and that they had all been shot in the head. When I neared the body that was positioned differently from the rest, I noticed a piece of paper jutting conspicuously from the breast pocket of the shirt. I slid it carefully from the pocket and held it aloft in the light. It read,

To the government,
What I have done is a terrible thing. There are no words to say the pain I feel. I wish I could have done something else. But we were all going to die because of you. You brought this evil to us and we pay the price because of it.
YOU DID THIS AND YOU WILL BURN IN HELL FOR IT.

I refolded the note and laid it gingerly on top of the pocket. As I did so, something glinted on the far side of his body. A large revolver was still clamped in the left hand. I started to reach for it, then stepped around the body, knelt beside it, and leaned closer. Even though the body didn't have a head, I half-expected it to reach out a hand or sit up and call me an asshole, at the very least. But it didn't. It just lay there as I pried the pointer finger off the trigger and wrenched the gun from its grasp.

I tossed the knife across the room and examined the revolver. It was a heavy caliber and obviously more than enough for my purpose. I emptied the shells onto a desk in the corner of the room, reloaded the only unspent round, then spun the cylinder because I'd seen it done in a movie once. As I readjusted the cylinder so that the unspent round would fire first, I considered writing a goodbye note.

> *Dear Government,*
> *I'm not with this crew, but I endorse the sentiment of their letter. Go* *fuck yourselves.*
> *Sincerely,*
> *Paul*

I leaned against the wall by the desk. For a while, I stared at what remained of the bodies. Five bodies, their brains shredded and rotting and their bowels mostly emptied as they decomposed in a dried pool of blood. The body that laid at odds with the other four must have been a man. The other four had been a woman and three . . . kids. I sunk to a crouch and winced at a twinge of pain in my head.

Father, age unknown, invited his family into his office. He was casual; there was nothing wrong. They followed him in. He waited until they were all inside, then shut the door and locked it. Mother, age unknown, looked at him questioningly, then noticed the revolver he had pulled from the back of his pants.

No. Honey, no, no!

The barrel thundered, and she fell. Her head was gone. The kids shrieked in unison.

Thunder. The youngest sank, and the screams were fewer.

Thunder. Another well-aimed shot, and the next youngest fell as the eldest stood frozen in place, terrified.

Thunder.

Father dropped the gun, and his ears were ringing so loud that he couldn't hear himself sob but he could still hear himself scream. He wailed uncontrollably as he crawled to the lifeless bodies of his family and mumbled apologies. He stayed there for hours. Eventually, he emerged from his stupor for long enough to arrange the bodies neatly in the middle of the room. Someone would come here someday, and they must know that what happened was not simple murder. It wasn't like that. He loved his family. He retrieved a pen from the desk in the corner and ripped a piece of paper from a notepad. As he wrote the note, he hoped the intended recipients felt every word. He hoped they felt his hatred. He hoped they would indeed burn in Hell. When he finished the note, he folded it, stuck it in his pocket, and picked up the revolver. He knelt at the feet of his family and pointed the revolver into his mouth.

Thunder. Father tucked his family into bed with the barrel of a gun, then fell asleep beside them.

My eyes started watering too much to ignore, so I held my head between my knees and let them drip. My shirt had fallen from my nose, but I didn't care. With the side of the gun pressed against my temple, I cradled my head in my hands and let the water flow. I knew I was crying, but somehow it didn't feel like it. Something in my mind felt different, almost foreign, almost numb. The sickness was taking over.

I waited for my eyes to stop watering so that I could at least kill myself with some small measure of dignity, but they wouldn't. Finally, I threw the revolver at the door and screamed. I stomped over to the desk, pulled out all the drawers, and emptied them onto the floor. Nothing. I left the room and made my way down the hall to the first bedroom I came to. Planes and birds adorned the wallpaper. I moved onto the next room, then the next, until I came to the master bedroom. I searched the nightstand, then the closet before I finally found what I was looking for: bullets.

For a long time, I hadn't cared about the source of the virus. There was nothing I could do about it, so there had been no reason to preoccupy myself with it. When Jack had told his tall tales about the government's involvement, I had shrugged it off and focused instead on the details that were more pertinent to me: their troop and equipment strengths. But when it came down to it, there could never have been any doubt as to the source of the virus.

It was no stretch of the imagination to think that the unethical experiments we knew about, from the illegal research of the last fifty years to the legal clinical trials of the present day, were only the tip of the iceberg, that there was infinitely more information we didn't know and would never know. I had no doubt that all the commissions, committees, and investigations were held only because the public finally found out about it. Then, the responsible parties covered their asses and threw less powerful men under the bus. But even if justice had been done before, the real culprits behind the South American flu would never be revealed. History is written by the victors, after all; this time, the victors were the people who survived: the people who knew it was coming and knew how to escape the inevitable fate of the rest of the world. I suddenly felt certain, more certain than I had ever been of anything in my life, that the government was to blame. Whether through direct action or inaction, they had caused the South American flu pandemic.

They had destroyed the world as we knew it.

Billions of people were already dead. I couldn't stop that; it was already done. I couldn't even avenge it; the government was stronger, more capable, and better supplied than I could ever be. They were beyond me. But I had an advantage because I had nothing left to lose, including my life. I could do more than write a note, blow my brains out, and leave my body to shit itself and rot. I could take my note to the government's doorstep and deliver it to them personally.

I searched the house until I found more rounds for the revolver, as well as two boxes of shotgun shells. I couldn't find a shotgun to go with them, but I took them anyway. I loaded some food from the kitchen into a few grocery bags and threw them into the cab of the truck, then tried and failed to raid the father's closet for clothing that fit me. His clothes were all too big for me, which was a shame; however inglorious he had been in death, he had been a dapper motherfucker when he was alive.

On my final trip out of the house, I returned to the room where the family had spent their last moments. As I strode through the room to the father's corpse, I couldn't help but imagine the scene as it must have taken place. I felt a molten fury as I retrieved the father's note, pocketed it, and made my way back outside.

Between the house and the truck, I was suddenly assaulted by the smell of rotting flesh. I looked to my left just as two teenage biters stumbled around the edge of the house. Their clothes were little more than tatters, and the flesh underneath was a mix of black, red, and a mucus-like green that was torn and otherwise severed in patches that hung open and flapped with each step. I hesitated to shoot them, since I didn't want to attract more attention.

"You lightweights better get on outta here," I said. "Scram!"

They paid my warning no heed. I wasn't sure why I had bothered to hope for a different resolution. I raised the pistol and relieved them of whatever consciousness they may have had left.

Fuck it. Time was wasting, and so was I.

30

It felt oddly like a road trip. Maybe it was because the journey promised to be arduous or because the destination wasn't set in stone. Maybe it was because I had a bag of beef jerky between my legs and was staring at the road like it owed me money. I veered haphazardly around abandoned vehicles and powered over approaching zombies as I chewed. I had no map, but I knew where I was going. Even if I got lost or became confused, all I had to do was follow the signs. The road led east to Interstate 79, which I would follow south, back to the city I had abandoned in favor of survival. I had taken the river route in my initial escape because it had been less risky, but survival wasn't even an option anymore.

Signs at a T-intersection indicated that I-79 was to the right. I veered left instead; I had a pit stop to make. A dog ran across the road in front of me, and a woman in a business suit appeared from where it had come. She stood there and watched me pass. For a moment, I thought she might have been an uninfected survivor, but I had no interest in company or small talk, so I accelerated past her without another glance. She probably wouldn't have liked much of what I had to say anyway.

It wasn't far to my destination. I couldn't help but smile when I finally caught sight of the sign: Rupert's ATV Sales.

I flashed a look in the rearview mirror, and though I didn't see anything, I knew the infected would not be far behind. I drove past Rupert's and turned into the driveway of the house just beyond it. I sped up and around the house, then mashed the brakes and immediately killed the engine. Any infected who had given chase would have undoubtedly seen where I stopped, so I didn't have much time. With the bags in one hand and the revolver in the other, I threw open the door and made a break for it. To avoid being detected, I ran with the flashlight off.

I paused at a wall of darkness that turned out to be the start of cornfield, then shook my head and plunged in. The rustling of the bags had seemed noisy on the way toward the corn but was almost unbearably loud when moving through it. Contrary to my expectation that I would be quickly surrounded and torn to shreds among the cornstalks, the field ended and I stepped out toward the backside of Rupert's. I sneaked over to a metal door on the back of the store, then set the bags down and looked around as I caught my breath.

My lungs felt raw. I wiped my nose on an arm, then retrieved a can of beans from one of the bags, ripped the label off, and used it to blow my nose. I listened for movement. Detecting nothing, I pressed the flashlight up to a small window and looked inside. As far as I could tell, there was no movement. I tried the door handle and pulled, but it didn't give or even rattle.

Between the store and the road was a house that was likely the home of the business owners. I ignored it and carried the bags around to the front of building. I glanced nervously at the road as I set the bags down and examined the front doors. They were mostly glass, but the metal frames were solid, and while I could break the glass without the risk of an alarm going off, the sound would still attract attention and greatly lessen the time available to find keys to a suitable ride. Even then, the metal of the doors would prevent me from leaving. I sighed and walked toward the house.

My patience gone, I strode up to a back door of the house, raised a foot, and kicked with all my strength. It crashed open and bounced back against the wall as I stepped past it into a cement-floored hallway. I closed the door, then pressed a box up against it to keep it from opening on its own. It wouldn't be enough to hold it shut if something tried to force its way in, but the door would at least look undisturbed. That was as much of a safety precaution as I cared to take.

I listened for a half second, then strode through the hallway and up a set of stairs to a kitchen. I searched the walls for a set of keys but found nothing. The drawers and cabinets yielded the same result, as did the living room and a small table by the front door. I walked down a hallway toward the rear of the house, then jumped at the sound of a violent impact somewhere deeper inside. I continued more slowly, then stopped again when the impact repeated from the other side of the door to my right. Whatever the source of the sound was, it was in that room. I walked past the door and to the end of the hall, then into what I hoped was the master bedroom.

A queen-size bed sat against the far wall. I took a quick look around the room, then made a beeline to a small, cluttered bedside table and retrieved a keyring from a pile of miscellaneous items. None of the keys were labeled, but it seemed a safe bet that one of them opened the store.

I started to head back outside, then stopped in front of the room from which the sounds had emanated. Something was obstructing the door from the inside, so I pocketed the keys and leaned my body weight against it. The obstruction shifted, and the door gave way. I stumbled into the room, then caught my balance and looked around, the revolver cocked and ready to fire. Someone groaned, and I followed the sound to the base of the open door. A pair of legs stuck out from behind it.

I closed the door and took a quick step back. There, lying on the floor was a nude, barely living zombie. Its eyes were no more than infected mounds on its face, its skin was an unnatural yellow shade, and its hair was falling out. It opened its mouth to groan again, and I could see that most of its teeth were broken. With one hand, it lashed out at nothing, then pulled its arm into its chest as the hand spasmed wildly. Something glinted in the corner of my eye, and I pointed the flashlight over to see a wheelchair sitting unoccupied in the corner.

"You poor, unfortunate fucker," I said aloud.

The zombie gave a halfhearted growl, then lashed out again. I stepped closer. Its head turned feebly toward the sound of my footsteps, and it growled again, quieter, as I knelt beside it. Suddenly, it lashed out at my face with surprising quickness. I dodged, narrowly avoided the blow, and fell onto my side. Before I could react, its claw-like hand fell and wrapped around my ankle, then pulled my foot toward its open mouth. I leaned forward and pistol-whipped it in the face once, then twice. The second effort struck it in the right eye, which popped and propelled a string of dark, viscous material past the door.

A wave of disgust and anger washed over me. I threw the gun across the room, sat up to face the zombie, and shoved the sole of my boot into its jaw. It groaned, opened its mouth, and tried to bite through the material. I stomped a second time, followed by a third, and it lost its grip long enough that I was able to pull free and push to my feet. As it reached for me again, I sidestepped its arm and brought my boot down into its throat. It made a strangled choking sound, and I stomped it again, then kicked its head against the wall and screamed. I kept kicking until it stopped moving, then I glared down at it and breathed heavily.

My breathing and heart rate gradually normalized, and I felt a return of my initial pity. A crippled person had become infected, lost its mind as it succumbed to the disease, then laid on the floor, utterly helpless, until someone had finally discovered it and stomped its face in. I used a blanket from the bed to cover the body, then retrieved the revolver and tried not to vomit as I wiped off what remained of the sludge from its eye socket. After extensive searching of the house, I finally found a shotgun, as well as a buck knife and a chainsaw. Though I didn't want to, I left the chainsaw behind and made my way back outside.

Once I entered the store, it took only a minute or so to find a large collection of keys in a back room behind a counter, then another ten minutes or so to match a key with what looked like the best ride: a hefty four-wheeler with front and rear racks. It took another fifteen minutes of siphoning gas from a truck out front before I felt confident I could make the trip in its entirety. When I had finished, I loaded the shotgun and my bags onto the racks, propped open the front doors, and sped out. Something or someone yelled from behind me as I drove off, and I had to force myself to ignore whatever it was.

I wanted to go back and kill them all.

31

Dawn approached as I neared Interstate 79, and after I had rumbled along the first mile or so of the highway, the sun finally emerged in all its benevolent glory. I had been right to take the river out of downtown rather than risking the highway. While the lanes heading south to Pittsburgh were almost entirely devoid of cars, the northbound lanes were an endless, bumper-to-bumper procession of windowed metal coffins. In some of the vehicles, heads turned slowly to watch me and hands scratched weakly against the glass. For whatever reason, some of the infected had remained in their vehicles. Perhaps they forgot how to open the doors, their favorite album was playing, or it was just too damn cold outside, even for them.

In my haste, I had not dressed appropriately for the weather. On more than one occasion, I considered hopping in one of the vehicles to warm up with the zombies. I tried to pull my sleeves over my hands, but my fingers still froze in the wind. When I reached relatively clear bits of roadway where the infected couldn't easily reach me, I shoved each of my hands down my pants alternately, despite the awkwardness and danger of driving with my left hand on the right-handed throttle. Sometimes I just stopped, shoved both my hands down my pants, and ran laps around the ATV to get my temperature up. I also kept warm by practicing good old-fashioned killing.

They mostly came from the other lanes to try and cut me off, but they were usually slow—not just slow compared to the four-wheeler, but slow compared to what I had grown accustomed to. Whether as a result of the cold or the extended effects of the infection, the zombie population as a whole had become far less capable. At first I veered around them when I could, then dismounted and took them out only when they left me little choice. As I continued on down the highway, I stopped to kill them more and more often.

With a head chop here and a bullet to the brain there, I told myself I was just doing it to keep warm and to help clear the road of potentially-lethal obstacles.

At first, that might have been true.

I slowed to a stop, shifted into neutral, and shut off the engine. Ahead of me was a pileup of vehicles that appeared to have veered across the median from the opposite lanes. Approaching me from both the pileup and the northbound lanes was a crowd of infected that would have been easy enough to outrun. Probably.

I hopped off and grabbed the shotgun from the front rack, then walked toward the nearest zombie as it stumbled toward me with uneven, unsteady steps. He looked like he had once been pretty well-off, but judging by what was left of his clothing and severed right foot, he had clearly fallen on hard times. Still, he was determined to give me a stern talking to, at the very least. As I neared him, he broke into a run, somehow propelling himself despite the missing foot. It might have been my imagination, but I swore I could hear the impact of bone on pavement. I aimed at his torso and pulled the trigger.

Click.

I looked down at the gun in bewilderment as the zombie continued toward me, then stumbled, took three large steps to try and catch himself, and fell to the pavement. He craned his neck to look up at me, and with a deep-throated growl, he pushed himself up onto all fours and scrabbled toward me even faster than before. I dropped the shotgun and grabbed the revolver I had tucked into the front of my pants. I almost lost my grip as the hammer caught on the waistband, then I jerked again and heard the fabric rip. I jerked a third time and the revolver came free, but the biter had already reached me and wrapped his arms around my legs. He turned his head and sunk his teeth into my lower thigh.

I screamed, fell, and landed hard on my back. My head hit the road, and my vision went black. I was stunned at first, but the pain in my leg forced me to attention. I swung a fist and landed successive blows on the side of the crazy's head. When I leaned forward to swing again, I saw another zombie closing in from only ten feet away. Before I could aim at it, I felt another shooting pain in my leg. I placed the revolver barrel against the crazy's forehead and fired. The back of his head exploded in a torrent of blood and brains, and as he slumped on top of me, I raised the pistol and fired into the chest of the other zombie. Its legs buckled, and it collapsed to the road.

I pushed the corpse off of me and scrambled to my feet, then grabbed the shotgun as other biters drew nearer. My leg throbbed as I ran back to the ATV. By the time I strapped the shotgun down and started the engine, five more